WE SOLDIE

Graham John Parry

WE SOLDIERS FEW text © GRAHAM JOHN PARRY

COVER ARTWORK © G. J. PARRY

All Rights Reserved

This is a work of fiction. The names and characters
are the product of the authors imagination, or are used in an
entirely fictitious context. Although based on real events any resemblance to actual incidents is wholly coincidental.

We Soldiers Few is
for my Wife and Family
with much love.

Novels by Graham John Parry

* * *

The Waves of War

In Time of Battle

Man of War

When D-Day Dawns

We Soldiers Few

Fighting Command

Table of Contents

Novels by G J Parry
Author's Note
1   Duty Calls
2   The Black Patch
3   Cold Steel
4   The Farm
5   Enemy
6   Battlegroup
7   Ruffians
8   The Barn
9   Panzer-Lehr
10 Grenadiers
11 Paulette Chalamet
12 Château Fontaine
13 To Hold
14 Stand To
15 Open Fire
16 Against All Odds
17 The Flanks
18 Kill or Die
19 A Fury of War
20 Hand to Hand
21 Gun Up
22 Hell Let Loose
23 The Raid
24 Carnage
25 Waves of War
26 A Reckoning
27 A Final Wave

Author's Note

History tells us of great battles fought and won by famous Generals, revered Commanders whose names echo long through the eons of time. But no matter the glories visited upon such illustrious beings those same distinguished leaders know exactly to whom they owe their victories.

It is to the heroic sacrifice of rank and file soldiers that the mighty Captain turns, be it as an Army of thousands or the warriors of a small fighting Platoon. For each hard-earned foot of land gained, the wise commander-in-chief never forgets his reliance on that most valuable of resources, the ordinary man.

This story concerns itself with just one of those fighting Platoons, and it is their courage, endurance and tenacity when faced with the ultimate challenge, that remains long in the memory, so many decades after the battle was run.

GJP.

> O Gods of War, we pledge anew,
> To hold our ground . . , we soldiers few.

1 Duty Calls

It was early June, 1944, when a Major by the name of Paul Wingham strode briskly through a rain soaked quayside in Portsmouth's Royal Navy Dockyard. The drizzle had stopped shortly before dawn but the black tarmacadam still glistened to the ripple of standing water. Wind blown grey clouds chased away to the east, glimmers of mid-morning sunlight reflecting off a harbour overcrowded with vessels.

He sidestepped a flapping canvas tarpaulin and set about negotiating a multitude of crates and boxes that lay strewn across the dock, some already piled high into bulging cargo nets. Many nearby wharves and jetties displayed similar sodden heaps and all awaited transfer into the next available ship's hold. Tall skeletal cranes had begun to swing cumbersome loads from heavy iron hooks.

A strident shout made him pause. 'Mind yourself!'

Wingham glanced round at the warning and found a docker pointing ahead. Not more than a few paces away, a slick sheen of iridescent oil had spread into an ever widening puddle, a dented fifty-gallon steel drum leaking from a split. He raised a hand in thanks and gave it a wide berth. The man grinned before bending to tug at a heavy looking steel hawser.

Paul Wingham shook his head in wonder. It was difficult to comprehend the enormous amount of equipment yet to be shipped across the Channel. Yesterday's seaborne invasion of Nazi occupied France, the so called long awaited "D-Day", had succeeded beyond all expectation. But it was because of that, this well anticipated need for ongoing re-supply had swung into action.

He dodged yet another coiled rope and tried to imagine how many other south coast ports continued to provide "Operation Overlord" with all the bewildering paraphernalia of ships, men and weaponry that were needed to reinforce the landings.

Wingham negotiated the last of the stacked cases, turned away from the edge of the water and strode smartly towards an imposing multi-storied red brick building generally referred to as Semaphore Tower. He moved through to the arched entrance and took the stairs two at a time. Up on the second floor he then hurried along the corridor to a door marked, "Commodore J. A. Pendleton, R.N., D.S.O." He knocked and stepped inside to be met by the incessant clatter of half a dozen typewriters. It was a busy typing pool staffed by six young Wrens immersed in paperwork. A couple of them glanced up at the handsome intruder and he nodded at their inviting smiles.

Sat at an isolated desk by an inner door, the lovely Jennifer Farbrace saw him enter and as First Officer and PA to the Commodore, beckoned for him to join her. They were old acquaintances, and with no more than a cursory acknowledgement he allowed her to usher him through to the quiet of the inner sanctum where he took a seat opposite old man Pendleton's large mahogany desk.

Already seated, Lieutenant-Commander Richard Thorburn, Royal Navy, nodded, the hint of a smile on his well tanned features. Wingham winked in return, a casual greeting between men who'd known one another from as far back as 1940. From the very first introduction, they'd instantly seen eye to eye.

The large white faced 'Smiths' wall clock chimed for 11.30 and the two officers leaned forward, anxious to hear the Commodore's verdict. Each officer had been summoned to await judgement on their previous day's action reports, and that day, Tuesday the 6th of June 1944, had already earned itself the privilege of being officially written up as "D-Day".

Major Wingham rubbed his chin and again reflected on how he'd hit the beach with the first wave of American troops to assault 'Utah' over on the right flank. His mission had then been accomplished with the able support of Richard Thorburn, strategically positioned off-shore in the destroyer H.M.S. *Brackendale*. Between them they had managed to fulfil a small but important role in that day's historic proceedings.

But Wingham was well aware that yesterday had come and gone, and this was a new day, which might cast an entirely different interpretation on the previous day's events.

Behind the large mahogany desk, Commodore James Pendleton, stocky, red faced, and sporting the very finest of traditional, grey-flecked, handsome beards, looked up from his paperwork, leaned back and nodded. Well versed in the ways of Combined Operations, his verdict on the completion of their latest mission was an important part of the debrief. He cleared his throat.

'Well, gentlemen. It appears the general consensus is that your mission was accomplished in exemplary fashion. Additionally,' he added, and cleared his throat, 'I've had credible eye witness confirmation that your target was indeed completely obliterated.'

Thorburn gave him a rueful smile. 'Might have been better if *Brackendale* had got away with a little less damage, sir.'

Pendleton chuckled and smoothed the heavy beard. 'Fortunes of war, my boy. Fortunes of war. You should have seen off that U-boat first time round.'

Thorburn politely inclined his head and accepted the point. The damaged U-boat had collided with H.M.S. *Brackendale's* bows in mid Channel and she was now tied up out of action awaiting repairs.

A knock on the door made Pendleton frown. 'Come!' he snapped at the interruption.

First Officer Farbrace appeared, her delightful young face troubled by a frown. 'Sorry, sir, but General Bainbridge is here.'

Before Pendleton could answer, the door was thrown wide and the formidable figure of General Scott Bainbridge marched in. Dressed in an immaculately presented full uniform, gleaming Sam Browne, obligatory scarlet flashes on his lapels, and displaying two rows of well earned medal ribbons, the old warrior strode across to Pendleton's desk. The face of tanned leather only served to highlight the most piercing blue eyes, a vivid scar running back across one cheekbone.

'Morning, James, how the devil are you? I'm a little pushed for time. Heard you were here, need to speak to Wingham. Rush job on.' He swivelled to face the Major. 'How's that wound of yours?'

Paul Wingham glanced sideways at Thorburn and raised an eyebrow before addressing the General. This was the man who had brought both Wingham and Thorburn together under the original banner of Special Operations.

'Not so bad, sir. Just a flesh wound really.'

Bainbridge dropped his briefcase onto the desk and perched on the corner.

'Sure? Not a hindrance?'

'No, sir. Just a scratch.'

'Right, Major,' Bainbridge said. 'I'll hold you to that because I'm sending you back to Normandy. Think you'll be able to cope?'

Before Wingham could answer, the General eyed Thorburn. 'I understand your ship is out of commission?'

Thorburn nodded. 'Yes, sir. Tangled with a U-boat.'

'Never mind, never mind. You wouldn't have been much use anyway. Not this time, probably too cumbersome for what's needed.'

Intrigued, debrief forgotten, Major Paul Wingham leaned forward, elbows on his knees.

Bainbridge delved into the briefcase and pulled out a buff coloured file. He waved it at Wingham before reverently removing a single sheet of foolscap.

'There's a village south of Sword Beach called Ranville. It's about four and a half miles inland and about six to Caen, which is south-west.' He walked across to Pendleton's large map of Normandy. He peered at it and then tapped a point south of Ranville.

'More importantly from your point of view, there's a farm just here that you need to get to. It's called the Farm Sainte Beaumont, abandoned by its owner. Now,' he said, and jammed his fists into the tunic pockets. 'That farmhouse is used as a place to exchange information and we're expecting someone to be there tomorrow.' He fixed Wingham with a piercing gaze. 'Tomorrow, Major. A bit short notice but we understand that the information is both vital and urgent. And bear in mind, whoever you finally get to meet is in a good deal of danger. They've quite literally put their life on the line.'

Wingham raised a finger. 'What about 6th Airborne, sir? They dropped all over that area.'

Bainbridge shook his head, the pale scar glinting. 'You'll appreciate communications are rather chaotic at the moment. We can't just ring round until we find someone.' He paused, staring at his feet. When he looked up it was with a faint smile. 'Also, Major, it's important that whoever I send over there can speak French. I seem to remember that's almost your first language.'

Wingham held up a hand and nodded, conceding the point. 'Of course, sir. Complicated.'

'Exactly. So here's what I want. In the first instance I need to get you to Ranville. The powers that be reckoned that the quickest and most reliable way to get you to France is by Motor Gun Boat. The weather over there wasn't that kind to the Paras so a fast boat was thought to be the answer.' He glanced at a window. 'Not that it's exactly anything to write home about today either. Now once ashore you'll get yourself down to the village and tie up with a Major

Lane. He's holding the outskirts on the left flank. There'll be a Platoon ready and waiting.'

Wingham stiffened to sit upright. 'Freddy Lane, sir? If it is we worked together in Scotland. Good man.'

'Yep, that's the chap. There's also a Sergeant Cartwright. He'll go across with you.'

Wingham pursed his lips and nodded. That was a big plus and he couldn't have asked for more. He and Cartwright were no strangers. He held up his finger again.

'What exactly are our orders, sir?'

Bainbridge came back to the desk. 'Simply put, find out what's so important. You'll have a radio to transmit information. Anything you deem urgent needs to get back to the top brass.'

Wingham took that on board and gave the faintest of shrugs. He looked over at Thorburn and smiled.

'Looks like a parting of the ways, Richard. But don't forget you still owe me that drink.'

The General interrupted.

'Not quite,' he said looking at Pendleton. 'I still need a boat, and a skipper.'

Thorburn wasn't backward in coming forward. As a Captain without a ship he'd already guessed he was facing a lengthy spell of administrative work and was quick to seize the opportunity.

'I'm free.'

Pendleton immediately shook his head. 'I'll not risk an experienced Lieutenant-Commander on such a wild escapade. Forget it.'

Thorburn thought for a moment before floating another possibility. 'Then might I suggest Lieutenant George Labatt. He's more than capable of skippering a Gunboat. *Brackendale* won't be ready for months so he won't be missed. In any case, the Channel is swarming with our ships, it's not very likely he'll encounter much in the way of the enemy. The least he can do is make himself useful.'

Bainbridge smiled. 'He does have a point, James. It would make my life a sight easier if I could count on this . . . , what did you say his name was? Labatt?' He rubbed his hands. 'That means we just need a boat.'

Pendleton gave an exaggerated sigh and tugged at his beard.

'Very well,' he said, and shook his head. 'Feels like I'm being steamrollered into going along with all this.' He reached for the telephone.

'Ahh, Benson. I need to get a message to *Brackendale*. No.2 repair basin. Ask Lieutenant Labatt to report to my office. Immediately.' He listened for a moment. 'Yes, thank you.' He gently replaced the handset on the cradle.

Bainbridge chimed in. 'Brilliant,' he smiled. 'Now, James, how about a boat? Got anything up your sleeve?'

Pendleton gave the three of them an exasperated shrug and raised his voice. 'Miss Farbrace! A moment if you would.'

The door opened and Jennifer popped her head round, delicate eyebrows raised. 'Sir?'

'Young lady, would you kindly make enquiries of Chief Petty Officer Swanson at the Gun Boat repair yard. Ask him if they have a serviceable boat, just for a day, no more. We've got a crew, a boat is what we need. If it helps tell him the request comes from Whitehall, the very top. Urgent.'

'Yes, sir.' She gave an assured nod and backed out.

James Pendleton went back behind his desk and eased his thickening waist into the chair.

'Gentlemen,' he said, waving an expansive hand round the room. 'Have a seat while we wait for our answer.' He offered his pack of Senior Service and they lit up, the General also content to sit and take a minute.

Thorburn breathed a veil of smoke and leaned back in the chair. 'The invasion, sir, how're things going?'

Pendleton let a smoke ring curl thoughtfully towards the ceiling. 'Better, Richard . . . , better. The chaps are expanding the beachhead now, pushing inland, and the reinforcements are building up.'

Wingham grunted agreement. 'I can vouch for that. Came through a lot of stuff down at the quayside.'

Bainbridge nodded in agreement. 'And I hear the RAF have the skies to themselves.'

They lapsed into a contemplative silence, cigarette smoke lifting to form a fine mist of blue at the ceiling. It was then that Wingham was struck by the need to have some kind of password exchange to identify his contact.

'General, sir. How will I know that I'm speaking to the right person at the farm?'

Bainbridge lunged to his feet and crossed to his briefcase. 'Sorry,' he said, fumbling for a sheet of paper. 'My mistake, all with your written orders, forgot to tell you.' He grinned sheepishly. 'Forget my head if it wasn't screwed on.' He handed the sheet to Wingham and returned to his seat.

'Read and digest, Major, read and digest. That won't leave this room.'

A knock on the door turned heads.

'Come,' Pendleton barked.

The door swung open and a rather shy Lieutenant George Labatt, cap under his arm, stepped hesitantly into the office.

'Labatt, sir. Reporting as ordered.'

Pendleton gave him a fatherly smile and looked to Thorburn. 'Richard,' he prompted. 'Maybe you'd like to explain.'

Thorburn stubbed out his cigarette and looked up at the young officer's perplexed expression. It wasn't every day a junior Lieutenant was summoned to attend on a Commodore.

'George,' he said kindly. 'How would you like to take command of a Gunboat?'

Labatt raised one eyebrow, disbelief showing on his usually smiling face. 'An M.G.B., sir? Me? When, sir?'

Thorburn glanced at the General.

'Today,' Bainbridge said, 'hopefully.'

Labatt eyed them all one after the other, then returned his gaze to Thorburn, a perplexed frown furrowing his brow.

'You're not getting rid of me, sir? I'm not leaving *Brackendale*?'

'No, George, not at all. If all goes according to plan, it's just for today.'

Labatt's normal grin returned to replace the frown of concern. 'In that case, sir, I'm ready.'

Wingham stood and offered his hand. 'You'll be my chauffer, Lieutenant. To French France as the saying goes.'

Labatt shook hands and if he was surprised by their destination it didn't show. 'Just say the word, sir.'

Wingham released the hand shake and fixed Pendleton with a frown. 'I'd like to be able to do that, Lieutenant, but that word is a bit slow in coming.'

Coincidently, there was a knock on the door and Jennifer strode in. With great formality she opened her pad and read from her notes.

'Sir . . . , I spoke to Chief Petty Officer Swanson who came up empty handed, so I mentioned Whitehall's involvement. He laughed and said something about spare parts, and the lack of. But he then directed me to the Motor Torpedo Boat yard. They have two M.T.B.'s available but without torpedoes. Supply shortage. All the Gunboats are either in use or too far gone.'

Bainbridge came to his feet. 'Same difference aren't they?' he ventured, and glanced at Pendleton. 'If it's alright with you?'

'I suppose it'll have to be. What about you, Mister Labatt, that a problem?'

'No, sir,' Labatt snapped, standing a little taller. 'Similar to the M.G.B.s, definitely not a problem.'

Bainbridge looked at his watch. 'Well, it's coming round to twelve-thirty.' He looked at Wingham and thoughtfully rubbed his jaw. 'Am I right in saying you completed your Parachute jumps?'

'Yes, sir,' Wingham nodded, remembering the training but wondering why Bainbridge asked.

'Good, that means there'll be no arguments over your choice of uniform. We need to get you kitted out, and warn Sergeant Cartwright. Time, as they say, is of the essence.' The General stood and gathered up his brief case. He glanced at Pendleton.

'Thank you, James. Awfully sorry about barging in like that but you can see we are in rather a hurry.'

Pendleton came to his feet and straightened his jacket. 'Never known you to be anything else, Scotty.' He nodded at Wingham. 'Good luck, Major. I have a feeling you're going to need it. And you, Mister Labatt. Do try and get back in one piece. It would be awfully bad form if you failed to return.'

Bainbridge led the way. 'My car then.'

And with that, they were gone.

Pendleton stepped out from behind the desk, walked across to the map and stroked his heavy beard. The gold rings on his cuffs gave off a dull gleam in the light from the window.

Behind him the door opened and Jennifer moved across to the desk, emptied the ashtray, and then began returning the chairs to their customary positions.

'Well, young lady, a penny for your thoughts.'

Jennifer Farbrace knew exactly how far she could go by way of criticising those in authority.

'Hare-brained,' she answered simply.

Commodore James Pendleton laughed, a rich, deep belly laugh that filled the office.

'My dear Miss Farbrace,' he chortled. 'How right you are.' He wandered back to his desk, added his signature to the two action reports and very deliberately placed them into his out-tray. He leaned back and stroked his full, grey-flecked beard. Hopefully, he thought, they wouldn't be the last.

2 The Black Patch

Far across the turbulent waters of the English Channel, in the dark interior of an old French barn, five badly wounded British Paratroopers took advantage of a lull in the German attacks to tend their injuries. For more than an hour bullets, tracer rounds and stick handled grenades had lashed at their flimsy defence. But they'd held on while their blood soaked smocks had turned a sticky dark red. Only now, with their meagre supply of ammunition rapidly running out, did they reluctantly admit to the thought of being overwhelmed.

Rifleman John Weaver, twenty-one, from Hastings, East Sussex, had been hit twice. As he'd fought the Germans through the remnants of a broken window, a 9mm bullet slammed into his left elbow. Seconds later a piece of red hot shrapnel struck hard and lodged in his ribcage. He no longer had the strength to hold the rifle but instead fired deliberate shots from a Paratrooper's last resort, his Browning pistol.

Defending the right end of the building from behind a half open door, Tim Sheridan, nineteen, also a Rifleman, had been hit in the jaw by a bullet from a Mauser. It had passed through from left to right, smashed his teeth and sliced away part of his tongue. With a broken jaw, unable to speak, and bleeding profusely, it was all he could do to summon the will to raise his Lee Enfield. Sheridan came from

Scarborough in North Yorkshire and doubted he'd live to see it again.

Lance-Corporal Daniel O'Sullivan, a twenty-two year old sub-machine gunner from Dover in Kent, had been on the receiving end of a stick grenade. The blast knocked him into a wall and punctured a lung. In the same instance a pebble thrown up by the explosion snagged his right eye and ripped it from the socket. Head bandaged and in considerable pain, vision blurred and breathing shallow, he lay propped against a bale of straw and waited for the inevitable.

Corporal Oliver Beresford, twenty-three, from the market town of Barnard Castle, had been hit both on the heel of his right foot and his calf muscle. He was losing too much blood. From the south facing double door he was able to see enemy troops taking cover in a ditch at the far end of a field. He was down to his last magazine in the Sten gun.

Sergeant Brandon Sinclair, twenty-six, a one time resident of Bury St Edmonds in Suffolk, sat leaning against the opposite side of the door frame. His left leg had been broken during his parachute landing, a compound fracture of the ankle. They'd strapped him up the best they could and given him a rifle to act as a crutch. The bones grated with every step he took. In addition an explosion had dislodged a large wooden splinter from an upright support. Whirling viciously through the air it had sliced open the back of his left hand. A chunk of wood had lodged deep and wouldn't stop bleeding. He too was almost out of ammunition. He glanced round at the others and wondered what more he could ask of them? They'd come together during the night, each man a stranger to the next. The drop had gone horribly wrong and they'd landed well wide of the drop zone. But they were all members of 6th Airborne and to that end knew how to fight. It had been a magnificent stand and by the time the Germans had pulled back many of their jack booted comrades lay dead in the rye.

Now the Paratroopers waited for the inevitable final attack, and they all knew where their duty lay. Do everything in their power to delay a German advance towards the beaches. Sergeant Sinclair looked away from his wounded men and stared at a stand of distant trees. Whatever happened next would prove costly for both sides.

Forty yards away from the barn, a sixth soldier lay hidden in a bush at the bottom of a hedge. He had neither a Sten gun, rifle or grenade, just a pistol. Nineteen year old Rifleman Harry King came from Huntingdon in Cambridgeshire. He'd lost his weapons after landing in deep water, surviving only by discarding their weight. He'd managed to evade capture but ended up spending the rest of the night shivering and alone wandering aimlessly through the fields of Normandy. Finally, bone tired, he'd crawled into the bottom of the hedge and closed his eyes.

He awoke in daylight to the sound of rifles and machine-gun fire. Germans were attacking the barn and he found himself mesmerised by the battle. Whoever was in the barn put up a great defence, but it was the better part of an hour before the Germans accepted they weren't making much headway and pulled back to reorganise. They left a good many dead in that field of rye. But Harry King was caught by indecision. If he tried to join whoever it was in the barn he would be hopelessly exposed to enemy fire. And if he tried to intervene with just a pistol his chances of making a difference to the final outcome were negligible.

Then from the far end of the field where a few spindly trees straddled a dirt road, a German armoured half-track rumbled out into the rye. In the troop carrier's open compartment a smartly uniformed young officer stood next to an NCO carrying a white flag and Harry immediately snatched a glance at the barn. There was no sign of an attempt to open fire and he turned his gaze back to the half-track. It advanced steadily until it was almost level with where King remained hidden, and then came to a grinding halt. The officer shouted at the barn.

'Englanders! Do you hear me?' His words were heavily accented but easily understood.

There was a long pause before someone answered.

'We hear!'

'Then listen well, Englander. My Kommandant demands your surrender. You are surrounded. It is foolish to die for no reason. There is no shame in it, you have fought well. You have five minutes to make up your minds.'

The rumble of the engine increased and the half-track steadily backed away to the far end of the field.

King glanced at his watch and guessed there were about four minutes left. He could vaguely make out the men in the barn but in no real detail. He watched a little longer, and then the sound of the returning half-track got his attention. The white flag was prominent in the back. It stopped more or less where it had originally halted.

The officer cupped his hands to his mouth. 'Well, Englanders. What is it to be?'

The reply came falteringly. 'What guarantee is there that we will be treated as prisoners of war?'

'Because you have my word, as a man of honour.'

There was a prolonged silence before a voice from inside called out.

'We have your word?'

'I have said so, Englander. The word of an officer in the Wehrmacht.'

There was another short pause and then came the answer. 'In that case we lay down our weapons. But we are wounded and walking is difficult.'

'Do not worry, Englander. My men will help.' The officer turned and beckoned, and Rifleman Harry King watched as thirty or so soldiers advanced out into the rye. He sank down to make himself small and held his breath. And it wasn't long before the German infantry arrived to stand in a loose semi-circle, weapons aimed at the barn doors.

A single Paratrooper hobbled out from the dark interior, hands held in the air. A German stepped forward to search him, found nothing and motioned for him to move over against the wall of the barn. The trooper had lost a good deal of blood, leaving him faint and disorientated, stumbling. It was all too slow for the German and he gave the Paratrooper a particularly vicious shove into the wall. And slowly, one at a time, four more wounded Paratroopers were poked and prodded out to line the wall, all in various states of distress, visibly carrying the scars of battle. Five or six Germans then went back inside and were gone for a number of minutes before one returned and reported to his young officer.

King guessed he was satisfied by the report because a minute later a second half-track rumbled into view at the other end of the field. As it drew closer he spotted two triangular pennants flying, one either side of the engine compartment. One of the flags bore the Nazi insignia of a black swastika presented on a white circle emblazoned on a deep red background. The other pennant was less distinct, portrayed overall in a drab brown with what might be some sort of regimental badge in the shape of a palm tree. The vehicle made a rapid approach then slowed. Four or five soldiers rode in the back along with one other who appeared older, appeared to carry more authority.

As the tracked carrier drew closer it could be seen the soldier wore the peaked cap of an Officer-of-Panzergrenadiers. It was topped with field-grey and banded in a dark green, and three discreet lines of lighter green piping edged the cap. Twin rows of silver-grey cord separated the gleaming visor from the dark band above.

The prominently displayed badge glinting above the peak was that of a silver Eagle clutching a Swastika. The officer's immaculate tunic bore the shoulder board insignia of a Major.

From Harry King's viewpoint, the most striking feature of the man's outward appearance was that of a dense, triangular black patch covering his left eye.

The half-track ground to a halt alongside the other vehicle and the newcomer was saluted. It was then that King noticed a difference in uniforms. From what he remembered of the briefings on enemy recognition, these newcomers wore the uniforms of Panzergrenadiers. And Grenadiers were primarily skirmishing infantry for tanks, professional to the core. King hoped they wouldn't begin a search of the surrounding area.

After a short conversation, 'black patch' dismounted and strode arrogantly across to stand in front of the prisoners. He obviously addressed them but King was too far away to hear any of the spoken words. The officer then walked back to his half-track, mounted up and spoke to his junior. There appeared to be a short argument before they exchanged salutes and the younger of the two reversed away, to be followed by more than half the Wehrmacht infantry. King estimated no more than five or six Germans remained in the semi-circle. As for the Paratroopers they lay in a pitiful bloody row and nursed their wounds.

As the young officer's half-track rumbled away into the sparse woods, the few remaining Wehrmacht guarding the Paratroopers slowly ambled away. The man with the black eye patch dug out a silver case, selected a cigarette and then accepted a flame from one of his underlings. He blew smoke into the breeze.

Then Harry King jumped. The explosive rasp of a Spandau machine-gun hammered. Glowing tracer slammed into defenceless British flesh. Blood sprayed, limbs torn apart. Agonised screams were lost in the harsh rattle of gunfire and a hail of bullets smashed bone and sinew, mercilessly chewing at shredded bodies. Defenceless Paratroopers died under the onslaught. Rifleman King watched in horror. These men were his fellow soldiers and were being betrayed, slaughtered in front of his eyes. He made an involuntary move for his pistol but sense prevailed. It would not help save the Paratroopers and the Panzergrenadiers would seek him out in minutes. He froze, unable to take his eyes off the massacre. The hot sting of tears welled up unbidden. He was witnessing the cold blooded execution of not only prisoners of war, but British prisoners of war already wounded in action.

The firing ceased abruptly, a haze of gunsmoke drifting from the back of the half-track. One of the nearby Wehrmacht infantry wandered over to take a closer look, raised two fingers and shook his head. Obviously not all were dead.

The arrogant black-patch tucked the cigarette in the corner of his mouth and clambered to the ground. Walking nonchalantly over to the dying Paratroopers he drew his Luger and stepped close. A Sergeant lay in a twisted heap his upturned face a mass of blood, only the eyes moved. The muzzle of the Luger was lowered to hover over the Paratrooper's nose.

The eyes blinked.

The gun fired. Sergeant Brandon Sinclair, with the back of his head turned to pulp, stopped breathing.

An agonised groan came from another Paratrooper. There were no signs of rank on the Englander's uniform and he lay in a bloodied heap against the wall. His breathing came as a loud hiss, lungs punctured, lips frothing pink. But it was the eyes that caught the attention, staring, unblinking. The lips quivered and another groan escaped the man's throat.

Again the Luger hovered in mid air, paused. The sharp crack echoed, and Rifleman John Weaver lost his life at the hands of a crazed German officer..

Satisfied, 'black-patch' holstered his pistol and strode back to the half track. He raised a gloved finger and pointed back down towards the scattering of trees. A general withdrawal began and this time the half-track made a wide turn through the rye before steering away.

Harry King grimaced as he saw the officer turn to an underling. He bared a mouthful of white teeth and laughed at a shared comment. King hugged the ground and watched them go. He remained motionless, giving the Germans plenty of time to vacate the area. After forty minutes he came to his feet and again checked the far end of the field. No sign of the enemy. He uncased his pistol and strode determinedly across to see the end result for himself

Nothing could have really prepared him for such a sight. The five Paratroopers lay where they were murdered. Blood ran down the wall, and more soaked the ground, and these defiant Paratroopers, men who had bravely faced down their own fears in answer to the ultimate challenge, here they now lay, blood all around.

King took a deep breath to steady himself and then began to find and collect each man's Identity Disc. It was a gruesome business but he felt the need to at least honour the dead by allowing their relatives to acknowledge their passing. As for himself, Rifleman Harry King swore to stay alive long enough to bear witness and report what he'd seen. The Paratroopers of 6th Airborne must be warned that capture by Panzergrenadiers could well end with the treachery of summary execution.

There'd not been the slightest attempt to comply with the Geneva Convention. So much for the word of a German officer.

In Portsmouth, it was later that afternoon when Major Paul Wingham emerged from a dockside warehouse having completed a total transformation. He was no longer dressed as a smart, well turned out Infantry Officer, but now wore a uniform of shapeless camouflage. Next to him strode Sergeant Cartwright, similarly attired in a shabby smock. Both were heavily armed and loaded down with enough provisions to see them through the next forty-eight hours.

A hundred yards along the quayside stood the waiting trio of General Scott Bainbridge, Lieutenant-Commander Richard Thorburn, and the young Lieutenant George Labatt. In the placid waters alongside, a Motor Torpedo Boat awaited their arrival and as far as Wingham could tell it was manned with an abundance of sailors. He saluted Bainbridge and with a nod to Thorburn, gestured at the boat.

'Got enough crew have we?'

Thorburn grinned. 'Volunteers, Paul. Had so many it was difficult to say no. But they're all needed, if not as crew, then to man the guns.'

Wingham shrugged with a smile. 'I'll take your word for it. Where d'you want us?'

Thorburn pointed to the flying bridge. 'You know Chief Petty Officer Falconer. He'll show you.'

Cartwright dropped down onto the foredeck and made his way back towards the bridge. Wingham hefted his pack onto one shoulder and prepared to follow.

Bainbridge leaned forward and held out a hand. 'Good luck, Major.' It was a firm handshake and Wingham nodded.

'Thank you, sir. If everything goes according to plan, I'll see you in forty-eight hours.' He grinned at Thorburn. 'Save some gin for when I get back.' They shook hands and Thorburn shook his head. 'No chance. We don't waste good alcohol on army types.'

Wingham chuckled, turned away and followed Cartwright onto the bows.

Labatt watched as they disappeared below and excused himself. 'Time I was away too, General sir.' He gave a quick salute and jumped down onto the quarterdeck.

Below decks, the Cox'n led the two soldiers aft into the small wardroom. 'Make yourselves at home. You'll not be disturbed. Not while we make the crossing.'

Wingham dropped his pack on a seat and propped his Sten gun in a corner. 'Thanks, we'll do our best to keep out of the way.'

The Cox'n nodded and turned for the bridge. Wingham pulled out his map of Normandy and spread it on the table. Cartwright leaned in and together they went over the route.

Up on the flying bridge, the Cox'n reappeared, eyebrows raised in query.

Labatt glanced round the boat, placed both hands on the screen and nodded. 'Start her up, Mister Falconer.'

With a grumbling cough the engines kicked into life, blue smoke swirling astern.

'Let go for'ard.'

A seaman unhitched the line and jumped onto the bows. The boat rocked gently.

'Let go aft.'

A rope snaked inboard over the stern rail, and an Ordinary Seaman followed. 'All clear, sir.'

Labatt settled his cap squarely over his eyes, grinned at Falconer, and gave the order.

'Slow ahead. Take us out, Cox'n.'

The boat burbled to the muted snarl of engines, and then as the engines increased in volume, gracefully peeled out from the quayside. Falconer put the helm over and with practised ease steered her away for the harbour entrance.

Labatt bellied up to the screen and looked down on the foredeck, admiring her sleek lines. He was in sole command of a Royal Navy Torpedo Boat, small, yes, but what a weapon. She was seventy feet from tip to toe, what they called a wooden hulled Vosper. He'd had a quick glance at the three powerful Packard Marine petrol engines, motors that in theory could help her achieve a top speed of thirty-seven knots all up. This particular boat had been fitted with a pair of 21inch torpedo tubes, a couple of pairs of half-inch machine guns and a 20mm Oerlikon. All in all, when loaded with torpedoes, she made for a formidable weapon. Not, he thought sadly, that he expected to use it as such, after all, today he was really only a glorified taxi driver.

'Permission to join you?' It was Wingham.

He looked astern and grinned. 'Feel free, sir. Plenty of room.'

Wingham came forward and together they stood watching as Falconer carefully conned the boat through the mass of moored shipping. 'Less of the "sir", skipper. I'm Paul and you're the captain, let's just leave it like that.'

Labatt gave him a sideways glance, a broad grin lighting up the boyish features.

'That's fine by me,' he said, and then allowed himself the luxury of enjoying his time in command.

Eventually, as they cleared the entrance to the harbour and then pushed out into the eastern arm of the Solent, the Cox'n increased power and headed south for the beaches of Normandy.

Major Paul Wingham took a firm grasp of the screen and grinned into the spray flecked wind. As the boat danced from one breaking crest to the next he leaned closer to Labatt.

'It's no wonder you agreed to volunteer. This is magic.'

Labatt narrowed his eyes into the spray. 'Wonderful,' he grinned. 'Bloody wonderful.'

The Cox'n allowed himself a quiet smile and made a great play of concentrating on the steering. The young Skipper was in his natural element and not every Naval officer got the chance to captain his own warship. A bit small, granted, but if it floated and could be put to sea then all was right with the world. God alone knew what he'd be like during the coming months. Bear with a sore head most likely.

The boat cleared Bembridge Point on the Isle of Wight and Labatt glanced at the compass.

'Steer one-seven-five, make our speed thirty-knots,' he said.

Falconer acknowledged. 'Steer one-seven-five, thirty-knots, aye aye, sir,' and he made a fractional adjustment to the wheel. 'Course one-seven-five, sir.'

'Very well,' Labatt said, and with the bows lifting to the thrust of the screws they settled down for the run south.

Wingham decided to stay up top. After yesterday's events, and with half an inkling of what was to come, he welcomed the exhilarating ride, his chin lifted to the wind.

It was later that afternoon, with the Torpedo Boat being guided skilfully through a mass of off-shore shipping that Labatt directed the Cox'n to slow their approach. It gave him chance to study the war torn beach. It turned out to be a not very deep strip of sand covered in the dark green camouflage of British vehicles. And he began to realise a lot of those military vehicles were battle damaged, charred shells broken and burnt.

Then Labatt suddenly jabbed a finger towards a five yard stretch of sand that had just been vacated by a landing craft.

'Get in there, Cox'n!'

Falconer gave the boat a short burst of power, whipped her round to starboard and at the last second brought her back to port. With a fierce scrape she landed her bows on the surf laden sands. Up the beach, and to both east and west as far as the eye could see, military hardware was stacked up waiting to drive inland. Soldiers by the thousand were filtering their way through the traffic and pushing off the beach into the French hinterland. But also, scattered indiscriminately at various locations along the strip of sand, lay the stark reminder of a bitter battle hard fought. The desolate wreckage of battered tanks and Bren gun carriers, intermingled with Jeeps and trucks shot up and burnt out gave evidence of the savage fight to win the ground. Casualty stations were inundated with the wounded. The battleships and cruisers that Labatt and Falconer had so diligently negotiated on their way in kept up a resounding if sporadic barrage, their heavy artillery lobbing great shells over head. The rattle of small arms fire could be heard in the far distance.

Major Paul Wingham nimbly made his way past the torpedo tubes and onto the foredeck, Bill Cartwright with him.

Labatt leaned over the screen with a grin. 'All the luck, sir.'

Loaded down with his pack and weapons Wingham waved a hand in acknowledgement, bent his knees and dropped from the bows into six inches of surf. He waded clear, waited for Cartwright, and called back to the bridge. 'God speed, Lieutenant. And you can tell Commander Thorburn not to forget that drink he owes me!'

Labatt gave him a broad grin and touched the peak of his cap in final farewell.

'Get us out of here, Cox'n.'

'Aye aye, sir,' Falconer said, and the three Packard engines roared to the increase of power. The M.T.B. seemed to lift bodily off the sands and took off astern. Forty yards out, Falconer swung the wheel, put her into full ahead and with the sea thrashing at the keel she forged out between a pair of incoming Tank Landing Craft and into deeper waters.

Lieutenant George Labatt glanced back at two small figures striding into the distance. Pushing his cap back off his forehead he pursed his lips in thought. Whether it was the waves of fighter-bombers flying in overhead, or wave after wave of landing craft making their approach runs to the beach, one thing he believed was certain. The war in the Channel had finally taken on a new direction. It was no longer just the preserve of the Navy and Air force, the battle for supremacy had moved on. A quiet smile touched his mouth as he recognised the true meaning of the latest developments.

It was the Army's turn to carry the torch, and in so doing, it would take with it the seemingly never ending, bloody waves of war. Labatt turned back to the screen and bent his knees to the boat's undulating rise and fall.

'Take us home, Cox'n.'

'Aye aye, sir,' Falconer answered, and with a nudge of the throttle the bows lifted, and as she powered up, they headed down the port side of three troop ships all disembarking their preordained quota of infantry soldiers into the small flat bottomed landing craft.

The bows thumped an oncoming roller and a sheet of salt laden spray smothered the bridge. Labatt wiped his face and grinned. This was the life, and he knew he needed to make the most of it. Might be a long while before *Brackendale* resumed her duties in the English Channel.

Wingham and Cartwright made it to a sand covered sea wall, clambered through the rubble of a damaged section and turned to look back out to sea. Labatt's boat had become a mere speck against the mass of shipping yet to unload their precious cargoes. The beach itself was organised chaos, a plethora of equipment causing massive congestion. And every now and then an enemy shell erupted in the middle of it all, the explosion causing considerable damage. Here and there the dark red-orange of flickering flames danced amongst steel wreckage. Columns of thick oily smoke drifted skywards, shrouding the scene in dismal grey.

Wingham turned his back to it all and pointed to the left.

'This way for now,' he said. A beach front road led off towards Ouistreham, exactly where he wanted to be. Once they'd cleared the town a road led due south to a couple of bridges and then it was just a short walk to Ranville. If Bainbridge's intelligence was correct, that's where he and Cartwright would link up with Major Lane.

With a fair few miles to cover they set off at a good pace, both knowing that finding the place in daylight would make their task a sight easier than thrashing around in the dark.

It was late that same night when Rifleman Harry King stumbled on a two man British Observation Post. He was lucky not to be shot at close range by the vigilant Paratroopers, alert to the slightest disturbance. As it was a short burst fired blind into the dark missed the intended target and his string of curses quickly convinced them of his nationality. It turned out they were fellow members of the 5th Parachute Brigade and as King wolfed down some shared rations, he relayed the tragic story of five brave Paratroopers. By daybreak the majority of 6th Airborne had heard of a massacre carried out under the orders of a Nazi officer wearing a black eye patch. No-one who heard that story was in any doubt as to its authenticity. It proved to be a timely warning.

3 Cold Steel

Dawn of the following day came swiftly to the land of Normandy, and far inland the orange glow of a rising sun brought warmth to the rich, fertile soil. It was a place where orchards flourished and cattle grazed rich pasture, and where peasant farmers made the sweetest cider and the softest cheese in all of France. At this hour, amongst the many isolated farms, womenfolk kneaded and baked their dough until that familiar warm aroma of freshly made bread drifted in the air. And from far away a cockerel crowed, a raucous cry that echoed on the morning air, and chickens pecked for their morning grain. Fat pigs grunted in their pens, and the bountiful fields of wheat, barley and corn waved soft in the passing breeze.

It was midsummer in northwest France and after a week of wild wind and rain the weather had set fair for a fine, peaceful day.

And yet, on this day in the June of 1944, there was no longer peace to be had in Normandy. Three days beforehand, as night had given way to the first grey of dawn, the savage fury of a bloody war had descended on this gentle, long forgotten land. From the shimmering beaches in the north an immense Allied army had stormed ashore to liberate Nazi occupied Europe. From a vast array of landing craft, thousands of soldiers had waded through the turbulent surf to fight their way forward into the teeth of implacable German resistance.

Now, on this third morning since the invasion began, a quarter of a million men bore witness to the brutal reality of a murderous war as Allied soldiers fought desperately to expand their tenuous foothold on the shores of northwest France.

But inland, well south of the fragile bridgehead, a lone soldier stood silent under the branches of a twisted oak. And beneath its dense canopy of serrated leaves, a thick tangle of hornbeam formed a comforting cloak of concealment. Away in the distance the muted thunder of heavy artillery resounded across Nazi occupied France, German guns to the south, Allied ships firing from out at sea. And vaguely heard were the resulting explosions as enormous shells found their targets.

The soldier ignored it all and took time to study the landscape ahead, motionless. He was in his element, a man to depend on, smoothly muscled yet strong, a man for whom leadership sat comfortably on broad shoulders. He carried himself with a natural ease, quietly confident, effortless. An overnight growth of stubble darkened the outline of his firm jaw, and the keen, sharp eyes were narrowed in concentration.

Major Paul Wingham, raised his binoculars and focussed the lens. The uniform he wore bore little resemblance to that of the Regular Army. Rather it was the shapeless smock of a Paratrooper, and the haphazard brush strokes of green and brown camouflage blended seamlessly with the surrounding vegetation. The rounded dome of an 'Airborne' helmet sat tight on his forehead, chin straps hanging free, and a string net stretched taut over the helmet had been carefully interwoven with a latticework of leaves. From a strap on his right shoulder a sub-machinegun hung loose and his ammunition pouches bulged with spare magazines. Grenades weighed heavy in the pockets of his smock and a Browning pistol sat holstered on his right hip. Comfortably sheathed on his left buttock a 'pig-sticker' bayonet and fighting knife lay ready to hand.

Wingham had been born in a place called Alderney, one of the Channel Islands. He learned to sail and grew up to become a fine fisherman, and therefore a valuable member of the small community. His schooling had included two terms at the Officers' Training Corps in Victoria College on the larger island of Jersey. In the early June of 1940, with the threat of a German invasion, Winston Churchill had agreed to evacuate all those wanting to escape to England. Wingham, along with his mother and father, boarded the last ship out of Braye Harbour and took passage to Weymouth on the Dorset coast where he left them to be looked after by relatives. His rapid completion of Officer Training became almost a formality, after which the young Second-Lieutenant Wingham joined the 2nd Battalion Sherwood Foresters on Home Defence duties.

Now, all these years later, 'Major' Paul Wingham raised his binoculars and took another long look at Normandy's tree lined fields. The trees he focussed on formed the northern edge of a dark wood, but immediately to his front two large fields separated him from his objective and gave cause for concern. Other fields spread out both left and right, but for Wingham time was at a premium, and it left him with no option but to cross that open ground. The one saving grace was a tall hedgerow that formed a barrier running down the right side of the fields. If nothing else it offered some background cover to the movement of his Platoon. It all went against his better judgement, but finding a safer route was out of the question. Wingham took one last look before lowering the glasses to his chest, and then turned his head.

'Sergeant,' he called in a fierce whisper.

Hidden amongst low growing hornbeam, Sergeant David William "Bill" Cartwright answered.

'Sir?'

Wingham waited for Cartwright to extricate himself from the bushes and grinned as the Sergeant emerged brushing dried mud from the collar of his smock. He cursed and wiped his heavily lined face clear of dirt.

'Bugger this for a game of soldiers,' he muttered, more to himself than for general consumption. He mumbled something unintelligible before raising an inquisitive eyebrow. Wingham met his gaze, the grin softening to a warm smile, glad that Cartwright had also been chosen for the mission. Aside from the formal relationship between officer and senior NCO, the two men had long since become good friends. Wingham nodded at the field.

'Not exactly what I had in mind,' he said, 'but I'm going to move out along that hedge, staggered formation. You and I take point, the rest to follow. Five minutes.'

Cartwright nodded, staring down at the distant trees. 'You think we'll have company down there?'

'I wouldn't bet against it,' Wingham said.

'Hope the bastards are asleep,' Cartwright snapped, with feeling.

Wingham agreed. 'Me too.' Then with the merest hint of a change in the tone of his voice he said, 'Let's have them formed up.'

'Sir,' Cartwright said in that deep gruff voice, recognising the shift in emphasis, and began passing orders to Section leaders.

Wingham slipped his binoculars back in the case and readied his Sten gun. He stifled a yawn, more tired than he cared to admit. It had been a hectic few days. After landing they'd spent some hours searching for Major Harry Lane's temporary Field Headquarters. Eventually they linked up with men of HQ Platoon, the same soldiers with whom Wingham had personally, naturally, had the most contact in training. Unfortunately, their platoon officer, Lieutenant Roger Jefferson made a bad landing and broke a leg. By chance the remainder of the Platoon had more or less survived as a unit. Only a few had not reported in. So with some adjustment in numbers to create three Sections of eight men, the Platoon now consisted of twenty-four highly trained soldiers, and one new officer, namely himself.

Cartwright reappeared from the undergrowth after only a short delay, his six-feet two inch frame poised for action. 'They're ready.'

Glancing round at the shadowy figures Wingham rubbed the stubble on his jaw. He and Cartwright were about to lead these Paratroopers into the back of beyond.

'Right then,' said Wingham, 'no time like the present,' and he took a purposeful step towards the field.

Moments later, eight camouflaged men, now transformed in their guise as Light Infantrymen, strode out from the edge of the tree lined rise and into the open. They walked single file, well spaced, guns poised. They were ten yards out into waist high rye and moving alongside the hedge when the next Section of men emerged from the trees and followed on. And finally, with the sun's rays slanting in from above the horizon, the remaining eight lightly armed Paratroopers filed out to join the line. The distant thunder of heavy artillery accompanied every step, and now and then the closer rattle of rifle and machine-gun fire echoed in across the fields. Wingham's small Platoon braced themselves for whatever lay ahead. No-one doubted they were back in the war.

Wingham led them on, forcing his way through tall stems. It was thick and clung to the legs, making each step an effort. He took a look behind. They advanced in good order, weapons up. For an instant he smiled. In the weeks leading up to the invasion, training had been hard, competitive. Looking at them now, the end result of a harsh regime, these tough, rugged soldiers were all he could wish for. It had been worth all the pain, all the mutterings and all the swearing and cursing. What emerged were men who brought to the battlefield a typical British belligerence. His only regret had been that during the last weeks of training he'd been called away to prepare for D-Day itself. It had been a specific operation that had required intensive training on the use of wireless telegraphy.

Cartwright brushed past Wingham and moved ahead, to be joined by two others, leaving Wingham centre rear. The Platoon moved steadily, each man wary of a possible unseen enemy.

As Wingham pushed on behind them he remembered there was something else that set this particular Platoon apart from all the others. A night exercise near the east coast of Northumbria had resulted in a requirement for passwords. Because the Platoon was operating independently, an unnamed but imaginative staff officer in the signals unit had come up with the codename of '*Ruffians*'.

The men had instantly taken to the name, later confiding to the local barmaids, and any other young ladies within earshot, that they were in fact the most handsome bunch of '*ruffians*' a girl was ever likely to meet.

The Platoon pressed on and long minutes passed before they reached the end of the first field, without incident. At the end of it Wingham tensed as he cleared the dividing embankment and followed Cartwright into the next field. There was an immediate sense of 'no place to hide'. This was lush pastureland for cattle, part meadow with wild flowers. Nothing grew taller than a man's calf muscles, and only a hundred yards away those dark green woods remained ominously quiet. Deathly quiet. He peered intently at the scrub undergrowth. The stillness became unnerving and his heart quickened. As hot as he was, a cold finger of apprehension ran through him. He put it to the back of his mind and took another glance round the Platoon. The last man stepped off the embankment. With a good deal of caution they pushed on staying tight to the hedge, the high foliage adding a shaded margin to the field. From the edge of the wood a pair of blackbirds winged their way skywards.

A single gunshot shattered the peace. A bullet punched the air and Paratroopers hit dirt. It was instantly followed by the violent rasping buzz of a Spandau. The tree line lit up with the stabbing flash of gunfire, Schmeissers, Mausers and light machine-guns adding to the din. Tracer ripped across the field.

But the Paratroopers had expected something of the kind and were well drilled. By chance they'd gone down in a slight fold in the ground and it gave them just enough cover to flatten beneath the direct line of fire. They laid down a withering wall of return fire and the accumulated marksmanship of well disciplined soldiers quickly began to make itself felt. Three Bren guns, one to each Section, thumped a steady stream of bullets into the undergrowth. The noise increased, rising in ferocity. Sten guns added to the battle, and riflemen hammered a hail of .303 rounds at the enemy. Shouts and yells filled the air and multi coloured tracer fizzed back and forth. The rain of bullets thrashed at the low growing foliage. The accumulated weight of gunfire began to take effect and the German firepower stuttered, no longer a continuous barrage.

Rifleman Henry Tipton of No.3 Section, from Seaham in Durham, raised his head. He lined up on the half hidden figure of a machine-gunner. A squeeze of the trigger and blood sprayed, the German collapsed. A second German dragged him clear, took his place.

But Tipton then made a fatal error. He held himself in that same raised position as he reloaded, pausing to pick out another target. A bullet found him. It slammed into the Paratrooper's left cheek bone, deflected, and buried itself at the base of his skull. Blood pumped and Tipton sagged. He was twenty and died oblivious to his surroundings.

The rattling crash of gunfire filled the air and Wingham tried desperately to make sense of the contact. What were they up against? How many? Seasoned troops or un-blooded? Lying flat on the short grass, the smell of the meadow filling his senses, he twisted sideways to peer at the tree line. Tracer whined over his head and he narrowed his eyes, his skin crawling in expectation of being hit, an instinctive reaction to such danger. But that glimpse of the bushes gave him vital information. There were at least two Spandaus stationed approximately twenty-yards apart and they had the Platoon neatly bracketed. At the same time No.1 Section's Bren gunner had latched on to the Spandau at two-o'clock, the enemy rate of fire noticeably reduced. And Wingham had three such Bren guns under his command, all hammering short, aimed bursts at the seat of tracer.

He risked another glance and managed to locate Cartwright. He was lying prone by the hedge taking aimed shots at the enemy. Between Wingham and the Sergeant lay the majority of the Platoon, enemy bullets kicking dirt all around. And Wingham knew it was no good lying out in the open exposed to German marksmanship, that could only end one way, and it wouldn't be pretty.

'Sergeant!' he yelled across the gap, the sound of his voice almost lost in the din.

Cartwright heard and looked over.

Wingham gestured at the trees and called. 'We need to outflank 'em. I'll take No.2 Section left, circle behind. We'll need covering fire.'

Cartwright raised a thumb indicating he understood. He shouted, his stentorian voice cutting through the noise of battle.

'No.1 and No.3 Sections! Covering fire for No.2! Make ready . . . . Ready?' He checked with Wingham who gave a thumbs up.

'Fire!'

Every gun in the hands of fifteen Paratroopers blasted a curtain of bullets at the low growing foliage. Germans ducked from the onslaught, some too slow to avoid the volley. The raking gunfire scoured the undergrowth, twigs and leaves and pebbles and dirt driven asunder. The enemy kept their heads well down.

Wingham made his move.

'No.2 Section! With me!' he yelled, and sprang to his feet. The Section rose as one, running hard, bent at the waist. Wingham led the way, angling in towards the trees. Behind them the gunfire rolled on, hammering at fleeting shadows hidden in the bushes.

Blowing hard, Wingham lunged inside the line of trees and pushed straight on to gain some distance before turning back towards the fight. He jumped a moss covered log, ducked beneath an ancient, leaning tree trunk and then paused in a partial clearing. The Section closed in around him, eyes questioning.

'We'll hit 'em from this end, flanking fire, clean the bastards out. Questions?'

Heads shook and the men looked to their weapons, changing partially used magazines for fresh ones, Lee Enfields replenished from five-round steel strip-clips.

He gave the order to, 'Fix bayonets,' removed his own from the scabbard and clipped the cold steel onto the Sten's housing. In moments an array of 'pig stickers' gleamed dully in the sombre light.

He gave them the once over, saw they were ready, and then turned to set off for the battle. He moved at speed but with his senses fully attuned to the dangers ahead. And when the first German rifleman came into view Wingham didn't hesitate and shot him twice through the side. He fell back into a ditch being used as a trench. A two man Spandau team were next in line, the gunner firing controlled bursts out into the meadow.

Wingham lobbed a grenade and gave the pair half a magazine of 9mm rounds. The grenade exploded at their feet in the ditch, lower limbs lacerated, more wounds inflicted by the Major's submachine-gun. The gunner rolled to the bottom of the ditch screaming with pain. Wingham finished him with bullets to the head. The man's assistant slithered sideways bleeding from the neck. He came to rest with one arm flopped over the chest of the gunner, a grotesque imitation of lovers entwined.

A startled German officer spun round at the grenade's explosion, sub-machinegun hammering at the intruders. A Paratrooper grunted and fell. The bullet hit his chest and smashed a rib, grazed a lung and then lodged in his heart. Blood trickled from his mouth, his breathing laboured, and in seconds he was dead.

A Rifleman fired from the waist and the officer stumbled backwards. The .303 round struck the man's midriff, the impact knocking him off his feet. Sprawled on his back he tried to raise the gun, and the Rifleman gave him another, this time aimed at the chest. As the Paratrooper moved closer a stick grenade landed. Wingham saw it and yelled a warning. The men dived clear of the grenade's proximity and the resulting explosion failed to inflict any harm. Then a Sten gun rattled and a German took the full force of a magazine. Another Rifleman pulled a pin and hurled a grenade along the ditch. It detonated on a bounce and flying shrapnel wounded two. One lost an eye, the other hit on the shins, his legs peppered with steel fragments. Paratroopers then made certain, both Germans given no chance to surrender.

Out in the sunlit meadow, Bill Cartwright recognised the instant the Spandau was silenced, the rate of incoming fire severely reduced. It was time to join the fight. He gave a tight lipped grimace and came up on one knee. Tracer snarled past his head. He flinched, ignored it and shouted. 'Bayonets!'

He gave them a moment to comply, tracer sweeping the ground.

'Up the *Ruffians*!'

He lunged to his feet and charged at the nearest trees, weaving as he ran. He thought he saw enemy uniforms and fired from the waist. To his left Paratroopers overtook him, a fusillade of gunfire aimed at the bushes. The right flank Spandau still spewed tracer across the meadow and a grenade went in from No.1 Section.

Cartwright slowed, waited for the explosion, and then gave the area half-a-dozen rounds. The grenade was well delivered and Germans died. Charging Paratroopers crashed into the bushes. Bayonets struck soft flesh, stabbing and twisting, and were tugged free. Bullets fired at close range, men on both sides injured and bleeding, the wounded desperately trying to crawl clear.

Wingham caught sight of a German kneeling at the base of a trunk, his sub-machinegun levelled at the oncoming Paratroopers. There was no time for careful aim and he hit the trigger while still only waist high. The gun juddered and two or three rounds struck low, the soldier's pelvis shattered. He screamed and dropped his weapon, writhing on the ground, splintered bone protruding from his waist. Wingham stepped closer, aimed, and put a bullet through his head. A splash of blood showed red.

Panicked Germans began to scramble from the ditch, retreating into the wood. Two of Wingham's Riflemen brushed past, pig stickers gleaming as they went after their prey. He saw Cartwright down at the far end jump the ditch and disappear into heavy undergrowth. Multi-coloured tracer hissed and whined in every direction. Another grenade exploded in the trees. Leaves fluttered. A Paratrooper stumbled backwards out of the bushes, hands holding his belly. He missed his footing and fell to the edge of the ditch. Wingham went to help and knelt at his side. He recognised Lance-Corporal Oliver Turnbull and could see he'd been shot twice in the chest. There was a lot of blood and the hands trembled. It looked like he'd been stabbed with a bayonet. Before Wingham was able to do anything at all, the man's breathing stopped, his eyes staring.

A bullet slapped at Wingham's smock and he ducked away, diving into the ditch. He landed in the bottom, turned and slammed his back against the far wall, Sten gun poised. A shadow flickered, a hint of grey, and he gave it a burst. There was a yell and a body crashed through the greenery. A pair of eyes beneath a German helmet peered down from the lip of the ditch, fear etched across the swarthy face.

Wingham calmly fired again and the soldier's face turned into a bloody mess. Wingham nodded to himself. One less German to worry about..

Distant shouts caught his attention, Paratroopers urging one another on, chasing the fleeing enemy. He pushed himself to his feet and winced at pain in his neck. He felt the area at the side and his fingers touched a sticky warmth. Blood was oozing from a wound. The gunfire faded to silence and he gave himself a minute, taking deep breaths. The Platoon began to filter back and gather on the open meadow.

Cartwright came along the ditch and raised a hand to Wingham's bloodied collar.

'You're wounded,' he said.

Wingham shrugged his hand away. 'Leave it, Bill, I'm alright.' He fixed Cartwright with a meaningful look. 'Casualties?'

'Near as I can tell, three dead, four wounded,' Cartwright said in a hushed voice. 'I gave orders to bring the dead back to the field.'

'Right,' Wingham said, 'let's get to it.' He clambered out from the ditch and pushed through low growing hawthorn. The last body was being carried out from the wood and he watched as they laid it reverently alongside the others. They stood back and moved away and Wingham went over to recover dog tags. He looked down at the bodies and swallowed. He knew all these men, had trained with them.

The first was that of Lance-Corporal Oliver Turnbull from Glasgow, and Wingham had watched him die, unable to help. Formerly of the Black Watch, and accepted for the Paras in late '43,

Turnbull had been struck twice by bullets to the chest and then taken a bayonet to the belly. He was twenty. Wingham retrieved his dog tag.

Next to him lay Rifleman Henry Tipton of No.3 Section, killed by a bullet through his cheek. An ex coalminer, he'd joined the Rifles aged eighteen, and had been Mentioned-in-Despatches during combat in Sicily. He became a Paratrooper in January '44. On the 1st of June he'd celebrated his twenty-first birthday. Another dog tag.

And lastly he found the body of Rifleman Fred Price, another member of No.3 Section. Price was a native of Cumbria and had made a living repairing dry stone walling to support his wife and baby daughter before being called up. He'd fought in Sicily and then the Italian campaign before joining 6th Airborne. He was twenty-three.

Sergeant Cartwright detailed four men to stand watch in the woods, and while the wounded were being tended, a burial party dug three makeshift graves. They chose to locate them in the corner of the field, four yards out from the hedge, where sunlight would warm their place of rest. A Paratrooper's helmet was laid gently at the head of each mound. It fell to Wingham to say a few words and when he finished they briefly stood with heads bowed in silence. Cartwright then quietly dismissed the Platoon.

Wingham lingered, three dog tags clasped in the palm of his hand. Cartwright came to join him and together they took a last look at the freshly turned soil.

'It's a sad thing,' Cartwright murmured.

Wingham swallowed hard and nodded.

'Yes,' he said at length. 'Might not have been my best decision.'

Cartwright raised his head and stuck his chin out. 'No choice though, was there? I'd have done the same.'

Wingham slowly let the dog tags slide into a pocket, eyes down. Those few words, especially coming from a man like Cartwright, helped alleviate the worst of his thoughts.

'Thanks, Bill, I appreciate that.'

'Simple truth is all,' Cartwright said, and stepped back from the graveside. 'I better see to the lads, see what's what.'

Wingham straightened and glanced at his watch. 'Yes, do that. Ten minutes and we'll have to move.'

'And the dead Jerries?'

'Leave the buggers. We don't have time. Someone might come knocking.'

Cartwright turned away with a nod and went to join the Platoon. Major Paul Wingham swivelled his head left and right to ease the ache in his neck.

In the end it took the Sergeant twenty minutes before he'd made certain the wounded were comfortable and that the reorganisation of the Sections was to his satisfaction. Where once there had been three sections of eight, they were now divided into sevens. As luck would have it, the injured turned out to be walking wounded, although one man had a calf wound that gave him a bad limp.

With a final check on the time, Wingham gave the order to 'move out', and in the shaded gloom of an ancient woodland, he and the remaining Paratroopers picked up the pace and pressed on to find their main objective.

4 The Farm

A few short miles north of the three freshly dug graves, the battle to push inland ebbed and flowed. Along a sixty mile length of ancient coastline, General Dwight D. Eisenhower's multi national invasion force slowly but inexorably began to expand their foothold on French soil. But the worry for Allied command was Hitler's ability to reinforce his front line with the Panzer Divisions he had in reserve. If they arrived in strength before a substantial build up of Allied armour, then the hard won precarious foothold might yet be lost. Thus far, a half hearted attempt by the 21st Panzer Division, followed by an ineffective counter attack by the 12th SS Division, had both been stopped and reversed. A well prepared defence of artillery and tanks by the Canadian's 7th Brigade had sprung a trap and inflicted substantial casualties on the German spear point. They withdrew in disarray and were ordered to take up defensive positions in the immediate vicinity of Caen.

But with the serious possibility of heavy German armour hanging in the air, measures were put in place to help weaken the impact of any German counter attack. As the next wave of Allied reinforcements fought their way inland, a senior staff officer with the British forces, recently landed on Sword beach, made specific inquiries as to whether any Paratroopers had been despatched to an isolated farm.

In the English county of West Sussex, at an old ramshackle cottage overlooking the friendly waters of the narrow Channel, a young woman opened her eyes and luxuriated in the warmth of an early morning sun. A gentle breeze stirred the yellow curtains hanging either side of her bedroom window and very slowly Mary slid her feet to the floor. A small sheepskin rug caressed her toes before she stepped onto the polished floorboards, cool on her heels. She tossed her head to settle her tousled hair, moved to the window, and smiled. It was the first morning for some time that the grey clouds had disappeared and the incessant rain had stopped falling. Honeysuckle Cottage always looked better when the sun's rays kissed the old thatched roof and turned it to that lovely shade of honeyed gold.

Leaning her elbows on the windowsill, Mary looked south towards the English Channel and guessed that somewhere over in France, her fiancé had probably already become mixed up in the fighting. Her copy of yesterday's newspaper, the Telegraph, dated Wednesday the 7th, assured its readers that the D-Day landings had proved successful and that the Allies had achieved a significant tactical success by managing to push inland by several miles. A heavy naval bombardment was assisting in pacifying targets further inland. She was not quite so naïve as to believe all that the journalists wrote but the BBC reported much the same so she assumed it couldn't be far from the truth.

After all these devastating years of war, Mary was excited by the news of that long awaited Allied invasion. At the same time her excitement was tempered by the fact that her fiancé, Chris, had parachuted into enemy held territory and even now might be lying hurt and in pain. The thought of his being killed was a step too far and definitely not something to dwell on.

'Mary!' It was her mother calling from downstairs.

'Coming,' she answered, reached for her gown and pushed her toes into the comfort of her carpet slippers. She went down the narrow stairs with her body turned slightly to make the descent easier, right foot leading. Almost at the bottom she stopped to listen. The heavy drone of aircraft engines filled the air, the stairs vibrating with the ever increasing noise. She ignored her mother pouring tea in the kitchen and rushed out into the garden. A glance overhead and the reason for the noise became self explanatory. Bombers. Too many to count, all headed south, the formations neatly silhouetted against the blue of the morning sky. She watched for a little longer, until the last of them became mere specks in the distance, and turned back into the kitchen.

'Sounded like a lot, dear,' her mother observed, basting a fried egg in the pan.

'As many as I've ever seen all together.' Mary said, cutting two slices of bread. She placed a slice on each plate and moved them to the table. Pulling out a chair she sat and waited for the eggs, her thoughts returning to foreign fields.

Her mother served up the fried eggs, and then before joining Mary at the table, moved over to the Welsh dresser. Very deliberately she turned on the wireless and as the valves warmed up the cultured voice of a broadcaster filled the kitchen.

"This is the BBC. Here is the nine o'clock news for today Thursday, June the 8th.

It is reported that Allied troops have captured Bayeux five miles inland from the beaches. Having penetrated that far our troops are now involved in heavier fighting. Air support is limiting the advance of enemy reserves and overnight our heavy bombers were deployed in great strength.

General Eisenhower yesterday went to the beachhead and met with General Montgomery.

That concludes this brief summary of our eight o'clock report. Further news will follow in the BBC's ten o'clock bulletin."

Music from the Light Orchestra followed and Mary began to eat. She caught her mother looking at her with questioning eyes but looked down to avoid answering. Any attempt to work out possible locations from such a limited broadcast would result in nothing more than sheer guesswork. She took another mouthful, chewed vigorously and then reached for her cup of tea. It was no good worrying over all that now, and anyway, there was work to be done. Chickens to be fed, the pigs to be cleaned out, Snowy, her Shetland pony to be let out into the paddock and the vegetable plot needed weeding.

That was more than enough to keep her mind from wandering. And she knew she was far from alone. Across Great Britain, and America and Canada, and many other far flung countries of the British Empire, thousands of mothers and daughters and fathers and sisters were in the same predicament. Betrothed too, she allowed herself, fell into a similar category.

No, she was far from alone in praying for Christopher's safe return. She took a last swallow of tea and changed from carpet slippers into her old Wellington boots. Knotting the dressing gown firmly round her waist she made her way out to the chicken coop. The business of greeting individual chickens and spreading corn quickly took her mind off the war. In the stable she let Snowy out into the small paddock, and the silver Shetland pony trotted playfully over to the nearest fence rail to be made a fuss of. Bob the dog, their three year old collie, padded over to sniff at the nearest posts.

Mary spread a little more corn and watched them peck. Whatever else was happening in the world, her animals were awake to the new day and needed feeding.

In Normandy, many kilometres south of Wingham's under strength Platoon, an elite Panzer Division, much favoured by Adolf Hitler, had not been released until late on the day of the Allied invasion. After much confusion the Fuhrer finally ordered the Division to vacate its holding station in the region of Chartres-Le Mans and move to reinforce 12th SS Panzer west of Caen. On arrival they were to prepare for an assault on British and Canadian advance positions. The Division, known simply as the Panzer-Lehr, only then began its forced march to reinforce Caen. It had set off at full strength with close to 15,000 men and boasting almost 240 Panzers. The total establishment included ten, 54-ton Tigers fitted with the deadly 8.8cm anti-tank gun, while the remaining numbers were made up of Panthers, Panzer Mk4's, Stugs and Panzer Mk3's. For the infantry, more commonly known as 'Panzergrenadiers', almost 300 half-tracks were used to transport them into battle, the only division to achieve total armoured protection for troops on the move.

Having advanced towards Caen during the remainder of daylight hours on the 6th, the Division proceeded to push on through the hours of darkness in an attempt to gain as much ground as possible. Wednesday the 7th found them exposed to ground attack by Allied fighter-bombers and casualties began to mount.

At the front of the third column of the Division's northerly advance, a twenty-one year old Unterofficier by the name of Jurgen Voigt, the driver of a Mk IV Panzer, kept his foot pressed firmly against the throttle pedal. With the coming of daylight on Thursday the 8th, and against all recent military doctrine, the Division was again ordered to proceed during daytime hours regardless of heavy air attacks. For Jurgen Voigt, hatch open and goggles clamped tightly over his leather helmet, it became a simple matter of maintaining what speed he could to maintain a healthy gap between himself and the Panzer behind, mainly to avoid collision in the event of aerial bombardment. Manoeuvring twenty-five tons of tracked armoured Panzer, at speed, in a tight formation was not to be recommended. Far better to maintain a gap of ten or fifteen metres between himself and those following.

The column rumbled on, engines growling, the steel tracks squealing on the paved surface. Voigt jostled with the steering levers, light tugs at speed, more forcefully when slowing to negotiate tight turns. Exhaust fumes from the half-tracks in front swirled back to encompass Voigt's driving position, the acrid taste bitter on the tongue. Travelling in column for this extended period had left him with a harsh dry cough.

But of one thing Jurgen Voigt was certain, the Panzers were urgently needed to stem the advance of the Allied army. And he was part of the Fuhrer's famous Panzer-Lehr, the most well equipped and up to strength Division in Rommel's entire mobile reserve. He was convinced there would be much for the enemy to fear when they came up against the best of Army Group West's armoured Divisions.

In a dense wood well behind enemy lines, Wingham came across a small clearing and decided to call a halt. The *Ruffians* had been on the move since late yesterday evening and if nothing else the wounded needed a break. A hot drink would be more than welcome.

He waited for Cartwright to join him.

'Time for a brew, and we'll check the wounded while we're at it.'

Cartwright nodded and crossed to the nearest Section leader.

'Pass the word, we'll have a brew.'

Corporal Jim Harrison grinned and turned to issue the order.

'Cup of char, lads. Get to it.'

Cartwright reached out and grabbed his arm. 'I want a picquet posted twenty yards ahead and another to the rear. And check on the wounded. Let me know what you find.'

Back packs were shrugged to the ground and men quickly gathered into small groups as the makings were unearthed, and a chosen few began the task of boiling water. Two men from No.1 Section were detailed off for picquet duty and both melted away into the trees.

Rifleman Chris Jamison, a twenty year old from Hastings, moved cautiously back along the path the Platoon had just negotiated. He found a well spaced couple of tree trunks, one of which had a chest high branch protruding horizontally to the right. Placing his Lee Enfield so it sat snugly in the fork he then leaned back comfortably against the other trunk. His pig sticker bayonet gleamed dully in the soft light and Jamison settled down to watch and listen.

The Sergeant rejoined the Old Man who was occupied studying his map, so without a word Cartwright set about lighting his own 'Tommy cooker'. He opted for a mess tin to make enough tea for two. Corporal Harrison came back to report that most of the walking wounded were managing well, only the 'calf wound' requiring two men in support.

A fallen tree trunk lay isolated at one side of the clearing, making an ideal place to sit, and when the Old Man eventually tucked away his map, Cartwright was able to offer him the mug.

'Cheers, Bill,' Wingham said and used his chin to gesture at the Platoon. 'I thought they did well.'

Bill Cartwright nodded thoughtfully. He took a sip of the hot tea and gave the Major a surreptitious glance. In his humble opinion, Major Paul Wingham hadn't done so bad himself. As in every unit, there were many officers who didn't really have a clue, too young, no common sense, a waste of time and effort. And then there was an officer like Wingham. First and foremost he led from the front, always where the danger seemed at its worst. And he never asked anyone to do something he wasn't prepared to do himself, no matter how lowly that task might rank.

He'd more than earned the respect the lads gave him, but not because of his rank. No, when they obeyed orders it was because of the man, the underlying decency with which he handled both himself and the *Ruffians*. From the outset Cartwright always knew he'd been right to attach his colours to Wingham's mast.

'Yes, sir,' he said in answer. 'Couldn't have asked for more.'

The heavy thump of canon fire rolled in from the north and they waited. A muffled explosion reached their ears.

Cartwright took another mouthful of the hot liquid. He glanced in the direction of the explosion. 'Wouldn't want to be on the receiving end of that lot.'

'No,' Wingham said thoughtfully. 'Let's hope they're making ground.' He reached into a pocket for cigarettes and offered the pack to Cartwright. They lit up and with a hot drink in one hand, smoke in the other, and with the morning sun flickering down through the high canopy, two battle hardened soldiers found a few minutes in which to relax and take stock.

Chris Jamison stiffened. He'd heard a metallic chink, something solid, and he peered hard at low growing bushes between a haphazard line of trees. Movement! Not a bunch of leaves ruffled by the breeze but a dark shadow, seen and gone. He squinted, convinced he'd spotted the enemy. And then, in his peripheral vision to the left, more movement, a fleeting glimpse, twenty yards away. He thought he caught the sound of a snapped twig and turned his head to the right, carefully. This time he clearly picked out the slow moving, well camouflaged figure of a German soldier, slightly hunched over, MP40 at his waist. The man was fifteen yards away and already three or four yards past Jamison's position.

A bead of sweat trickled out from behind his helmet and Jamison bared his teeth. He slid the rifle back from the fork and swivelled round to his right. But now he was caught in two minds. If he fired, the other two would be on him before he could reload. He made a decision. Take out this one with his bayonet and then alert the Platoon. He moved. Bent at the waist he crept into the undergrowth and closed the man down. He was two strides behind him when the soldier sensed something and hesitated. Jamison took a final step forward.

'Psst!' he whispered harshly.

The German turned, startled, mouth open to shout.

Chris Jamison lunged with all his strength and the pig sticker punched into the man's throat. What had almost been a shout of alarm turned into a death rattle and blood pumped. His submachinegun fell as both hands reached for his neck, eyes bulging. His weight began to drag down on the bayonet and Jamison twisted hard, skewering the man again. The eyes glazed over and the hands collapsed, and the Paratrooper wrenched the bayonet free. Blood sprayed and soaked his rifle, hand and forearm glistening red. The German tumbled backwards into leaf litter, soundless.

Breathing hard, Jamison whipped round to face the other two, lifting the blood streaked rifle to his shoulder. He aimed at the nearest, side ribcage, made certain he was on target, and squeezed. The crack of the rifle sounded loud, recoil thumping his shoulder. The bullet struck and knocked the man sideways. An involuntary reaction made him pull the trigger of his sub-machinegun. The gun hammered in automatic as the soldier fell, a clear warning to the Platoon.

The last German went to ground, hidden in the green of the undergrowth. Jamison cursed and went down on one knee, searching. The crash of Paratroopers running to join him made him call the alarm.

'Steady! We've got a live one hiding!'

The noisy approach quietened, stealth replacing the dash. All went quiet and Jamison froze, peering ahead.

A shout. Then a gunshot, and a voice in English. 'He's dead.'

The Sergeant called. 'You all right, Jamison?'

Jamison stood and walked forward.

Cartwright appeared, Sten pointing at the ground. 'You hurt?' he asked as he saw the blood.

Jamison shook his head and gestured toward the German. 'No, his blood,' he said and wiped the bayonet with leaves. 'Made a bit of a mess.'

Cartwright took a closer look at the German and nodded his appreciation.

'Well done, Jamison. Nice work.'

And with that the Paratroopers slowly returned to the clearing, one man slowly walking backwards to check no-one else was coming up from behind.

But now there could be no outstaying their welcome and all too soon it was time to move.

Cartwright tipped away the dregs. 'Let's be having you,' he called. 'We don't have all day,' and the Platoon came to their feet. A quick check and they moved off, single file, well spread, no unnecessary noise.

It was a while later when Wingham caught a glimmer of daylight between thinning trees and after thirty minutes of tramping through dense woodland he raised a hand. The Platoon came to a watchful halt.

'Bill,' he called in a hushed voice.

Cartwright came up from the rear. 'Sir?'

'Let them rest. I'm taking a look ahead.'

'Right, sir. Need me?'

Wingham gave him a sideways grin. 'You volunteering?'

'I might,' Cartwright said, tilting his head as if making up his mind. 'Just this once.'

'In that case, be my guest.'

Cartwright's rugged face broke into a lazy smile and he turned away to issue orders. They left the Platoon with two men standing guard while the remainder spread out to relax.

Wingham led the way, their boots muffled by long decades of soft leaf litter. Ten yards from a sunlit field of corn, both men dropped to their hands and knees. They covered the next couple of yards on their bellies and slowly worked themselves inside a tangle of hornbeam. Wingham uncased his binoculars and eased up onto his elbows. He pursed his lips and pressed his eyes to the sockets. And there, at the far end of the field, sat a large, imposing farmhouse.

He settled down for a thorough examination.

5 Enemy

Five miles to the right of where Wingham and Cartwright lay hidden in that clump of trees, German elements of the 21st Panzer Division had regrouped as per Rommel's orders and set up a fresh defensive perimeter around the City of Caen. Two of the Division's Panzer Regiments had lost a combined total of more than twelve Mk4 Panzers when their initial armoured attack, hurriedly thrown in against the British landings, ended in failure. Over five-hundred Panzergrenadiers were either killed or taken prisoner and another three-hundred were wounded in combat. The 12th SS Panzer Division, arrived late in support, and then stunned by the appearance of so many Allied tanks, also suffered serious reversals.

Quickly realising it was a lost cause, General-Feldmarschall Erwin Rommel ordered the Panzers to withdraw and create an impregnable stronghold. It was imperative that the Allied advance be delayed for as long as possible in order that the next nearest armoured division, the elite formation known as 'Panzer-Lehr', should arrive in a timely manner to reinforce the front line.

With the majority of landline communications sabotaged by the French Resistance, and more recently, destroyed by Allied bombing, the supporting Panzer division was now contactable only by wireless telegraphy transmitted over the airwaves. This required the use of time consuming coding and decoding via the wheeled 'typewriter'. As an extra safeguard, and with battle conditions in mind should there be an Allied invasion, Rommel had established a secondary, secret location that utilised morse signalling as a means of contacting Berlin, Paris or besieged field commanders.

At this critical moment, and in order for Rommel to better understand what he was facing, he instructed his 21st Divisional Commander, General-Leutnant Edgar Feuchtinger, to gather whatever 'in the field' intelligence he could acquire.

To that end, a message was despatched to one of Feuchtinger's Panzergrenadier Regiments, the 126th, ordering its Commanding Officer to reconnoitre north and east and report the extent to which British Paratroopers and supporting armour, if any, had encroached.

The Regiment's Bavarian born CO, was a man who'd survived North Africa and won a Knights Cross in heavy fighting at the Battle of the Kasserine Pass. Personally honoured by Rommel, the then badly wounded 'Major' Heinrich Kohlberg, was promoted Colonel and rewarded with a posting to the City of Caen in the quiet backwaters of Normandy. He'd quickly become extremely fond of French cooking, and with his newly won rank and the authority that went with it, he took full advantage of his senior status. Over indulging himself for the last twelve months, a noticeably overweight Kohlberg refused to be dissuaded from his craving.

On this, the third morning since the Allied invasion, at a place called the Château Fontaine southeast of Caen, and even though the distant sounds of heavy artillery could be heard through an open window, Kohlberg rose late and indulged in a leisurely wash and shave. Having then dressed in his now rather tight uniform, he then descended the grand stairway to the marbled hallway below and made his way along to his south facing office.

Waiting beside the table stood his most trusted officer, the hard faced, jack booted, twenty-eight year old, Capitan Thomas Buschmann. His heels clicked together with formal respect.

'Good morning, Herr Oberst. I have already ordered coffee.'

Kohlberg smiled and rubbed his hands. 'Morning, Thomas.' He nodded at the big bay window. 'I see the weather has improved.'

'Jawohl, Herr Oberst.'

Kohlberg gestured to a chair. 'Sit, my friend.'

As they settled at the table, Kohlberg took a tentative sip of the strong black coffee. He licked his lips and carefully replaced the cup.

'Have you any news, Thomas?'

Buschmann pointed vaguely towards the oversized oak desk. 'The wireless room brought orders from General-Feldmarschall Rommel. They have been decoded.'

'Good . . . , that will be good. I will see to them shortly, after breakfast, I think.' He looked round and raised his voice. 'Talking of breakfast, what can we expect today?'

Buschmann picked up a fork and banged on the table, in case the cook had not heard.

There was a noticeable increase of activity in the kitchen and then Buschmann leaned back with a lecherous smirk on his lips. A young serving girl brought a heavily laden tray to the table and leaned to slide it on. Her low cut top did little to hide the soft swell of her breasts and he looked across at the Colonel and winked.

'A fine serving, Herr Oberst, is it not?'

Kohlberg gave an enthusiastic nod, fully aware of the Capitan's meaning. She placed the plate between his knife and fork and turned to retrieve the tray. Buschmann made no attempt to hide his thoughts and made a point of staring until she blushed. She gave a small curtsey and quickly left. He laughed and turned his attention to the meal.

They enjoyed a breakfast of the finest lightly charred bacon, two sausages, tomatoes, and two large fried eggs, all washed down with a glass of red wine. In Kohlberg's opinion, the meal would have been even more palatable if Paulette, the beautiful French maid who normally served table had been present. Her uniform did little to hide well rounded breasts, the frilled, white cotton blouse exposing an exquisite cleavage when she leaned to the table. Likewise, the short-ish skirt allowed for a good view of her long shapely legs. He'd not bedded her yet but she'd accepted kisses on her cheek and a wandering hand, and he thought it only a matter of time. Sadly she'd been reported missing.

Still, he mused, this new girl, this buxom young blond by the name of Angélique, appeared ripe for the taking. Her curves were all woman and when she came to clear the table she leaned in close and exposed her ample young tits. Kohlberg glanced at Buschmann, gave him a wink and a suggestive grin, and then reached out a hand to caress Angélique's well rounded rump. She giggled. Encouraged, Kohlberg eased his chair out from the table, wiped his mouth with a napkin and indicated his vacant lap. She feigned reluctance, slanting her pretty face to one side and touching a finger to her glistening red lips. He reached for a hand and she snatched it away, laughing at his obvious frustration. Annoyed at her refusal to accept his request he came slowly to his feet, as if to leave, but then lunged to trap her against the table. She squealed. With an arm clamped round her waist, he roughly mauled the soft tits with his free hand and forced his lips on hers.

Angélique half resisted, attempting to pull away, but then relaxed and let him have his way.

Kohlberg felt the young woman submit to his overpowering strength and eased his grip, pulling away from the savage kiss. Her face no longer wore the coquettish smile and her eyes reflected an inner fear. It was his turn to laugh. She'd thought it was all a game. No longer. Before the day was out he would have this woman. None of her teasing. He would have her brought to his room, and then they could play games, his games. And there would be nowhere to hide.

He let her be and turned away, a crooked smile distorting his heavy jowls. She would more than make up for Paulette's absence, of that he was absolutely certain. He stepped across to the tall ornate windows and in the warmth of the morning sun lit a large cigar. Behind him he heard the girl sort the table.

Thomas Buschmann had remained seated while the Colonel had abused the girl and felt he'd missed out. He stood and moved round to the far side of the table. As she came back for the coffee cups he stepped in behind her, reached round to grab her breasts and planted a kiss on the nape of her neck. She made no attempt to fend him off and he slipped a hand inside the blouse. It all lasted less than a minute but he enjoyed every second before he let her go. He patted her backside and walked over to join the Colonel.

Angélique tugged her skirt straight and tucked her blouse back into the waistband. Trembling from their unexpectedly rough advances she finished clearing away the cups and saucers and carried them to the kitchen. Tears came unbidden and she hurried through to the coolness of the walk in larder, out of sight. She found a handkerchief and dabbed her eyes, slowly regaining her composure. How she hated that fat bastard. Yes she had flirted with him, smiled and giggled at his suggestive wandering hands, and yes, she probably had exposed too much of her ample breasts. But the job paid well and she was given a food allowance, vital when it enabled her to help support her mother and father.

And that Capitan Buschmann was no better, younger and fitter, yes, but no less a filthy swine for assuming he had a right to her body.

She dried the last of her tears, patted her hair into shape and walked back into the kitchen. She wondered if Paulette had been in the same predicament? Is that why she'd not turned up for work today? They hadn't talked much but what little time they'd spent together had convinced Angélique that Paulette probably wouldn't have had much time for that fat bastard. Yes, she thought, Paulette had probably decided enough was enough and left. Maybe it would be better not to serve table tonight, give it a miss. Dinner for Kohlberg and two of his young officers could start as late as half-eight and not finish until after dark. Not an ideal time to be a lone woman wearing provocative clothing in the presence of liquored up soldiers.

Colonel Kohlberg relished the cigar but eventually, to the distant grumble of heavy artillery, he reluctantly turned to his desk. Not that the Château was the Colonel's personal choice of residence. It had been General-Feldmarschall Erwin Rommel himself who had chosen this roomy but unostentatious building as the ideal location for his most eastern radio communications centre. Rommel called the Château his "camouflage", a deception that was "hiding in full view". If needed it had the signalling strength to act as an emergency transmitter to reach any and all of Army Gruppe B's mobile forces, also Paris, or the Führer in Berchtesgaten. A powerful array of aerials linking an inestimable number of radios called for round the clock watch keeping and more than a Kompanie of soldaten tended the needs of a few specialist Wireless Telegraphists. Rommel, remembering Kohlberg from his days commanding the Africa Korps, decided the Colonel would oversee signalling operations and suggested he make it the headquarters of 126th Panzergrenadier Regiment. Heinrich Kohlberg was well aware that a 'suggestion' from the likes of Erwin Rommel needed to be accepted as a command.

And so, on this the third morning of the Allied invasion, it was 09.00 hours before a fat man named Heinrich Kohlberg eventually opened the decoded order from Rommel's headquarters. The communiqué had come via his own Divisional Commander, General-Leutnant Edgar Feuchtinger.

Kohlberg clamped his teeth around the hand rolled Brazilian cigar, read the order and dropped it thoughtfully onto his desk. He scratched his heavy jowl and nodded to himself. He believed he had the ideal candidate for such an undertaking. The only complication was, what strength? A cold grin spread across the flabby features. He would make a few enquiries as to exactly how his Regiment was currently deployed before making a commitment, but he felt sure he had the answer. Kohlberg heaved his bulk out from behind the desk and turned to Buschmann.

'Thomas . . . , I believe Major Kruger is currently in charge of the Regiment's disposal. Am I correct?'

Buschmann slowly nodded. 'He is, Herr Oberst.'

'Good,' Kohlberg said quietly, 'very good.' He drummed on the desk. 'You will report back to your Regiment, Thomas. I have other duties for the Major. I need you to keep an eye on things, especially Major Fredrickson. I worry about Fredrickson. As my 2i/c he spends too much time in Caen.'

'Jawohl, Herr Oberst,' Buschmann said, clicked his heels and wheeled away, barking out a string of orders for his staff car.

Kohlberg nodded in approval and meandered back to his desk. He placed a call to the switchboard and decided he would wait for the telephone to ring before informing his chosen officer of what was required. His face twisted into a crooked grin. The 'Desert Fox' had called for answers. It was fortunate indeed that Colonel Heinrich Kohlberg could ensure that men from his very own Panzergrenadiers were sent out to gather the information.

Paul Wingham lowered the glasses and breathed a sigh of relief.

'That's it,' he said, and passed over the binoculars.

Cartwright studied the place for a full minute, before handing them back. 'Sure?' he asked.

Wingham smiled, much as a teacher might when confronted with a disbelieving pupil. He raised his binoculars and again studied the large, stone built farmhouse.

'Yep,' he said. 'The "Farm Sainte Beaumont." Positive.'

The building sat at the far end of the cornfield, on ground that appeared level with his present position. He estimated the range as three-hundred yards. It looked deserted, but he well knew appearances could be deceptive. In front of the house a long, low dry-stone wall with a wooden gate separated the house from the field. Facing him on the lower floor a wooden door hung askew from a solitary hinge, and on either side of the gaping entrance, windows were framed by faded white shutters. More importantly he took careful note of three upstairs windows overlooking his position. Behind jagged shards of broken glass, scraps of faded blue curtain swayed gently in the early breeze.

To his immediate left an overgrown ditch ran down along the side of the fields towards the farmhouse and he took a moment to thoroughly assess its potential. Nearest to him the ditch faded into a thicket of brambles where a sprinkling of red poppies drooped amongst the swaying grass. A sheen of overnight dew, not yet evaporated under the sun's warming rays, still glinted off their petals.

Wingham lowered the glasses, and careful not to make any unnecessary movement, repositioned himself for a more detailed examination. Satisfied all was well, he again raised the binoculars and continued his surveillance. Twenty yards to the right of the farmhouse was the brick made end of an outbuilding, possibly a barn, with a high wall joining the two structures. Where the wall met the barn's brickwork a solitary mature beech tree softened the angular structure. He moved the glasses left of the house, and there, partially hidden behind a tall thick hedge, he found the low roof of another outbuilding. He could just make out what appeared to be a rusting tubular chimney protruding from the roof tiles. It had what appeared to be a 'Chinaman' style cowl on the top. He continued to study the entire layout, convinced that this was the target he'd been ordered to find.

Lowering the binoculars, Wingham glanced to his right. 'Too quiet. Let's have the Platoon up here, deploy 'em either side and sit tight.'

'Fine by me,' Cartwright said, then squirmed backwards out of the thicket and slithered away to relay the orders.

Wingham hid a grin. The Sergeant was twenty-nine, of medium build, and as sturdy as an ox. The level blue eyes could fix a man with a withering stare, but underlying that tough exterior was a soldier of immense generosity. He was a man of few words but those offered were always to the point, and few words or not, men took notice of Sergeant Bill Cartwright.

In five minutes the men had strung out in a concealed line and all was quiet.

Cartwright came back and crawled into hiding. 'All done.'

Wingham nodded and then, looking at the overgrown ditch to his left said, 'Get Miller for me.'

The word passed down the line.

Private Joe 'Dusty' Miller had made himself comfortable in a grassy hollow. His modified .303 Lee-Enfield sniper rifle gave him the advantage of a telescopic sight, and he had it aimed through a hawthorn bush at the upper windows of the farmhouse.

From his left he heard a hushed call from Corporal Steve Dexter.

'Dusty!'

Miller sighed. 'What?'

'The Old Man wants you.'

Miller gave another sigh, drawn out, exaggerated.

'Bleedin' hell, no peace.'

But inwardly Miller could guess at why he'd been called, pleased with the thought. He relaxed the rifle and slithered backwards out of the hollow, careful to keep the bush between himself and the house. Six feet back into the cool shade of the trees he came up to his knees and slowly stood. With the rifle held loosely across his waist he loped off through the undergrowth. A minute later he found Wingham lying in bushes, binoculars up and focussed on the farmhouse.

He dropped to his haunches. 'You wanted me, sir?'

The Major beckoned him alongside, and belly down, Miller crawled forward to join him.

Wingham pointed to the ditch. 'Think you can get in there without being spotted?'

Miller gave it a long look and wondered if there'd be room enough inside? He glanced at the house, at the upper windows, and then looked back at the overgrown ditch. He thought he could make it, but not with his rifle. Finally he nodded.

'I can give it a try. Sten gun would be better.'

Wingham inclined his head. 'Have mine,' and he slipped the sub-machinegun across.

Miller passed him the rifle, checked the Sten's magazine and accepted a spare. He tucked it into a pouch and looked up.

Wingham met his eyes. 'I want to know if we can get a Section down there, and if so, how close we'd be at the other end?'

Miller pursed his lips knowing that this wasn't something a man could hurry.

'Might be a while, sir.'

The Major gave him a wry smile. 'No change there then, Miller. Just remember we're waiting for an answer.'

Miller bared his teeth in response. 'Slow but sure, sir. Slow but sure,' he said, and began to crawl backwards. At a safe distance he came to his feet and turned. He took a few paces and heard Wingham give a soft warning.

'Miller . . . , go careful.'

The sniper touched his helmet in acknowledgement and gathered the Sten to his waist. A faint smile came to his lips. He was back in his element, off to stalk the enemy.

Wingham looked at his watch. It showed 10.21.

Hidden inside the cool, dark interior of the old French farmhouse, two German Panzergrenadiers in mottled camouflage kept watch from an upstairs window. After much deliberation they'd chosen the bedroom situated centrally above the open door; it tended to give a better overall view of the northern approach. A tattered blue curtain helped dim the interior. They were stationed there as an Observation Post for the 126th Panzergrenadier Regiment, a unit belonging to the 21st Panzer Division. The pair of Grenadiers were acutely aware of imminent danger. No newcomers to war, they were both veterans of the Russian campaign. In the late August of '43, the pair had been wounded in the final retreat from Kharkov, and following evacuation and then treatment in a hospital on the outskirts of Hamburg, they found themselves posted to the 21st Panzer Division stationed near Caen.

Now, with what looked like the long predicted Allied invasion, they were once again at the forefront of combat. Recent information indicated that British forces in the immediate area were lightly armed Paratroopers, although further reports stated that Allied tank units had successfully expanded the Allied bridgehead. Part of 21st Panzer's Armoured brigades had already tangled with the British near the coast. News came that the Panzers failed to make an impression and had fallen back to defend Caen.

Hans Gruber, the older of the two, tensed, gripping the stock of his light-machinegun. As sunlight warmed the damp corn, something had glinted on the tree line.

'Edge of the trees. I see movement.'

Senior Rifleman Konrad Meyer peered along the length of his Mauser. The rifle sat propped on a pillow on a small dressing table in the shaded confines away from the window. He took time to study dark recesses below the dense greenery, where tree trunks met low growing foliage. He found no hint of movement, and raised the lip of his steel helmet.

'For me, there is nothing. No sign. Are you sure?'

'Ja. Warn the others.'

Meyer cursed and spat on the floor. 'If you say so.'

'I do, now go.'

Reluctantly, Meyer backed away to the door in the corner, stepped out into the narrow corridor and clumped down the bare wooden staircase. In the hall below he stayed well clear of the open front door and moved through to the large flag stone kitchen. Slipping out of the back door, he crouched low to ensure he wasn't seen above the wall, and hurried for the barn doors. They were closed but not secured and he pulled at a pitted iron handle. The heavy oak door groaned as it swung outwards and he stopped it moving as soon as he could squeeze inside. He stepped into the dark interior, his nostrils twitching to the stink of cattle dung. He called quietly.

'We have company.'

He detected movement near a small window let into the far wall and a young Panzergrenadier appeared from behind a stacked pile of hay. Seventeen year old Walter Hasse kicked his way through the straw. The size of his rifle made him appear even younger than he was.

'Where?' he asked.

Another movement caught Meyer's eye and the Austrian born Sven Zimmermann came over with his MP40 machine-pistol held high across his chest. In the dim light a white scar gleamed, extending down the gaunt face from left eye to jawbone. He was a veteran of Rommel's Africa Corps, very experienced, and should by now have been promoted. But his habit of drinking too much, coupled with persistent womanising, had seen the chance taken away. The wound had left him with a permanent sneer.

'Hans saw movement in the trees,' Meyer explained.

'How many?' Zimmermann snapped.

'None that I could see . . . , but he was in no doubt.'

Zimmermann tilted his head, obviously making up his mind. 'Then we must prepare. If Hans said he saw something, it must be so.' He glanced at the youngster.

'Get back to that window, boy, and you keep those eyes wide, hear me?'

Walter Hasse swallowed and nodded. 'Jawohl,' he said, a tremor in his voice. He turned away through the hay.

Zimmermann caught Meyer's eye and shook his head. It showed his doubt in the youngster's capabilities, but he chose not to speak of it. Instead he gestured with the gun. 'I found a stable door. It opens into a horse meadow and I see much of the trees beyond.'

Meyer gave him a twisted grin and spat. 'Then we are a fortress, no? Who would attack such well defended walls?'

The irony was not lost on Zimmermann. 'Of course, the swine only have a few thousand soldiers.' He gave a high pitched cackle, mocking his own poor joke. 'So much for a Calais invasion. Are we to bear the brunt? Again?'

Meyer inclined his head on one side. 'You could always go back to the Russian front.'

'No, my friend,' Zimmermann said, a sombre note in his tone. 'I think the British will suit me better.' He began to turn away for the stable door, but glanced back over his shoulder.

'Have you warned Höch ?'

Meyer shook his head. 'Last on the list, and then all we do is wait, no?'

'Ja, we continue to wait. Always we wait. Go,' he insisted, 'warn Höch.'

Joe Miller arrived level with the point where the ditch began, just beyond the thinning tree line. He came to a halt and dropped to his hands and knees. A willow tree fringed the corner of the field, elegant branches drooping low to the ground. He crawled towards the thick trunk, went left of its roots and down on his belly. Three feet ahead and covered by the branches of a bramble bush he could just make out the sides of the ditch. The bush sprawled haphazardly across the intervening space.

Miller grimaced. It wasn't what he'd particularly want for cover but beggars couldn't be choosers. He slowly raised his head until the roof of the farmhouse came into view. From his current position it lay at two o'clock, and the bush was both tall and dense enough for concealment. He checked the Sten's safety catch, wrapped the sling round his right forearm, and wriggled forward. A bramble snagged his right shoulder and he froze. With the fingers of his left hand he reached across and awkwardly peeled it away, gently allowing the thin branch to spring back to its original position. Satisfied that the bush remained largely undisturbed, he pushed forward and allowed himself to slide head first into the ditch.

The sniper landed in a three-inch slime of green water.

He swore under his breath. His left forearm had disappeared up to his elbow. Somehow he managed to prevent the Sten from touching the surface. For a moment he lay and cursed, a stream of choice words whispered with venom. But for all that, his eyes were taking in the hedge above the right wall of the ditch. It hung unevenly overhead and appeared to give ample cover for a man to negotiate the gulley. Ignoring his sodden arm, Miller spun his legs round and tentatively eased a pair of booted feet into the ooze. Beneath the surface the bottom seemed firm enough and he gave it an exploratory test. Bent double from the waist he ventured forward, and at that moment he relaxed. This was where the old skills of his youth came to the fore. Stalking game in Scotland's great estates was all about stealth of the highest order, and Miller's expertise put him high on the list amongst his peers. Seldom had a day passed without 'little Joe' arriving home to give his mother something for the pot.

Alert for the slightest sound, he pushed on. After fifty yards the green slime gave way to cloying mud, and then changed again to stones and pebbles. All the while he took good care to stay low, frequently pausing to stop and listen. And it was hot work. In the confines of the ditch rivulets of sweat ran down his forehead from beneath the helmet. Occasionally he took a moment to check his whereabouts in relation to the house, wary of watching eyes. He made slow progress, but by his own estimate he'd already covered a good percentage of the distance and was maybe only seventy or so yards from the farmhouse's end of the gulley.

Then mid-stride, something made him pause, his foot poised, dangling in the air.

He sensed danger, a premonition, and quietly lowered his foot. Up ahead the ditch turned a little to the right, enough to obscure whatever lay beyond. And instinct warned him of a hidden threat.

What now? Time was moving on, the Old Man waiting. He looked around and his gaze settled on the left bank of the ditch. Long meadow grass waved in the breeze above, enough to give some cover against an unsuspecting guard. Any German waiting round that corner wouldn't be watching the open meadow grass, the ditch being the obvious approach. And in any case, the windows of the farmhouse overlooked the other side of the hedge.

Miller took a deep breath, straightened to his full height and hoisted himself silently up and into the lush grass. Sten gun in his right hand, he snaked forward, moving slow, elbows and toes, boot heels low. Six feet, eight feet . . . . And there in the hollow lay a German soldier, his rifle aimed at the kink in the ditch.

The sniper lowered his head and inched backwards, knowing that he now had all the answers Wingham needed. With care the gulley was easy and with only one lookout at the end, of no real consequence. As he let himself gently back down into the ditch, Miller smiled. That old sixth sense had served him well. Bent at the waist, senses alert, he began to retrace his footsteps.

He made short work of the return leg, found the Old Man, and reported what he'd discovered.

'Well done, Miller.'

They swapped weapons.

'Take a breather,' Wingham said, and Miller slumped at the base of a convenient tree. He took a mouthful of tepid water from his canteen and settled back, eyes closed.

6 Battlegroup

Senior Rifleman Konrad Meyer made it to the opposite end of the house and hesitated at the corner of the building. In front of him lay a vegetable garden bordered by a dense hedge at the front. A picket gate allowed access to the fields of corn, and the ditch where Höch stood guard began ten metres from the gate. But using the gate meant open ground and Meyer wondered whether Höch had used that way or found another means to get into the ditch. He studied the garden hedge, where it turned to the right away from the fields, and thought he saw a gap. It would mean crawling on hands and knees, but better than being out in the open. He slung the Mauser cross-wise over his shoulder, shook his head in annoyance, and went down on all fours. Why he needed to warn Höch was beyond him. The man was on guard duty, surely he didn't need warning?

A sharp stone dug a knee and he winced. Taking more care he pushed on through a patch of onions, followed by two rows of potatoes, before squeezing past a ripening trellis of peas. Ahead of him the hedge gave way to sparse twigs, and by the obvious signs of damage, he guessed Höch must have forced a passage through this particular break.

Hugging the damp ground, Meyer forced the thin branches apart and emerged onto a narrow path close to the ditch. He scurried across on his stomach, dodged a ragged bush and lay panting at the entrance to the overgrown ditch. His eyes widened and he stared in disbelief.

Höch had turned to crouch, rifle raised, finger on the trigger. 'You, my friend,' Höch growled, 'are lucky to be alive. Are you relieving me?'

Meyer grinned sheepishly and slid down to join Höch.

'No, not yet. I come to warn you we have company, at least that is what Gruber thinks.'

Höch spat from the side of his mouth. 'What does Gruber know? The man is half blind. He sees twigs move in the wind and it is the enemy. No it is not! It is just an old man hallucinating.'

Meyer shrugged. 'Believe what you will, I am only here to give warning. He may be right.'

Höch eyed him warily and then pointed down the gulley. 'I have seen nothing, as you can see. You are welcome to stay if you wish.'

Meyer licked his lips and thought how much more shelter the solid stone farmhouse offered if it should come to a battle.

'Nein,' he said, shaking his head. 'I will return to Gruber. We have a good view from up there.'

Höch stuck his jaw out. 'As you wish, it is of no matter to me. Just remember to relieve me later.'

'Of course, one of us will come.'

Paul Wingham moved back into the depths of the trees and unfolded his map.

'Bill,' he called softly. 'Here a minute.'

Cartwright slithered back from the low shrub and moved to join him. He knelt. 'Sir?'

Wingham prodded the map. 'Here's the farmhouse. If Jerry are in there, we'll clear it.' He rubbed his jaw. 'I want No.2 Section with me and we'll use the ditch down the left side of the corn fields. I'll have No.1 Section out on the right flank, use what cover they can find, circle round.' He frowned in thought. 'No.3 Section to go left, have them stay within the trees 'till they hit this farm track.' He traced a finger along a line. 'Then follow it to where it intersects the other track beyond the house, here,' and he pointed to where one joined the other. He paused, mulling it over. 'That way, with No.1 Section round the back, all avenues are covered.'

He looked up, eyes narrowed. 'If we come up against stiff opposition and we have to fall back, the rendezvous will be here in the woods, as good as anywhere. It'll give us a fighting chance. After that, if it really goes tits up, every man for himself.' He gave Cartwright a searching look. 'What do you think?'

'Sounds fine to me.'

Wingham checked his watch. 'If you brief the others, I'll see our Section know what we're doing.'

Cartwright nodded and moved off.

Wingham watched him go, folded the map, and pursed his lips. Wouldn't be long now.

Close to the city of Caen, at a quaint hotel in the small provincial town of Colombelles, Major Carl Kruger of the 126th Panzergrenadier Regiment turned to answer the telephone on his desk.

'Kruger,' he said sharply.

The switchboard operator was familiar with his brusque manner. 'I have the Colonel for you, Herr Major.'

'Then put him through!'

There was a click followed by the voice of Oberst Heinrich Kohlberg.

'Is that you, Carl?'

'Ja, Herr Oberst, what can I do for you?'

'Rommel requires information on enemy movement. Do you have men scouting to the north?'

Kruger frowned before giving his reply. 'We had a small number in Ranville but decided to withdraw. There were many casualties. I have not heard since. But I left Grenadiers manning an Observation Post near Escoville at an abandoned farm.'

'How many?'

Kruger took a moment to quell his annoyance at the abrupt questioning.

'Not many. It is a small unit, five men.'

'Then we must check on them. British Paratroopers have seized the bridges over the Caen Canal and Orne River. Take your Kompanie and scout to the northeast. Rommel wants numbers. Where they are, who are we against? If I am to move the Regiment, I too need accurate information.'

'You wish me to deploy an entire Kompanie?'

'Ja. Is that a problem?'

Kruger hesitated. His normal reconnaissance patrol was a nine man section. 'No, Herr Oberst. No problem.'

Kohlberg grunted. 'Good, I want reliable reports, not the nonsense spiel of childish Leutnants. Get them moving.'

'Now?' Kruger queried.

'Exactly.'

'In daylight, Herr Oberst? You want us to move in daylight? Enemy fighter-bombers are everywhere? We risk many casualties.'

After a lengthy pause the Colonel spoke very softly, barely audible.

'Major Kruger,' he hissed. 'Are you questioning Rommel's orders? He demands action and I am not here to sit on my hands. You will obey orders. We may lose many more if we do not move immediately!'

Kruger heard the note of exasperation creeping into the Colonel's voice and took a deep breath before answering.

'As you wish, Herr Oberst.'

'Exactly, Kruger. As I wish!'

The telephone line disconnected and the Major slowly replaced the receiver. Fat bastard, Kruger thought, and looked straight at the wall map. There were three plausible routes to choose from, all of them open to aerial attack. Not that they would be exposed for long, the distance was a mere ten or so kilometres. Kruger took a deep breath and leaned his fists on the desk. As far as he knew that ridge of higher ground had not yet been infiltrated by the British, no report had come back from the farm. Any lightly armed parachutists could be quickly disposed of and he could then push north on a broader reconnaissance front. His problem lay in extricating his Kompanie of Panzergrenadiers from their current defensive positions. They were scattered throughout the town's northern perimeter and well concealed from aerial observation. Given the choice he would have preferred to move at night, but orders were orders. Yesterday's reconnaissance patrol had convinced him of the need to be hidden during daylight hours. Enemy fighter-bombers roamed freely although none had spotted Kruger's small patrol. He'd taken cover in a small wood that straddled an old farm track and had remained undetected. He smiled at the memory. A bunch of enemy Paratroopers had been on the receiving end of Kruger's ruthless impatience. By the time he pulled out he was confident the Englanders were no longer a threat.

Straightening from the desk, he reached for his cap and patted it into place, and then gave the highly polished peak a cavalier tug over his one good eye. The left eye socket was covered by a triangular black patch, a legacy of an attack on Tobruk. A tall man, Kruger carried his authority well. And the Knights Cross, prominently displayed under his chin, reflected past glories, and men respected the honour.

With a final glance round the office, he checked his Luger, picked up the sub-machinegun and then strode out through the foyer and down the steps to the town square. An officer looked up and saluted.

Kruger acknowledged the salute. 'Oberleutnant Lehmann?' he queried, not quite certain of the man's identity. There'd been a small batch of newly recruited officers arriving in the past couple of weeks.

Lehmann snapped his heels together. 'Jawohl, Herr Major!'

'You are in my Kompanie, yes?'

'I joined five weeks ago.'

'Good, good,' Kruger said, remembering. 'You were on Rommel's staff were you not?'

The officer's enthusiasm could not be denied. 'It was my honour to serve the General,' he said, his eyes glinting.

'Well, Oberleutnant Lehmann, you now have the greater honour of serving me. I want my Kompanie of Grenadiers. You will bring me four half-tracks and have the rest of the men in trucks. We move to join battle. And I also need Unter-Offizier Schwartz to report here immediately. Thirty minutes, you hear?'

Lehmann clicked his heels and snapped up a salute.

'Jawohl, Herr Major,' he said with a grin. 'The British have picked the wrong fight.'

Kruger nodded and the man moved off at a brisk pace.

From an upstairs balcony overlooking the town square, a Regimental staff officer leaned on an ornate scroll balustrade and looked down at Kruger's back.

Moments earlier Hauptman Thomas Buschmann had vacated his staff car and entered the hotel. He mounted the stairs to the upper floor and stepped out on to the balcony. Buschmann held a deep dislike of Major Carl Kruger. There was nothing remotely likeable about him and in Buschmann's opinion the man was an arrogant fool, one of Rommel's inner circle and too quick to criticise the efforts of others. They had crossed swords many times during their careers, and Buschmann was not one to hold back if he thought he was right. And many times Colonel Kohlberg had sided with Buschmann, to the extent of showing his contempt for Kruger's suggestions.

But now it appeared Kruger had been selected for armed reconnaissance, Kompanie strength, which would indicate he could expect trouble. Buschmann smiled. The arrogant swine might meet more than his match, and in that case there was always the possibility of a field promotion being awarded to the next most deserving officer.

He straightened up from the balustrade and turned away for his office on the ground floor. There were Regimental books to bring up to date.

Out on the square, Oberleutnant Lehmann could be heard shouting instructions. But the sound of his voice was then drowned out by the howl of aero engines and a pair of ME109's thundered north at tree top height, gone from sight in seconds. Kruger didn't envy the pilots their mission, they'd be lucky to make it back.

As the fighters receded into the distance he heard the muffled coughs of engines being fired up and smiled his satisfaction. Troop carriers were the lifeblood of Panzergrenadiers, the essence of their trade. They were 'motorised infantry' purposely designed for fast deployment with Panzers. He thrust his hands behind his back and waited, it would not do to show impatience. After all, these soldiers were combat veterans and their loyalty to Major Carl Kruger had never faltered.

Two motorbike riders swung into the square, pulled up outside the bank, and prepared to marshal the Battlegroup into order. And the Panzergrenadiers began to assemble. Sub-machine gunners, riflemen, mortar teams, and heavy-machine gunners. From a number of side streets half-tracks growled and squealed their way over the cobbles, and Kruger picked out the pennants fluttering on his own command vehicle. He marched forward and mounted the cab. In a haze of exhaust smoke the formation began to take shape, eventually completed by the arrival of six canvas covered wagons laden with Grenadiers. In a few short minutes 228 Grenadiers had formed up to await his orders.

Unter-Offizier Schwartz appeared at the cab door. 'Herr Major?'

Kruger smiled down and opened the door. 'With me, Schwartz. There is work for you this day.'

The man nodded and clambered aboard.

Kruger let him settle and gave him a wink. It was only two weeks since Kruger had managed to prise Schwartz away from Kapitän Dressler of 'B' Kompanie. For some time rumours had swirled around the Regiment that a 'killer' had joined their ranks and Kruger made a point of finding out more.

Unter-Offizier Otto Schwartz had been born and raised on the banks of the River Weser outside a small town called Nienburg. In the February of 1941, on his eighteenth birthday, he'd been recruited into the Wehrmacht and immediately shown a natural ability with a rifle. Within two months he'd been awarded the prestigious title of 'Marksman', and then joined the Light Mountain Infantry as a Senior Ranger. In both the Russian and Italian campaigns he proved his worth as a sniper, racking up a formidable fifty-two kills before two American tanks caught his unit crossing a ravine east of Salerno and wiped them out. Schwartz was wounded in the leg but managed to escape after hiding in a disused culvert. In December '43, having been passed fit but left with a slight limp, he joined the 126th Panzergrenadiers to complete his recuperation.

Kruger gave him a final glance and noted how the sniper's rifle was so carefully cradled. He made a fine addition to the Major's personal itinery.

Finally, the two motorbikes came off their stands and were kicked into life. Legs swung over saddles, goggles settled. Both riders wheeled round and took station ahead of the Major's half-track. They looked back, waiting, blipping throttles.

Kruger settled his eye patch and straightened to his full height. He grasped the leading edge of the armour plating, and deliberately raised a gloved hand. A final check on his newly assembled battlegroup, and a slow grin spread across the haughty features. The gloved fist changed to a single raised finger, and his forearm began to rotate. Engines throttled up in anticipation, then he whipped his arm down and pointed east.

'Forward!'

The subdued roar of engines rose to a thunder, and in a cloud of reeking fumes the heavily armed Kompanie headed for an insignificant farmhouse near an ancient stand of trees.

7 Ruffians

Major Paul Wingham passed word for No.2 Section to assemble for a briefing. He then strode deeper into the woods until he estimated there was enough vegetation to hide them from prying eyes. In a small clearing he felt for his pack of cigarettes, tapped one out and lit it. He waited while they gathered round. They wandered in one at a time, weighed down with all the accoutrements of war, everything the 'planners' had decided a man needed to survive in enemy territory. There were six of them in total, and they were all good at their job. Some had fought in Italy, others had helped drive Rommel out of North Africa. One had been evacuated at Dunkirk.

Wingham waited for them to settle, reassessing their capabilities. In reality, they were a bunch of misfits, self-reliant, and when the right occasion called for it, very violent. He'd once heard an unguarded remark in the Officers Mess accusing them all of being a 'bunch of ill-disciplined '*ruffians*', so word of their nickname had obviously spread, but, and Wingham hid a smile, they were *his Ruffians*, and that counted for a lot.

Corporal Steve Dexter ambled across and knelt on one knee, right arm resting on the Sten gun slung from his shoulder. At the ripe old age of twenty-six he'd packed in a lot of war. Dunkirk, Egypt, Sicily and Italy, and when the word went out for volunteers to join a new elite unit of Paratroopers, he hadn't hesitated. A proud Welshman, in a previous life he'd been a stevedore in Cardiff docks. He was a hard-bitten, uncompromising veteran.

On the Welshman's left, the stocky, blue eyed, Lance-Corporal Jed Tulloch came and sat cross legged with his back to a tree. At twenty-two years of age he was lean and hard, a man who could march for hours without complaint. He'd been born and brought up in the smoke grimed streets of Jarrow, in Newcastle-Upon-Tyne, and before joining up Tulloch had honed his muscles with hard graft as a drayman for Newcastle Breweries. Through force of circumstances during a battle in Italy, it had fallen to Tulloch to assist a badly wounded signaller, and he'd taken to the intricacies of operating radios without so much as the bat of an eyelid. Now officially the Platoon's Signaller/Radio Operator, Wingham felt lucky to have him. The man was cool under fire and, importantly for a soldier in his position, Jed Tulloch knew when to keep his mouth shut.

Private Frank Tillman stood with his back to the trunk of an oak tree. A giant of a man, he was broad shouldered and narrow at the waist, and it was rumoured he had muscles in his finger nails. His formative years had been as a butcher's assistant in Leeds, but his prime duty now was Bren gunner for No.2 Section. The weapon stood on its butt between his feet and both huge hands rested on the muzzle. He was the undisputed champion on a Bren, and for all his threatening appearance, his disarming smile made him a popular companion. Someone somewhere had called him 'Lofty' and the name had stuck.

And then there was Private Keith Brennan, an entirely different kettle of fish. He'd just turned twenty on D-Day and couldn't wait to get to grips with the enemy. Short in stature and with a fresh-faced boyish complexion, he'd quickly acquired the nickname of 'Angel'. Quite why, could only be guessed at, but the betting was on a shortened version of 'Angel of Death'. His youthful appearance made a mockery of his true nature. Although he'd been issued a Sten Gun for this particular patrol, his favourite weapon was a fighting knife that he kept in pristine, razor sharp condition. Wingham had heard gruesome tales of Brennan's willingness to use it at close quarters. Sergeant Cartwright had recognised a useful talent when he saw it, and eventually persuaded 'Angel' to join the Platoon. And the ex bricklayer from Richmond in Yorkshire, had fitted perfectly. The knife glinted as he ran a thumb along the blade.

Joe 'Dusty' Miller came and stood behind them, his rifle cradled over the crook of an arm.

The last to settle was Private Mike 'Red' Stratton. With a shock of flaming red hair and a temper to match, he was a tall, rangy, angular faced regular who's entire being was centred on life in the army. He'd joined on his eighteenth birthday, six years previously, and had been with the 1st Battalion, The Rifle Brigade, before volunteering to join the Paras in early '44. He'd twice been recommended for promotion to Non Commissioned Officer but refused to accept, citing the duties and responsibility of being an NCO as too much of a burden. Again, it was Sergeant Cartwright who'd singled him out as an exceptional soldier and persuaded him to join No.2 Section. And the ex barrow boy from Smithfields meat market, born and brought up in London's Old Kent Road, soon proved his worth.

Wingham cleared his throat and eyed each of them in turn.

'Right,' he began. 'Miller found a Jerry guard down the far end of the ditch.' He pursed his lips and rubbed the bridge of his nose. 'So it looks like they're in the farmhouse. Could be just an Observation Post, small unit on watch, might be more. But that's our objective. I'm sending Corporal Harrison's Section round the back via the right flank, and No.3 Section will be over to the left. As for us,' and he grinned, 'we're going down Miller's ditch.' He paused and stubbed out the cigarette with his boot.

'We've no option but to shoot the guard. That'll wake the rest of them and from there on in it'll be assault and clear the building.' He looked at Tillman. 'The Bren stays here to give covering fire. If they're behind those windows you know what to do.' He glanced at each man in turn. 'If we run into trouble, we rendezvous back here. After that, every man for himself.' He looked them over. 'Questions?'

Brennan raised a finger. 'What if I took out the guard, sir?'

Wingham nodded to show he appreciated the offer. 'You mean with the knife?'

Brennan gave a wicked grin, and flipped the blade to catch the hilt. 'Got to keep me hand in, sir.'

Wingham smiled, thin lipped. 'But not this time, not enough cover,' he explained, to soften the refusal. 'I'm sure you'll find a use for it.'

Brennan grunted his disappointment and sheathed the knife, head down.

'Anything else?' Wingham asked, and gave them a moment before looking at his watch. 'Good, get ready. We'll move in fifteen minutes.'

They began a weapons check and he did the same, going through the routine of guns and spare magazines. He released the Sten's magazine, pressed his thumb on the first round, felt the pressure on the spring. Satisfied, he snapped it back in place. He noticed Tillman shouldering the Bren gun and disappearing towards the edge of the field. A few minutes later, Cartwright rejoined them. 'They're ready.'

Wingham again peered at his watch. Two minutes until Harrison's Section made a move. He watched the seconds tick by but then averted his eyes. It would happen soon enough. He glanced at what should be familiar faces, and yet, at this precise moment in time, they were almost unrecognisable. Weapons ready, tense with expectation, each man alone with his thoughts. Waiting was never easy.

Another check of his watch. It was time. He caught a movement in the trees on the right flank, and with a brief sway of undergrowth, No.1 Section melted into the trees. Over to his left the last of Corporal Dave Greene's lads departed from sight, and he met Cartwright's eyes.

'Ready?'

Cartwright set his teeth in a tight grin and turned to face the men. 'Right, gentlemen. Shall we?'

Miller hefted his rifle and moved out first. Stratton fell in behind, and Wingham joined third in line. Tulloch came next, staying close with the radio, then Cartwright, Brennan, and finally Corporal Steve Dexter brought up the rear. They moved in silence, single file, weapons ready. Within minutes Miller reached the near end of the ditch, dropped to the ground and bellied across out of sight. One by one they followed him down into the green slime, and then bent at the waist, headed on beneath the overhanging shrubs.

Out on the right flank, the seven Paratroopers of No.1 Section took a wide detour through the trees. Corporal Jim Harrison, twenty-three and from Fort William near Ben Nevis in the Scottish Highlands, fanned them out in line abreast and then probed forward. Decomposing leaf mould muffled their footsteps. When the trees began to thin, and with the farm outbuildings just visible through the undergrowth, Harrison stopped and ordered his men to wait. He scouted forward until he found a convenient thicket from where to study the stone built barn. Then moving with great care, he eased inside the mass of tight knit branches until he could see all that he wanted.

As he settled on one knee, a flurry of bird wings made him pause, and he glanced up to see three pigeons fly away and circle round to the broader canopy behind. It reminded him of home and the forests where he used to spend hours exploring the foothills. Harrison was the first born, with two brothers and a young sister. The small cottage where he was raised, homely as it was, had felt cramped and overcrowded, and as much as he loved his family, when the opportunity arose he volunteered to join up.

Ignoring the flight of the pigeons he concentrated on the buildings. With the exception of one small window the dark grey wall was featureless. But what caught his interest was a large paddock to the rear of the property enclosed by a line of trees. At a rough guess he judged the trees to be nigh on three-hundred yards away, an ideal location for surveillance. Not so good if he had to attack over the open ground.

But the Old Man had ordered the Section out there as a backstop and that's what he'd get. He turned away and slipped quietly back into the depths of the trees. He gathered the Paratroopers to him, briefly explained the layout and where they were moving to, and then set off on the last leg.

Inside the barn behind the small window a young Grenadier of the 21st Panzer Division sat staring nervously at the trees outside. A few pigeons had suddenly taken flight from the branches of an old oak tree. It had startled him, but there was no repeat performance and now all was still. Young Walter Hasse screwed his eyes shut, rubbed his face, and again stared at the trees. He began to wish he was anywhere other than in this isolated farmyard with enemy soldiers prowling the woods. He repositioned the rifle and slid a finger inside the trigger guard. For a seventeen year old boy in a man's uniform, the movement brought with it a sense of comfort, a sort of protective shield against an unseen enemy.

Over on the left flank Corporal Dave Greene and the lads of No.3 Section had made it to the rutted track. Bounded by hedges it offered good cover against prying eyes. What Greene wasn't so keen on was the fact it blinded him to any nearby Germans. He looked round and picked out Private Dan

Clayton, the twenty-year old from Crystal Palace in London.

'Dan!' he called quietly.

Clayton came forward. 'Corp?'

'Take the left side and watch out for anything beyond that hedge.'

'Right,' Clayton said and crossed the track.

Greene beckoned the others to him. 'Bren gun to hang back behind Clayton,' he said, giving Private 'Dinger' Bell a meaningful look.

The twenty-one year old Bren gunner nodded and gave a thumbs up.

Greene eyed the rest of them. 'We go up the right.'

He found Lance-Corporal 'Nobby' Clarke. 'Me first, you bring up the rear.'

Clarke inclined his head and grinned. 'Tail-end-Charlie, that's me.'

Greene smiled. 'Yeah,' he said, knowing Nobby well understood the value of the two NCO's staying apart. If one copped it, the other took command. 'Alright then,' he said. 'Let's move.'

And so the seven Paratroopers pushed forward.

Inside the ditch at the edge of the corn fields, Wingham watched Miller drop to one knee and raise a warning hand. He held his hand shoulder high, head craning forward as if listening.

In response Wingham swept his left hand back in a downward arc, and those behind him froze. He waited for the sniper to react, one way or the other. Seconds ticked by, and then Miller lowered his hand and looked back with a nod.

Wingham pushed forward past Stratton to close the sniper and whispered. 'How much further?'

Miller glanced over his shoulder. 'Fifty yards to the German, thirty before he sees us. There's a slight bend to the right,' he said, pointing ahead. 'That's where he'll spot you. I'll need three minutes to get in position.'

Wingham pursed his lips. 'Right. You go up top and I'll distract him. Sure you can take him?'

Miller gave him a wicked grin. 'When have I ever not, sir? I'll take him.'

'Okay then, whenever you're ready.' He turned to Stratton. 'When Miller opens fire we move. Pass it back.' Stratton nodded and Wingham steeled himself to become the point of contact. Looking along the ditch, beyond Miller's stealthy movement, he tried to envisage the inevitable moment of exposure. It would have to be quick and yet long enough to fully attract the man's attention.

Wingham swallowed and moved forward, eyes firmly fixed on the sniper's back.

At the back of the farm, in a line of trees at the southern end of the paddock, Corporal Jim Harrison and the men of No.1 Section took up positions ready for action.

Senior Rifleman Konrad Meyer thought he saw something behind the hedge down to his right. It might have been the breeze ruffling leaves, but with Gruber's certainty over enemy activity he was quite prepared to believe he'd seen British soldiers.

'The ditch,' he said as a warning.

Gruber gave a sarcastic grunt. 'Oh . . . , so I am maybe correct now, no?'

Meyer refused to be drawn. It was enough that he'd spoken up.

Gruber scratched an ear, watching. 'Höch will sound the alarm.'

'Ja, if he's awake,' Meyer said. 'Is it not time to send the youngster with a report of enemy soldaten?'

'And what would he say? We have seen none, only suggestions. How many? We have no answer. We must be certain of their strength.'

Meyer thought it over and lapsed into silence. They could only watch and wait.

Miller found the spot where he'd last climbed out of the ditch and glanced back at Wingham. The Major was coming on a few paces back. Miller ignored him and concentrated on clambering out. It was awkward with the rifle, not wanting to get dirt smeared onto the breech. He made it onto his belly with no mishap and edged left into the tall grass. With the rifle cradled in the crook of his arms, and using elbows, knees and boot toes, Miller snaked forward.

Five yards and he caught sight of the German's helmet, a glimmer of dull grey, just the very top. The sniper grinned, snugged the rifle to his shoulder and slipped the safety off. He squirmed forward a touch more, slowly raised his head until more of the steel helmet became visible, and waited for the next move.

Wingham had his back pressed firmly to the side of the ditch. Another look at his watch showed the second hand just sweeping the three minute mark. He felt his heart pumping and licked dry lips. He hoped fervently that Miller was ready.

Wingham crouched, steeled himself, and lunged into the open, out! . . . , two seconds . . . , and back!

The solitary crack of a Lee Enfield split the morning air. A second or so went by with no return fire and he risked a glance. The Grenadier lay slumped to one side, helmet askew, the muzzle of his Mauser buried deep in dirt. A dark patch stained the collar of his tunic.

With no time for finesse Wingham shouted, 'Now!'

Stratton went past at the double.

Bullets slammed the hedge, slashing leaves, stripping the branches. Wingham flinched, moving fast. He heard the distinctive buzz of a German Spandau. Footsteps pounded behind him. Miller jumped into the ditch ahead and ran on. The deeper thump of a Bren gun joined in as Tillman reacted. Rifle fire interspersed the sound of machine-guns and tracer whipped the bushes. Bullets kicked dirt. Stratton and Miller made it to the end and Stratton jumped over the dead Grenadier, then leapt up out of the ditch.

'Through here!' He was halfway into a hedge. Miller went right and took a prone position aiming at the upper windows. The rifle cracked.

Wingham gathered himself and lunged for a hole in the hedge. He dived through and tumbled to a stop. Stratton nudged him.

'They can't see us here, sir,' he said, pointing at the house. There were no windows in the gable end.

Wingham came to his feet, Sten gun poised. 'Bring the others over,' he said and eyed the corners of the building. The Bren gun chattered, a short burst. A Spandau replied tracer whipping across the cornfield.

The remainder of the section made it across, Miller and Cartwright last to arrive. Cartwright raised an eyebrow.

'Anyone hurt?'

'No, Sarge.' It was Stratton who'd answered for all of them. Tulloch was knelt cradling the radio to his chest, and Brennan ran a thumb down the blade of his knife. Miller just grinned; he'd added another 'kill' to his tally.

Cartwright narrowed his eyes at the single storey building with a stovepipe chimney. 'We'll check that first,' he said, and gestured for Stratton to join him. The pair split up, left and right. Miller moved to cover them, rifle aimed at a faded oak door.

Wingham watched and waited, safety catch off. They went wide, circling round, but staying within the protection of the gable end wall of the farmhouse. He saw Cartwright pause and nod to Stratton.

Stratton thought he could move up behind the open door and glanced back at Cartwright, who gave another nod, encouraging him on. Stratton paused, finger on the trigger, and then sneaked a brief look inside. No obvious sign of occupation. He pulled back, took a breath, then thrust himself through the open door and slid left into the corner. Rifle poised he took in his surroundings. It was a workshop. Down the far end a steel door stood ajar, fields beyond. A blacksmith's forge sat near the left wall, the hearth extinguished, cold. A pewter grey steel anvil sat nearby, the weight supported on a large base of tree trunk. Assorted tools of hammers and tongs hung from racks, and woodworking saws and planes and chisels lay strewn across a workbench.

Two windows were let into the right-hand wall and overlooked the southern approach.

Stratton eased out from the corner and took a few steps further in. There were no enemy lurking inside. He relaxed his finger from the trigger and returned to the door. Outside in the fresh air he gave Cartwright a thumbs up and dutifully followed the Sergeant back to where the Old Man waited.

Paul Wingham dropped to one knee and gestured towards the house.

'We'll go in the front, tight to the wall, grenades first. Mind the rear windows when we get in there. No.1 Section might not wait to check who we are.'

They nodded.

'In that case gentlemen, I suggest we get to it'

Cartwright pointed to the corner of the building. 'With me,' he said, and made a move.

Back in the tree line Lofty Tillman watched as Cartwright slid along the front wall, Stratton close on his heels. They approached the open door and then Stratton stepped away from the wall, a grenade ready. But as he did so, Tillman spotted movement in the upper window. He inched the muzzle right and hit the trigger. The Bren juddered, and a stream of bullets shattered what was left of the window. The frame, glass and curtains exploded to the impact of a half dozen .303 rounds.

Stratton's grenade went in and detonated, smoke and dust boiling from the door. Cartwright fired a short burst from the Sten and lunged inside, disappeared from view. Stratton crouched and followed.

Tillman changed mags and scanned the upper windows. Whatever had caught his attention was no longer a threat. He watched and waited.

Hans Gruber had been struck by two bullets from Tillman's Bren. The first hit his throat, cut the larynx and exited close to the base of his skull. The second ricocheted off the machine-gun and ploughed into his breast bone, deflecting down to his heart. He died gurgling blood and slumped against the rear wall.

Leading Rifleman Konrad Mayer had been aiming for the Bren's smoke when a bullet penetrated his left eye. It blew out the back of his head, dead before he hit the floor. Blood dripped slowly down the wall to leave a deep red trail.

8 The Barn

Wingham made a lunge into the farmhouse and coughed on the taste of cordite. He squinted through the dust at Cartwright who stood braced looking up a flight of stairs, Sten gun chest high, and Wingham moved towards him. Then he saw Stratton at the top, one foot on the landing. It looked like they were coping, so he turned to Brennan and pointed left to a closed door. Brennan pushed past and Wingham raised his Sten. Brennan reached the door, flattened to the side and reached for the handle, looking back for approval.

Wingham nodded. Brennan turned the handle and shoved hard. The door slammed open and Wingham burst in, going left. Brennan went right, and then they both paused. Two vacant leather armchairs faced a large empty fireplace, and a sloped writing desk sat near a tall rear window. A couple of rugs softened the bare floorboards. There were no Germans.

From somewhere upstairs a door banged. Silence. No gunshots.

'Stratton?' It was Cartwright calling.

'Two dead,' Stratton answered from overhead. 'Looks like Tillman's work.'

Wingham relaxed. 'Alright,' he said, and moved back to the hall. 'Let's check the other rooms. And get Tillman to join us.'

Cartwright nodded and walked warily to the front door. He raised a cautious hand and beckoned towards where he thought the Bren gunner lay in hiding. Upstairs another door banged as Stratton went through the rooms. Brennan moved towards the right hand end of the dwelling and stepped down to a flag-stoned floor. Wingham could make out a row of pots and pans hanging above a wood burning stove. He followed Brennan and then snapped a warning.

'Mind that back door! Harrison's lot are out there.'

Brennan stepped out of the possible line of fire and then very slowly showed himself to the hidden Paratroopers. When there was no firing in response he looked round, eyebrow raised.

Wingham said, 'We need to take a look at the barn. Where's Miller?'

'Here, sir,' said the sniper. He was in the hallway. Behind him came the tall figure of Tillman, Bren gun slung over his shoulder. He was being ushered in by Cartwright.

Wingham called up the stairs. 'Stratton?'

There was no reply.

'Stratton!' he shouted.

'Sir?' The man from the Old Kent Road sounded a long way off.

'Where are you?'

'In the loft, sir. There's a south facing window.'

'Good, stay there and keep an eye out. We're going for the barn.'

'Sir,' Stratton acknowledged, and he could be heard moving across the attic floor.

Wingham stepped over to the back door and, about to move outside, was abruptly halted by his arm being grabbed. Miller squeezed by with a grin.

'Sorry, sir. Me first.'

Cartwright also shoved past. 'Not your call, sir, you being commanding officer and all that.'

Wingham felt the smile come to his lips and dutifully waited his turn. By the time he got outside, Miller had made it halfway along the adjoining wall and Cartwright was ten feet to his left, closing in on a pair of large solid oak doors. With Dexter, Tillman, and Brennan following well spread out, Tulloch brought up the rear, and they advanced cautiously across the open yard.

Inside the barn near the stable door, Sven Zimmermann prepared for the inevitable. He'd heard the firing and guessed at the outcome, his scarred face twisting into a grim smile. Gruber had been correct, the British had come. But they were not the fanatical Russians of the Eastern Front, these soldiers were only soft Englanders with little knowledge of hard battles. He would show them how a Panzergrenadier could fight. To his mind there were no thoughts of surrender. If this was the beginning of the end for the Fuhrer's Third Reich then he had no wish to be living on in a subjugated Fatherland. Much better to die with purpose than languish in some prison camp where sub-standard soldiers fed scraps to the defeated.

He checked the magazine of his sub-machinegun, made certain the MP40's spare mags were easily accessible and laid four of his long-handled grenades within reach. He made himself comfortable behind a thick oak support beam and waited, eyes glued to the big pair of doors. For a moment he thought of warning the youngster, then decided against it. The boy had never seen war close up and if he, Zimmermann, tried to warn the lad, he might panic. The last thing Zimmermann needed was a frightened child flailing about to no good purpose.

Now was the time for an older, wiser head. He cocked the weapon. Let the British come.

Sergeant Bill Cartwright crept up to the barn doors and reached for the iron handle on the right side. He waited for Brennan and Tillman to close up and gave them a terse, 'Ready?'

They both gave the faintest of nods and he looked at Wingham. The Major met his eyes. 'Your call,' he said, and lifted the Sten.

Cartwright hauled at the handle and as the dry rust encased hinges squealed in protest, the heavy barn door swung wide. Brennan crouched and threw himself in to the left, an old stone trough giving him some cover. Lofty Tillman went right and dropped to a knee, a large wooden cart affording him some protection. Silence greeted them, and both men peered into the darkness, eyes adapting to the gloom. Tillman shifted his weight and settled the Bren.

With the pair of them now watching the interior Cartwright decided he'd waited long enough. He darted in, bent double. Four yards and he dived to the floor, immediately rolling right. A sub-machinegun opened up from the far end of the barn, bullets scything past his head. Tillman rattled off a short burst and Brennan fired from the trough.

Cartwright squirmed forward towards some wooden slats that formed the walls of a cubicle filled with hay. He wriggled up onto his knees and glanced over the top. Another fusillade of enemy bullets and he ducked.

'Anybody see that bastard?' he asked.

'No,' Tillman said, 'but its coming from near that stable door.'

Cartwright heard Wingham call. 'We're going round the outside. Keep them occupied.'

'Right,' Cartwright said, brought up his Sten and sprayed a few rounds at the far end. The Bren gun hammered, and Brennan let off a few rounds.

While they gave covering fire, Cartwright leaned a little to his left in an attempt to locate the German, but with no luck. He cursed, willing the man to return fire. But then he took a breath. Just keep the man's attention and let Wingham sort it out. He swayed back, checked an ammunition pouch and freed off another magazine, leaving it to jut out by a third.

A bullet raked his right forearm, a burning crease ripping through smock and battledress. The simultaneous crack of a rifle came from his right. The hit made him almost drop the Sten, pain lancing up his arm. But he reacted instinctively, spinning right and emptying half the magazine into deep shadows. An agonised scream followed and he heard a thud as a body fell. He changed mags for the one he'd freed off, crouched on his haunches. There was a groan from the darkness, an almost childlike whimper. Behind him the Bren gun barked, five or six rounds.

Cartwright gritted his teeth against the pain from his arm, and then moved towards the sound of harsh breathing. The muted light from a low set window showed the shape of a form lying face down in straw, a rifle still clutched in the right hand. The man's breath became shallow accompanied by a faint whistle. Cartwright kicked the rifle clear and then bent lower. The breathing stopped.

Wingham rounded the far end of the barn and gestured for Miller and Dexter to spread wide into the paddock. From within he heard the stammer of an MP40 and the subdued echo of Tillman's Bren answering. He edged closer to what looked like a stable door, both halves clipped back. Inside, the darkness acted as a barrier, and Wingham knew he was at a disadvantage. Too close to that opening and he'd be silhouetted against the daylight.

Sven Zimmermann had begun to feel very alone. The Englanders had him outnumbered and it was his belief that the youngster was already dead. If he made the slightest move a dozen bullets peppered the wooden stanchion. One had already evaded the wood and struck his waist, passing straight through the soft flesh. Trying to bear weight on that side was painful and he almost stumbled. The blood flowed freely and he hoped not too much sweat stained clothing was trapped in the wound. If he survived this encounter he would prefer not to die of a gangrene infested injury.

And what of Höch, Gruber and Mayer, he wondered. Already meat for the carrion? Probably. He sank slowly to one knee, wincing as his side reminded him of the wound. He chose a stick grenade and readied himself to lob it the length of the barn. It would give them something to think about, might even injure one of them. A sharp pull of the cord and with his right hand he lobbed it the length of the barn. A machine-gun hammered and a bullet smashed his right thigh. The grenade exploded. He gasped at the pain and drew himself back behind what little shelter the oak beam provided. Blood flowed freely, his uniform soaked, and he knew he'd not be able to put weight on that leg.

He cursed and swore and raged at the Englanders. His frustration boiled over into recklessness and he reached for another grenade. A quick tug and he hurled it at a mound of hay near the large doors. The explosion started a fire and thick smoke billowed. He lifted his sub-machinegun and waited for his prey to bolt.

The Bren gun thumped into action, a stream of bullets seeking him out, and a Sten gun added to the chaos.

Zimmermann grimaced and returned fire, shooting blind, aiming loosely at the far end. Then the enemy firing stopped and he frowned. Silence.

Why?

Too late he turned to a noise behind. He swung the gun but never managed to pull the trigger. A Sten gun chattered and his chest erupted. Blood gushed. The impact drove him backwards and fluid welled up into his throat. He choked, coughed, and then finally, Sven Zimmermann drowned in his own blood.

9 Panzer-Lehr

Wingham recognised the moment of death and looked up at the other end of the barn. 'Douse those flames,' he called. 'Too much smoke.'

Brennan rose to his feet, grabbed a nearby bucket and plunged it into the trough. It took three goes before the flames were finally under control. Tillman kicked straw to check for embers.

Wingham turned to Miller. 'Bring in the other Sections.'

Miller nodded and set off across the paddock.

Then Tillman called. 'Sir, Sergeant Cartwright's hit.'

Wingham and Dexter headed for the big oak doors. They found Brennan and Tillman removing Cartwright's smock and rolling up his battledress sleeve. There was a bloody furrow in his forearm. Brennan cleaned it the best he could, careful to remove a few sodden traces of cotton fibre. He then dusted the wound with sulphanilamide powder before producing a field dressing. He unsheathed his fighting knife and Cartwright growled.

'Whoa, sunshine! What you doing with that?'

Keith Brennan grinned and winked at the others. 'S'all right, Sarge, just cutting me bandage to length.' He sliced it neatly and wrapped it well.

'There,' he said, pleased with his work. 'That should do for now.'

Cartwright examined the bandage, exploring it with his fingers. 'Nice,' he said.

Wingham nodded and grinned. 'You're supposed to dodge 'em, Bill.'

Cartwright half smiled and shook his head. 'It wasn't the one you shot,' he said, and gestured with his chin. 'It was this bastard here. Took me by surprise.'

Wingham frowned and looked beyond the shadowed stall. He made out the inert body of a Grenadier and stepped across to inspect. Bending low he turned the body over and, in the poor light from a window, leaned in for a closer look. He studied the face for a moment and pursed his lips.

'Did you get a good look at him?' he asked.

'No, I just emptied the mag.'

Wingham chuckled. 'Have a look,' he offered.

Cartwright folded down the sleeve of his tunic and shuffled across. He stood, looking down, and then shook his head in disbelief. 'A bloody school kid. I almost let a bloody school kid finish me.' He turned away in disgust.

But Wingham paused and took another look. Is this what had become of Rommel's elite? How old was he? Sixteen . . . , seventeen at most. Still had spots. It seemed like confirmation of what they'd all been told leading up to the invasion, a soft underbelly manned by old men and youngsters. He kept his thoughts to himself and rejoined the others.

A commotion outside the barn doors caught his attention and he walked into daylight. The seven men of No.1 Section were gathering.

'Miller said for us to join you, sir,' said Harrison

Wingham nodded. 'I've left Stratton in the farmhouse. Take over and keep your eyes peeled. This little episode might have woken someone up.'

'Right, sir,' Harrison said, 'but there's nobody south of us at the moment. I made sure before we came in.'

'Very well. And Miller?'

'Went off to find No.3 Section, sir.'

'All right,' Wingham said. 'There's a couple of dead Germans upstairs. Might be a good idea to get them out.'

'Sir,' Harrison nodded, and led his section towards the kitchen door.

Cartwright appeared, adjusting the right sleeve of his torn smock, teasing it into something that resembled a uniform. He grinned sheepishly.

'Not quite King's Regulations.'

Wingham smiled. 'No, Sergeant. More like a rag and bone man.' He looked down at his own smock and grimaced. Dried green slime from the ditch covered his chest, knees and boots scuffed with mud. He didn't really have the right to criticize. And most of his Section were in the same boat.

To Cartwright, he said, 'I'm going to do a quick assessment of the layout. You okay?'

Cartwright straightened. 'I'm fine. I'll check on the lads.'

Wingham took him at his word and swung away. A defensive perimeter was next in order.

Twelve miles south of the farmhouse, in a sprawling forest near a place called Bretteville-sur-Laize, a German NCO clambered back onto his twenty-five ton Panzer IV and manoeuvred himself into the driver's seat.

Unterofficier Jurgen Voigt made himself comfortable and then fired up the 12 cylinder engine. He revved it, held it for thirty seconds and let it slowly come back down to idle. A satisfying rumble came from the rear mounted, 300 horsepower engine.

Hidden in the mass of trees, what had recently been one of the most well equipped of all German armoured divisions in Normandy, Panzer-Lehr prepared to resume its advance in support of Caen's defence. As feared, the Division's march west in the daylight hours of June the 7th became an Allied fighter-bomber free-for-all as the pilots rampaged across the French countryside.

In the space of a few short hours Panzer-Lehr lost two King-Tigers, by air to ground rocket attack, three Jagdpanzer IV hunting tanks, bombed, five Panther tanks, three self propelled Sturmgeschütz assault guns, seven Puma eight-wheeled armoured cars and as many as one-hundred and fifty trucks, halftracks, fuel bowsers and scout cars. Casualties amounted to seven hundred of which almost half were killed.

Crucially, the aerial attacks achieved a much greater effect than first appreciated. Delay. Panzer-Lehr was delayed by hours, a delay that Rommel knew his forces could ill afford. Every hour that slipped by without such a powerful heavy armour confronting the enemy allowed the Allies to expand their bridgehead and threaten his left flank. And the distance between the Le Mans secondary holding area and Caen was one-hundred and forty kilometres. In an attempt to make good the kilometres lost in daylight, Panzer-Lehr pushed on through the night, but as dawn came on the morning of Thursday the 8th of June, the majority of the Division had still not reached their allocated rendezvous in the southern approaches to the City of Caen.

Having had a one hour halt to refuel and make good any urgent repairs, Voigt's Panzer joined the cacophony of the two-hundred plus Panzers currently starting their engines.

By mid morning Jurgen Voigt found himself once again on roads lethally exposed to rocket firing fighter-bombers causing further damage and chaos amongst the leading elements. Watching the tanks ahead on the receiving end of such attacks was enough to make Voigt wish he'd joined the infantry. Better then being cooped up inside a burning coffin.

But try as they might, British and American fighter aircraft were unable to stem the flow of such a widely dispersed armoured formation. And Rommel, initially frustrated by their lack of progress, began to realise that even Allied air superiority could not stop the Panzer-Lehr. Fortuitously, his foresight in ordering the placement of an underground communications centre at the Château Fontaine now proved to be a life saver. Rommel was able to maintain a personal connection with the division's Commander. He was persuaded that only something totally unforeseen, something completely unpredictable, could prevent his prized Panzer Division from finally driving the Allies back to the sea.

Voigt tugged his left stick, hard, and brought the Panzer round to the left. A blackened tank blocked his path, wisps of curling smoke lifting in the still air. As he drove past the wreck he smelt the burnt out shell, an acrid choking stink that stayed long in the nostrils. He pressed harder on the accelerator pedal to increase speed, to quickly leave the destruction behind.

Then in his headphones, the excited voice of Oberleutnant Berthold Hoffmann came over the intercom.

'Voigt! We must move ahead and join Major Fischer to form Reconnaissance Groupe Zwei. Fischer is ordered to probe north-west of Caen and we go first.'

Once again Panzer-Lehr was on the move.

On the road out from Colombelles, the leading elements of Major Kruger's battlegroup had been forced to halt at the edge of a bomb crater. It encompassed almost two thirds of the narrow road.

Exasperated by the delay, Kruger jumped from his half-track and furiously strode up to where two young officers were arguing over their next move.

'What,' Kruger demanded, 'are we doing?'.

The older of the pair shrugged his shoulders and spread his hands. 'It is deep, Herr Major,' he complained, pointing at the crater. 'The half-tracks will not manage it.'

Kruger took a deep breath. He held it before slowly letting go.

'Herr Leutnant,' he said pointedly. 'Do our men not have shovels?'

'Ja, but they are trench tools.'

Kruger scowled. 'But they *are* shovels, are they not?'

The man nodded.

Kruger gave the peak of his cap a decisive tug. 'Then you will have your men fill this hole. Fifty of them if necessary. Do I make myself clear?'

The two officers exchanged looks, glanced at the crater, and then back to Kruger. It dawned on them he was serious.

'Jawohl, Herr Major!' they acknowledged, saluted in unison, and hurried off to shout orders at the nearest bystanders.

In minutes, a dozen Panzergrenadiers began shovelling mounds of dirt back into the crater. Small shovels they might be, but by the time fifty men frantically dug and scraped to fill the bowl, it wasn't long before Kruger felt certain his half-tracks could negotiate what had rapidly become a shallow depression.

'Enough!' he snapped, and clambered up into the leading half-track. Sweating men stood back in relief, praying that they'd done enough. He tapped the driver on the helmet.

'Forward!'

The man engaged gear, throttled up, and drove hesitantly towards the sunken pit. The vehicle slowed as the front wheels dipped to the slope, but as the caterpillar tracks found purchase the driver accelerated smoothly before eventually wrestling the half-track triumphantly out and onto the far paved surface.

Kruger shot an elated glance at the two young officers and swung down from the cab.

'That, my young friends, is how we Panzergrenadiers rise above such setbacks.' He flicked a speck of dirt from his jacket and tugged it straight. 'Mount up,' he ordered. 'The enemy await.'

Gratefully, Kruger's men folded away their shovels and retook their seats in the waiting transport. Ten minutes later the entire unit, including the six-wheeled trucks, had made their way through the freshly filled crater, reformed in good order and hurried on for the outskirts of Escoville.

Major Carl Kruger looked at his watch, squinting with his one good eye. Twenty minutes up this road and he would divide his force to encircle the farm.

10 Grenadiers

Wingham decided to inspect the workshop, see for himself. It formed an obvious left flank position, with the added advantage of not being too remote from the main house. He entered through the faded oak door and slowly walked the length of the building. The two south facing windows immediately caught his attention. They were ideal for enfilading fire, particularly once the enemy had closed to within two-hundred yards, perfect for a Bren gun. He moved past the bench towards the old blacksmith forge. An old pear-shaped leather bellows sat at the rear, the extended nozzle directed at the base of a few long dead coals. Scrappy twigs of kindling lay in a box near the north wall and a leather apron hung from a wrought iron scroll. The anvil gleamed dully in the subdued light and its pointed horn gave a menacing appearance to the steel block. He pushed past to the far door of rusting metal and stepped out into bright sunshine.

Straight ahead in the distance, beyond a meadow of bright coloured flowers, an apple orchard filled the horizon. To his right, looking south, a wide swathe of cultivated lawns led down a long grassy slope to a large cornfield. A faint smile creased his mouth. Given a choice of defensive positions, this had to be amongst the very best. Two or three men and a light machine-gun could make a mess of any approaching infantry. Wingham leaned against the warm brick and reached for a cigarette. He drew smoke and gazed for a moment at the sun drenched orchard. The rows of trees, he thought, were laid out with fine precision.

A movement caught his eye. He thought it might have been a hare, a fleeting shadow between apple trees. But there was more to it than that. He straightened from the wall and freed the Sten from his shoulder.

Vague as yet, the movement appeared to be someone on a furtive approach through the orchard, moving discretely from tree to tree. He cocked the Sten, watching, looking for others. None that he could detect. He frowned, trying to figure out what he was looking at. A lost Paratrooper dropped wide on D-Day? A German trying to surrender? But then as the shape reached the edge of the orchard and stepped into the open, he narrowed his eyes. It looked like an elderly woman.

She walked slowly with measured footsteps, head down, face in shadow. Her calf length peasant skirt had seen better days, faded now and threadbare. A shabby black shawl covered her head and hung from her shoulders, partially concealing a cream open-necked blouse. Wingham thought she was late middle-aged, a little stooped, weary. Certain there were no others in sight, he lowered the muzzle of the gun, a little, and walked to meet her.

Drawing closer, the elderly woman lifted her head and Wingham stopped in surprise. His initial impression of a worn, tired woman was a long way wide of the mark. She was young, vivacious, no more than mid-twenties, raven haired and dark eyed, and with a flawless complexion. She came to a standstill, hesitant. He remembered he was in France.

'Mademoiselle?' he prompted quietly.

'No,' she said, emphasising the denial with a shake of her lustrous black hair. 'I'm English.'

He pursed his lips and wondered why Bainbridge had been so insistent on a French speaking officer. He met her probing eyes. 'I was expecting somebody French.'

A faint smile showed a glimpse of her even white teeth. 'So you were not sent to find me?'

He thought about that. 'Not specifically. My orders were to wait until contacted.'

'And you are who, exactly?'

Despite himself he grinned at her forthright questioning. 'Paul Wingham, Major.'

She touched a thoughtful finger to her chin. 'Well, Major Paul Wingham, consider yourself contacted.'

He remembered the need for an exchange of passwords. 'In that case,' he said, 'may I ask your name?'

She tilted her head and gave him a sideways look. 'You can ask,' she said teasingly. 'Which name would you like? There are a few to choose from.'

'Try me, I can't keep calling you mademoiselle.'

'All right,' she said at length, 'how about . . . , Jill?'

'Did you bring a pail of water?'

She laughed. 'No, but Jack did.' She reached out a hand. 'I'm Sarah.'

With the simplicity of a nursery rhyme their identities were satisfied and he took her small hand in his. Her shake was surprisingly firm.

'Sarah suits me fine. Now would you mind walking to the farmhouse? We can talk there. Standing out here in the open is not exactly my idea of fun.'

Sarah giggled and half curtsied. 'Why, kind sir, how can a young maiden refuse such a gallant invitation.' She waved an airy hand. 'Show me the way.'

Bemused, Wingham turned and gestured towards the workshop door. 'Through there for starters. We can get to the house from the other end.'

She smiled, inclined her head and walked past him. Wingham turned again for a final check on the orchard, took a few backward steps with the Sten raised, then gave it up to follow her. He felt a little out of his depth. It wasn't quite how he'd imagined this would all pan out. On the other hand, he now had a woman to worry about. As pleasant a diversion as it was, he prayed to God that she would impart her information and disappear to wherever she'd come from.

Private Joe Miller crept silently towards a mound of low lying boulders that topped the slight ridge overlooking a shallow valley. He'd already found No.3 Section and relayed Wingham's instructions. Corporal Dave Greene had immediately set off for the house. But Miller decided he might be more useful taking a dekko at the countryside that lay between the farm and Caen. With that in mind he'd pushed south at a tangent until spotting the well weathered slabs lying about seventy yards on from the tree line where No.1 Section had waited at the back of the paddock.

Squeezing between two of the rocks he slowly raised his head. There before him, beyond a low lying basin that formed broad flood plains around the River Orne, Miller found the distant outline of Caen's rooftops. A faint smile teased his lips and he brought the Lee Enfield forward for a closer look through the telescopic sight. He found that the built up heart of the city was no more nor less than he might expect of any conglomeration of buildings. Tiled roof tops, chimneys, church spires, and in one area, what appeared to be a solidly constructed water tower. Disappointingly, the roads were invisible, hidden within the maze of ancient houses in tightly woven streets. Cursing his luck, he wriggled forward until he managed a better view of a small town this side of the Orne. The name eluded him, but as he studied some of the buildings he thought how old-world were some of the hotels and banks with their arched colonnades and grand porticos surrounding what at first glance appeared to be the main market square.

Miller repositioned himself and began scrutinising a few roads leading in and out of the suburbs. He discovered one that meandered towards him, and followed it with the rifle's telescope. The road wound its way between lush acres of wheat and barley, and here and there orchards of ripening apples brought soft colour to gentle slopes.

And then to his astonishment, he picked out a column of mechanised infantry. Partially shrouded in dust and fumes, there were half-tracks and canvas backed wagons pushing up the road towards him. A pair of motorbikes led the way. Miller scoured the half-tracks for any evidence of officers. He could see troops riding in the open and wearing the distinctive camouflaged uniform of Panzergrenadiers. The numbers involved indicated at least company strength, a hundred men or more. He retraced the road back to the town. No sign of tanks. Refocusing on the leading half-tracks he latched on to the third vehicle in line and a grim smile creased his lips. Two triangular pennants flew, one either side of the bonnet. The more striking of the two flags fluttered bright red in the breeze, a circular splash of white displaying the Nazi's black swastika. The other pennant was less distinct, a drab brown with what might be a regimental badge in the shape of a palm tree.

Miller blinked and licked his lips, and then raised the 'scope to dwell on the troop compartment. Swaying to the motion of the vehicle he found an officer wearing full parade uniform, his leather gloved hands grasping the top edge of armoured plate. The highly polished peaked cap glinted in the light, and then Miller tensed as he picked out the incongruous sight of a black eye patch being worn over the man's left eye. The recent story of a brutal execution had filtered through to Lane's headquarters, and quickly putting two and two together, Miller also guessed the man in his scope might well hold the rank of Major. He wished the rifle had a longer range.

Another minute passed while he studied the column, and then having memorised all that he needed, Miller wormed his way back from the boulders and took off to warn the Old Man.

11 Paulette Chalamet

On the eastern outskirts of Ranville, at one of 6th Airborne's newly established battle headquarters, Major Freddy Lane was trying to asses how well his perimeter was holding. The meagre force at his disposal had been scattered by a surprise counterattack from the Germans, and having pushed the Paratroopers back from the middle of town, the enemy had then broken off the engagement. To add to his predicament an order delivered by messenger had seen him lose another twenty-four men to some foolhardy mission deep behind enemy lines. The only saving grace in that instance was that the Platoon was being led by the reliable Major Wingham. But Lane's problems didn't end there. He was yet to establish radio contact with Brigade and had no idea when, or if, he might get any form of tank support.

'Sir!' came a call from outside the house. 'Colonel's coming.'

Lane straightened away from the small map and moved to greet the towering figure of Colonel Douglas Rees-Morton. He was a man you didn't quickly forget. Wide set level eyes, strong nose and with a purposeful jaw. They met in the hallway and Lane gave him a respectful nod. They both appreciated the lack of formality. Saluting between all ranks had been forbidden while Allied formations were in close contact with enemy units.

Officers quickly became prime targets for enemy snipers.

The Colonel nodded, grim faced. 'Right, Freddy, what do we know?'

Lane took him through to the living room, showed him the map and waved a vague hand.

'Not much. We've been forced to withdraw to this side of the town. Jerry had a sizeable presence in there. We lost eight dead and at least as many wounded. We're holding a pretty thin line . . . , skin of our teeth.' He pointed to three separate buildings that straddled the road into town. 'I've got men here, here and here.'

Rees-Morton eased his helmet, giving himself time to take it in. 'Well, that's something. Did you manage to get that Platoon out?'

'Last night,' Lane nodded. 'About 20.00 hours.'

'Good, how many?'

'Twenty-five all told.'

'And who's in charge?'

'Major Wingham, sir.'

The Colonel raised both eyebrows. 'Paul Wingham?'

Caught by something in his tone, Lane said, 'Yes. Anything wrong?'

'No . . . , not specifically.'

Lane wondered where this was headed. 'I didn't have any say in the matter. General Bainbridge sent him. Last minute thing, in a torpedo boat, with Sergeant Cartwright. You have your doubts, sir?'

The Colonel smoothed his moustache. 'Well,' he said at length, 'I always thought he could be a bit of a loose cannon. Doesn't always stick to orders.'

Lane gave the Colonel a pointed look. 'That, sir, might be exactly why the General suggested he take it on.'

Rees-Morton blinked. 'You think so?'

'Definitely. That mission is as difficult as it comes. The farmhouse is about two miles south of here behind enemy lines. The General would have needed an experienced man, a man he trusted. If the agent does make contact then he'll be up to his neck in it. Sergeant Cartwright is his 2i/c and between the pair of them breaking a few rules would be par for the course.'

The Colonel thought about it before conceding the argument.

'Yes,' he said quietly, 'you're probably right. And Cartwright's a good man. Solid you know. Shouldn't be too inflexible should we?'

'Not in this case, no sir.'

'All right, then, let's hope he knows what he's doing. Heard from him yet?'

Lane shook his head. 'No not yet, but I can't get in touch with anyone else either. I was praying for some armoured support. Radio operator's doing his best.'

Rees-Morton smiled, thin lipped. 'That's why I came, Freddy, to let you know. There's a squadron of tanks on their way. Should arrive late morning.'

Lane straightened and pursed his lips. 'Thank Christ for small mercies. But if Jerry mount a major attack before then . . . , it'll be a bit touch and go.'

The Colonel hesitated before answering. 'Hold as long as you can. If you have to fall back, keep to the road. That's where the tanks will appear.'

Lane tilted his head and grimaced. 'As long as they don't take us for the enemy.'

That,' said Rees-Morton, 'would not be at all proper.' He grinned. 'Not at all.' He straightened his helmet and glanced at his watch. 'Sorry, but I have to run, orders from on high.'

'Yes, sir. Thanks for coming. We'll do what we can.'

The Colonel met his eyes and nodded. 'I know you will, Freddy. And don't forget to keep your ear out for Wingham's lot. They might not be many in number, but few as they are they're a vital component in all this. Good luck.' And with that, he was gone.

Major Freddy Lane sighed, turned back to the map and again cast an eye over the detail. Wingham's Platoon was uppermost in his mind. But just for once he wished that Bainbridge, or someone in the know, anyone, would tell him what was so bloody important about their mission. Being told they were a 'vital component' didn't really cut the mustard, not when it came to sending men on a possible one way ticket.

Studying the map he tried to fathom out what his next move might be should the Germans launch a counter attack.

Up in the loft of the farmhouse, Tulloch switched on the radio and tuned in to the day's frequency. He'd brushed away a mass of spiders and cobwebs from the rafters, removed a few roof tiles and then positioned the set beneath the opening before attaching the longest length of aerial. Headphones on, he pressed the microphone's 'send' switch and tried Brigade's call sign.

'Hello, Baker-Able, this is Dog-Two, over.' He released the switch to listen for a reply. What he actually got was a scrambled mass of calls filling the airwaves. He'd never heard the like, everything from Company level through to the Naval forces off shore. He checked the frequency and retuned, carefully. He repeated the call. This time, for ten seconds only the uninterrupted hiss of static met his ears. He tried again.

'Hello, Baker-Able, I say again, this is Dog-Two, over.'

The steady return hiss suddenly crackled into life and a metallic voice cut through the airwaves.

'Dog-Two, this is Baker-Able, over.'

Tulloch hesitated, he really needed the Old Man.

'Err . . . , Baker-Able, this is Dog-Two, stand by. Out.'

Wingham ushered Sarah into a deserted room with a few faded sticks of furniture scattered against the walls. The single broken window overlooked the south lawn that blended into the fields beyond. Spider webs clung to the corners of the ceiling.

She swivelled a wooden chair away from the wall and perched, selected a cigarette from a crumpled pack and flicked a lighter. With a slow curl of blue smoke, she crossed her legs and arched an eyebrow in query.

'You seem surprised, Major. Did they not tell you it would be a woman?'

'No, not once, and it was deemed vital I speak French. Not quite such a necessity as they thought.'

She smiled, a mischievous, almost apologetic smile. 'I had to get a message to London and to keep my identity as secure as possible I elected to wrap it all in French.' She drew on the cigarette and blew smoke at the ceiling. 'Do you approve?'

Wingham shrugged. 'It really doesn't matter whether I approve or not. What matters is that you tell me why you needed to make contact.'

She nodded and a small frown wrinkled her dark eyebrows. 'There is a pretty little Château in the valley to the south of here,' she began. 'It sits in the middle of an ancient wood and is almost hidden from view.'

Warming to her subject Sarah uncrossed her legs, leaned forward and stared at the wooden floor. 'It is called the Château Fontaine, innocent in appearance, but it hides an important secret.' She looked up from the floor and caught his gaze, eyes glinting.

'Go on,' he prompted, intrigued as to what she knew.

She sat back and teased the hair from her neck. 'There is a wine cellar, half the size of the ground floor, but no wine. At the beginning of May, a German soldier of the highest standing came to visit. General-Feldmarschall Erwin Rommel came to have lunch with Colonel Heinrich Kohlberg of 126th Panzergrenadiers. The Colonel uses the place as his headquarters.'

Wingham held up a hand to interrupt her. 'How do you know all this?'

'Until yesterday one of my other names was Paulette, and Paulette worked there as a waitress.'

'And now?'

'Never again,' she said vehemently. 'I will never return to the Château Fontaine.' She took a lungful of cigarette smoke and blew it at the ceiling.

Wingham caught the glint of anger in her eyes, a look of pure hatred reflected in the set of her jaw. It struck him something very untoward had happened to Paulette, but he let it pass.

'So . . . , about Rommel. What happened?'

'When the General left the Château the wine was taken out and lorries took it away, to Paris I think. In the next week many crates arrived and were carried into the cellar. We were forbidden to go near the cellar. After that, a new intake of men arrived, kept themselves to themselves, and their duties were always in the cellar. Then two weeks after Rommel's visit German engineers arrived and put up tall aerials on the outside of the Château. A day later a company of Waffen SS set up in the grounds and security became much tighter. Even the Colonel had to show his papers.'

Wingham guessed what was in the cellar. A large array of aerials could only mean radio communication, probably with multiple transmitters. If the cellar had become a signal station, under Rommel's direct orders, then Sarah's information was of utmost importance. No wonder Bainbridge had been so keen on the patrol.

Sarah stood and squashed the cigarette butt under her foot. 'One night I passed by the open door. The cellar was brightly lit and I saw three large radios on a long bench. One had a small screen with an orange display and three operators sat with headphones making notes.' She looked away to the window. 'I heard one of them say they needed to get a message to the armoured division of Panzer-Lehr. Another said the 12th SS Division had called for help.' She turned to confront him.

'I speak fluent German, Major, and I've been trained in wireless telegraphy. Of one thing I am certain, the Château Fontaine must be destroyed.

That's why I am here, and I need your help to do it. Without it I fear your soldiers will have a bad time trying to hold off three armoured divisions. But if we can destroy Rommel's method of communicating with his Divisional commanders then their battle plans will fall apart.' Her eyes glinted with determination. 'Think of how many lives it will save.'

Wingham gave a gentle smile. 'I will try,' he said, meeting her level gaze. 'We've not yet been able to make contact with anybody, certainly not 6th Airborne.' He pulled the map from his thigh pocket. 'Can you show me the location?' He moved over to a mahogany dresser and spread it out. Sarah bent over it, scrutinising the detail. 'There.' She pointed a well manicured finger at a dark shaded oblong.

He dug out a pencil and ringed it. 'Right,' he said. 'Pity we can't see it.'

'Oh but we can,' she laughed.

The laugh was a little shrill and Wingham realised how crucial this had become for her.

'If we go into the attic,' she said, 'you'll be able to see for yourself.'

He frowned. 'You sure?'

'Definitely. I could see this farm from the Château's top floor. The window in the roof.'

Wingham took a long deep breath. He wanted time to digest all this and see for himself without having to explain things. 'What will you do now?' he asked.

'Me?' It was her turn to smile. 'I'm with you. Just give me a weapon. I can look after myself.'

There was something about her reply that made him look again at this beautiful young woman, a hard edge to the bland statement. He almost wanted to believe her; wanted to be able to give her a Sten gun and let her get on with it, not have to worry about her.

He hesitated with his answer, not willing to commit to her joining their ranks.

'You don't believe me do you, Major?' She stepped close and held out her hand. 'Your Sten, I'll show you.'

He slipped it off his shoulder and reluctantly passed it over.

'Watch,' she said, and began stripping the weapon into its component parts. In less than a minute a well practised routine resulted in the seat of the chair displaying a neatly dismantled sub-machinegun. As the last piece was placed on the seat she gestured with a hand and tossed her head.

'There,' she snapped, hands planted defiantly on her hips 'Can you do better?'

Wingham thought he probably could but had no reason to press the point. She had proved she knew her way round guns and that was good enough. He dodged the question.

'I need to find our radio operator, see if he's made contact.' He bent to the chair and without hurrying, reassembled the Sten. Finally, he clipped in the box magazine and slipped the strap over his shoulder.

'Right now,' he said, 'the only spare weapons I have are German. Rifles or machine pistols. You know how to use those?'

She gave him a confident nod.

'All right, Sarah-whatever-your-name-is. If I make contact with headquarters, do you have a codename? How do I convince them you're telling the truth?'

The ebony eyes latched on to his and held. 'You tell them I am Paulette Chalamet and I was born on January 12th, 1919.'

'Good, now let's find you a weapon while I see what I can do.' He stepped out onto the landing and led her down creaking stairs. Outside in the cobbled yard he found Lofty Tillman cleaning his Bren. He looked up, surprised by the woman's presence.

Wingham gave a brief introduction and instructed Tillman to find her a German weapon.

'Yes, sir,' Tillman grinned and met Sarah's gaze. 'This way, love. Fancy anything in particular?'

Wingham hid a smile. There were no airs and graces with the man from Yorkshire. He was salt of the earth; a gentle giant with a bigger heart. He hefted the Bren to his shoulder and led her off to the kitchen before heading for the front door. Wingham watched them go, eyes narrowed in thought. Whatever happened now he couldn't just abandon her, so she may as well make herself useful.

12 Château Fontaine

Bill Cartwright strode into the sitting room with its large open fireplace and took a long look out of the south facing window. He had a good view down to the trees beyond the paddock, and an even better view of the ground from dead ahead round to the workshop on his left. He caught a glimpse of Miller making a loping run from the row of poplars across the paddock and guessed it must be important. The sniper didn't expend unnecessary energy unless it was vital. Cartwright made for the kitchen to meet him.

Miller staggered to a halt in the trampled garden, out of breath, and Cartwright held up a hand. 'Whoa, what's all the rush?'

'Jerry!' Miller struggled to catch his breath. 'Panzergrenadiers, a company at least.' He grabbed a lungful of air.

'How far?'

'Mile and a half, no more. Half-tracks and lorries.'

'Right,' Cartwright said, 'I'll tell the Old Man. Now get yourself up the loft, you'll like it up there.'

Miller stood firm, not moving. 'There's something more, Sarge.'

Cartwright took note of the sniper's tone, concern written across the man's face.

'Go on then, let's have it.'

'My telescope gave me a pretty good view of an officer leading the way.' He hesitated and shuffled a foot in the dirt.

'And?' Cartwright urged.

Miller raised his eyes. 'The bastard was wearing a black eye patch.'

Bill Cartwright gave a slow nod. They'd all heard the story. If they tangled there'd be no quarter given.

'I'll pass it on,' he said, and they went their separate ways.

On the road east from Colombelles, Major Carl Kruger signalled for the column to halt. To his left, at the place he'd decided to split his force, a cobbled lane forked off to the north. Two half-tracks and three trucks would take this lane and check the woods beyond the farmhouse. If all was clear his orders were for Oberleutnant Hans Schröder to establish a line of encirclement in case any British Paratroopers were inside the house. He turned and waved a long finger at the column, directing the secondary echelon to take the new route. Schröder led the way in his half-track and the allocated wagons peeled away in line astern. As they veered onto the cobbles Kruger again raised the gloved fist.

'We go!' he shouted above the noise of the engines, and chopped his arm forward. The half-track lurched ahead, gathering pace, the remainder of the column close on his heels. Kruger stared intently at the road in front, particularly at the hedge to his left. He remembered that somewhere along here, not far, a wide wooden gate gave easy access to the fields south of the farmhouse. And sure enough, minutes later, one of his motorcyclists was sat across the road. The man pointed and Kruger grinned. There on the left a gate of five solid wooden rungs, two metres long, barred entry to a field of corn.

'Open it!' he demanded.

The man dismounted, strode to the gate, and after a brief struggle to disengage the iron hasp, walked the gate round into the field. He stood staring through his goggles, waiting for the Major to move.

Kruger braced himself and glanced at his driver. 'Turn in, schnell!'

The half-track growled and clawed round into the standing corn, chewing the ripening ears under its tracks. Kruger let the driver advance sixty metres and then stopped to allow the other half-track time to take station. He called for Oberleutnant Lehmann, then uncased his personal pair of Carl Zeiss binoculars. With his one good right eye he focussed on the farmhouse. But even through the magnified lens the building still appeared distant, the detail small, inconclusive.

'Herr Major?'

Kruger lowered the glasses and found Lehmann stood to attention by the cab door.

'I want thirty Grenadiers, Lehmann, extended line out front. Now.'

With a formal nod the officer snapped his heels and made off for the trucks. Tailboards clattered and men tumbled out, then hurried forward between the vehicles to form a skirmish line twenty metres ahead.

Kruger looked at his watch. Schröder should have radioed in by now, why the delay? He glanced at the radio operator intending to have the man call

Schröder but decided to give him more time. There was no knowing exactly what was inside the woods. He looked round the assembled force and nodded his approval. Skirmish line out front, and half-tracks purring in readiness, and the trucks holding station as his main force. He scowled at the sky. So far, he thought, their luck had held. No Allied aircraft had made an appearance. . . , yet. He reached for a cigarette, flicked the lighter and drew smoke.

With the sun warming his face, Kruger gambled on not being spotted from the air and he and his armoured Panzergrenadiers waited, ready to advance. Soon.

Wingham was about to look for Tulloch and his radio when Sergeant Cartwright came marching round the corner.

'What's up, Bill?'

'German column. Coming up from the south. Miller says they're Panzergrenadiers.' He paused and held up a warning hand. 'And one of their officers is wearing a black eye patch.'

Wingham stared at him, taking the news at face value. He wondered if the *Ruffians* had a chance of pulling out. 'How long before they get here?'

Before Cartwright could answer they both heard the ominous sound of tracked vehicles pushing through the trees past their right flank, beyond the barn.

Cartwright gave a wry grin as he answered. 'Anytime now I should think.'

Wingham smiled in return but worried his lower lip. 'Question is, will the bastards keep moving? Might be headed for Ranville.' He rubbed his unshaven jaw. 'You saw the woman?'

'I did. Is she the reason we came?'

'Yes. Part of the French underground, but she's English. I have to get word to 6th Airborne. Has Tulloch made contact yet?'

'He's upstairs, rigging up some weird and wonderful aerial system.'

Wingham removed his helmet and ran a hand through his hair. 'I think,' he said slowly, 'I may be about to call for artillery.'

Cartwright frowned. 'You think we really need it?'

'For the woman. I'll explain later.'

'Sir!' The shout came from overhead. It was Miller at the loft window.

'What is it?'

'Germans!' he shouted, and pointed south beyond the trees.

Wingham, well aware of enemy movement passing his right flank, wasn't sure he'd heard correctly and cupped a hand to his ear. 'Say again!'

'Jerries, sir. In the bottom field!'

Cartwright waved an acknowledgement. 'They've split up.'

'Sod it,' Wingham said. The rattle and squeal from tracked vehicles still echoed in, but now the sound came in across the fields from the north, the front of the farmhouse. And then, in the wood where the Platoon had begun their attack, the noise came to an abrupt halt. Cartwright looked up, mouth tightening.

Wingham met his eyes. 'Buggered!' he said. 'Well and truly buggered.' He shook his head. 'Bloody surrounded.' It was stating the obvious but somehow it needed saying, aloud.

Cartwright agreed. 'That we are.'

'Right.' Wingham said. 'First things first. I'll find Tulloch, you organise the men.' Cartwright turned away but Wingham stopped him.

'Sergeant,' he said, an urgent authority in his call. Cartwright looked back.

'If they attack we have to hold. You must give me time.'

Cartwright stiffened to his full height. 'Major, sir,' he said very deliberately. 'If that's what you want, that's what you'll get.'

And with that assurance ringing in his ears Wingham nodded and they parted company.

Wingham got side-tracked by No.3 Section moving into defensive positions around the front of the farmhouse. Corporal Dave Greene requested Wingham's approval for the sighting of their Bren gun. A brief look confirmed what appeared to be an ideal location and he gave his agreement. From the corner of his eye he caught sight of Tillman giving Sarah a few spare magazines for the MP40 she held. He gave them a curt nod and then he was in the front door and taking the stairs two at a time. He threw himself up the loft ladder and emerged to find himself bent double under the eaves of the roof. Miller was watching the fields from the window, Tulloch had the radio over by the north elevation.

Wingham crossed to the window and focussed his binoculars on low ground to the south. He carefully searched the boundary of a distant wood and found what he thought must be the Château. A tall building, it sat discreetly amongst even taller pine trees. White walled and with a high round turret, the grey tiled roof reflected the sombre style of French design. At this range there was no sign of aerials but Sarah's explanation of the layout coincided with what he could see. If he got her confirmation an artillery strike would be the obvious choice. He lowered the glasses and turned to Tulloch.

'You in contact?'

'Yes, sir, just this minute. Wait one and I'll get them back.'

Wingham grunted impatiently.

'Hello, Baker-Able, this is Dog-Two, message, over.'

'Send, over.'

Wingham reached for the mic. 'Baker-Able, this is Dog-Two, get me Sunray-Minor. Over.' There was a distinct pause before the reply.

'Dog-Two, wait out.'

It took two minutes and then Wingham heard the voice of Major Freddy Lane.

'Sunray-Minor here.'

Wingham collected his thoughts.

'This is Dog-Two. Contact made as ordered. I have map co-ordinates for you, over.'

'Go ahead, over.'

Wingham gave him the grid reference and then said, 'Contact insists this location must be destroyed soonest. Suggest heavy artillery, over.'

There was a pause, airwaves full of static. Then . . . . 'Dog-Two, this is Baker-Able. Date of birth? Over.'

Wingham chose his words with care, speaking slowly and clearly into the mouthpiece 'One-two . . . , oh-one . . . , one-niner, over.'

'Baker-Able, Roger. Do you have a visual of target? Over.'

'Dog-Two, yes, over.'

'Baker-Able . . . . Wait out.'

Minutes passed, too many, and Wingham called them up.

'Hello Baker-Able this is Dog-Two, over?'

Static. . . . No answer. He gave it another thirty seconds.

'Hello Baker-Able this is Dog-Two, over.'

Static, a hiss, and then a click. 'Dog-Two, this is Baker-Able, Sunray-minor. Wait one-five minutes. I say again one-five minutes. Acknowledge, over.'

Wingham understood Lane would need time to set up a fire mission. 'Dog-Two, Wilco out.' He passed the mic and headset back to Tulloch and made for the ladder. First things first, he needed Sarah to verify the target, just to be on the safe side.

He found her stood at the kitchen table with a German sub-machinegun and in the process of inspecting the inside of the barrel.

'Sarah!' He was deliberately brusque, abrupt. This wasn't the time for pleasantries. 'We're in contact with Brigade. I need you in the loft . . . , now.'

Her ebony eyes narrowed to meet his, the pink of her tongue pinched between white teeth. She made no effort to question his demand, but nodded. and slipped the gun over her shoulder. 'Whenever you're ready.'

'With me then,' he said and made for the stairs. She followed close on his heels.

In the loft he turned to assist her off the ladder. Her grip was strong and yet that smallness of her hand reminded him of her vulnerability. Outwardly tough she might be and well versed in soldierly ways, but beneath the rugged exterior, a woman nonetheless.

'Mind where you put your feet,' he warned and guided her to the window. Miller had moved to the side, perched on one knee, the rifle cradled in his arms.

Wingham pointed to the valley. Once you knew where the place was, even with the naked eye the white walls were just discernable through the trees. 'Is that your Château? In those woods?'

'Yes.' She spoke softly, with a slow nod. 'That is the Château Fontaine.' Her words came with a great deal of bitterness.

He glanced at the time. Another seven minutes before Freddy called again. From the corner of his eye he snatched a glance of her beautiful profile, the dark hair falling gently down cheek and jaw, long lashes, her eye glistening.

Lifting the glasses he brought the focus in closer and panned down the field of corn. The force of Grenadiers held station, not moving, a slight haze of exhaust fumes drifting from the vehicles. He hadn't the faintest idea of why they remained immobile, but right now it was a vital breathing space.

The radio came to life. 'Hello Dog-Two, this is Baker-Able. Over.'

Tulloch answered. 'Dog-Two, over.'

'Baker-Able, your request agreed. Big Boys not yet available. I am informed ten minutes, over.'

Wingham rubbed his eyes in thought. If the Germans attacked before then the chances of observing any hits on the Château were negligible. He reached for the mic. 'This is Dog-Two . . . , we have Panzergrenadiers closing, over.'

'Sunray-minor, can you hold long enough? Over.'

Wingham blew out his cheeks. 'Dog-Two, you'll know in ten minutes, over.'

There was a pause before Lane came back. 'Baker-Able, I'll try and gee them up. Out.'

Long minutes passed for Wingham and the girl but finally Lane came back to them. 'Baker-Able, fire mission ready. Repeat coordinates, over.'

Wingham dug out the map and traced his finger across the intersecting grid, eastings then northings, and came up with a six figure reference. It was as good as he could do with the map he had. He made a note down one side and passed it to Tulloch. 'Send that.'

Tulloch glanced at the numbers and passed them through. He listened intently to the reply.

'Dog-Two, Wilco, out.' He looked at Wingham. 'One round for ranging, sir. They'll wait for your correction and fire another. If that's on target, they'll fire for effect, high explosive.'

'Very well,' Wingham said, and lifted his binoculars to the Château. A minute passed and then came the sound of a single shell ripping through the air. He tensed, expectant. A distant orange flash and a rolling ball of dirty grey smoke rose short of the target.

'Up two-hundred.'

The correction was sent and Wingham waited. A second shell whipped overhead and the resulting explosion obliterated the foot of the building's ornate front entrance.

'On,' he said to Tulloch. 'Fire for effect.'

'Baker-Able, this is Dog-Two.' Tulloch's voice had gone up a notch. 'On target . . , fire for effect. I say again . . , fire for effect, over.' He listened for the answer and then said, 'Dog-Two, out.' He looked up easing the earphones. 'Twenty rounds high explosive, sir.'

Wingham glanced at Sarah and she gave a thin smile. 'I can't wait,' she said and leaned forward in anticipation. Her waiting didn't last. Arriving from five miles north, the harsh shriek of shells from a battery of 25 pounders whistled over and the Château erupted in a flash of thumping high explosive.

Shattering blasts blew walls to fragments, scything through the roof. A parked wagon half full of ammunition took a direct hit, instantly adding to the inferno, lethal missiles exploding in random chaos. White phosphorous sprayed and burned, melted flesh, dissolved bones. Caught in the mayhem, men of the Waffen SS died in agony, torn apart by the brutal fury of British guns. The crew of an anti-aircraft gun near the Château's main gate abandoned their position and sought shelter in a ditch. The last man was too slow. The next shell detonated and hurled him ten metres. It impaled him on the stump of a branch. His broken remains twitched in the pulp, an involuntary convulsion as he died.

Against a neatly trimmed hedge leading to the ornate gardens, a second half track had been demolished, the remnants burning freely, wreathed in smoke. An officer's body lay nearby, face down in the grass, savaged by fragments of exploding shell. Dark blood dripped into glistening pools.

Inside the crumbling Château, and nursing a deep wound to his right thigh, Kohlberg crawled the floor in trembling terror. His desk had taken the worst impact of a plunging shell, but the pressure wave caught him and slammed his bulk against the wall. Shrapnel sliced his leg. The destruction was mind numbing, and in total shock he mumbled in disbelief. He'd survived the war in Africa, proclaimed his continued allegiance to Rommel, believed in Hitler's assurances of how the Third Reich would rule for a thousand years. But now Colonel Kohlberg, favoured recipient of a Knights Cross, realised for the first time as he coughed in the choking dust, that his life probably hung by a thread. Ears ringing, almost blind, he crawled on.

The office door had been blown off its hinges and he dragged himself into the corridor. A glimmer of daylight showed to his left and he headed for what he hoped was the exit. The constant thunder of exploding shells blotted out all else from his thoughts, praying only that he might make it to fresh air. For a moment he pressed himself into the base of the wall, cowering from the lethal barrage. A section of roofing gave way above him and a timber slammed into his back. His spine shattered in a misery of white hot pain and he screamed in torment, unable to escape the house of death. He wished it would all end.

The artillery's final salvo ripped into the grounds of the Château in a hurricane of explosive force. A communication from Panzer-Lehr to Rommel's headquarters, in the process of being passed via the signals section at the Château Fontaine, suddenly ceased mid transmission. With that break in communications the immediate threat of German forces dealing a decisive blow to the Allied invasion faded.

For Colonel Kohlberg there was one shell too many. It exploded close by and he incinerated. As the smoke drifted clear through the maze of tall pines and hedgerows, only the decimated skeletons of men and guns remained, burning softly in the cratered earth. Annihilated.

Buried beneath the Château's weight of broken masonry, the cellar lay crushed and silent, pulverised bodies strewn amongst the dark rubble. At a critical moment in Adolf Hitler's defence of the Third Reich, a vital link between German High Command and Panzer Divisions manoeuvring in and around the City of Caen had been broken.

Three kilometres to the south of Château Fontaine, the young waitress called Angélique stood in the doorway of her parents home and watched the last of the shells explode on and around the Château. She trembled, shivering at her lucky escape. It was only forty minutes beforehand that she'd left to walk home. But even as she watched the violent destruction she felt an uncertainty replace the relief. Her job no longer existed. Yes, she could look forward to days without the attention of the Colonel and his underling, but her parents could no longer rely on her financial support.

Gradually, the immediate shock of what she'd witnessed began to wear off and Angélique even managed a tremulous smile. In her heart of hearts she felt a certain elation at the Château's destruction. For the first time the war had come close and a small smile came and went. It looked as if the Boche would soon be running. Maybe it was time to polish up her English.

13 To Hold

In the attic of the farmhouse, Sarah looked on with bitter satisfaction, her mouth compressed into a grim line. This was the culmination of eighteen months work. All through that time she had lived not only with the fear of discovery but in the full knowledge of what terrors she would have to endure. During the last three months, four of her female colleagues had been arrested by the Gestapo. None had been heard of since and the conclusion had to be drawn that they'd been tortured and killed. Sarah had known who they were from the outset, but they had all been ignorant of her role within their organisation.

She began to cry.

Silent tears welled up and trickled gently down her cheeks. Her relief at seeing the total destruction of Château Fontaine couldn't be put into words. It left her feeling numb.

Wingham reached out a hand to her shoulder. 'Okay?' he asked gently.

Sarah nodded, brushed away the tears and managed a half smile by way of reassurance.

He patted her arm and turned to Tulloch. 'Call 'em up.'

'Baker-Able, Dog-Two, over.'

'Dog-Two, this is Baker-Able, send, over.'

Wingham took the mic and listened through one headphone pressed to his ear. 'Target destroyed,' he said, emphasising the words. 'I say again, target destroyed. Over.'

There was a short pause. Then . . . 'Hello Dog-Two, this is Sunray-Minor. Roger. Time to come home, over.'

Wingham glanced out of the window and shook his head.

'Dog-Two, those Panzergrenadiers are camped on our doorstep. Over.'

'Any sign of tanks? Over.'

'Not yet, over.'

'Can you withdraw? Over.'

'Dog-Two, slim chance, over.' There was a prolonged silence before Lane came on again.

'I have armour arriving for a push south. Over.'

Wingham thought that sounded promising. 'How long, over.'

'Midday-ish. Over.'

Wingham glanced at his watch. That was still an hour off. He tried a last alternative.

'Baker-Able, this is Dog-Two, artillery still on call? Over.'

'Sunray-Minor. Sorry, they've been re-tasked on a priority shoot.'

'Dog-Two, air support? Over.'

'Sunray-minor, doubt it. We can't get any for ourselves. Over.'

Wingham ran his tongue over his upper lip and made up his mind.

'Baker-Able, this is Dog-Two, we'll dig in. Over.'

'This is Sunray-Minor. Your decision, Paul. Sorry we can't get there sooner. Good luck. Out.'

Wingham handed the headset and microphone back to Tulloch, his mind racing. Uppermost in his thoughts was the safety of the Platoon. Casualties were inevitable, he could only try and keep them to a minimum. Freddy had said, 'your decision', and Wingham shook his head. Easy for him, not so bloody easy up at the coal face. In the end, he thought his duty lay with the men. He should have seen it coming, and it was another mistake. Two in one day. Maybe he'd lost his touch, it had been a fair while since Italy. He reached out a hand to Sarah.

'Come on, we're finished up here.'

She nodded, took a last look through the window and then followed him to the ladder. He let her go down first and made a move for the hatch, and with a parting 'Stay sharp,' to Miller and Tulloch he dropped down the ladder to find Cartwright.

His second-in-command would need to know the outcome.

Dusty Miller, watching from the loft window, spoke from the corner of his mouth, 'Take a look.'

Tulloch glanced over. There was something in the sniper's voice, different. He discarded the headset and shuffled across beside him.

'Christ all bleedin' mighty,' he mouthed. 'We gonna fight that lot?'

'Could be,' Miller said. 'See that leading half-track? Officer in that one, the one with the eye patch. Saw him down on the road but the bastard was out of range.' He ran a finger down the telescopic sight. 'Standing up like a soddin' Prima Donna. Just asking for it.'

Tulloch nibbled his bottom lip. He'd been in his fair share of battles, but most times without fully realising what he'd been up against. Not till after the event anyway. No wonder Miller had sounded different.

'Hope the Old Man knows what he's doing,' he ventured, and moved back to the radio. Before replacing the headset he checked the Sten and made sure it was within easy reach. In the semi-darkness of the loft he licked dry lips and listened to the airwaves. For a minute he heard the insistent hiss of static and then switched off. No point in wasting battery power.

Tulloch sank onto his backside, cradled the Sten, and waited.

At Honeysuckle Cottage the wireless in the kitchen came alive to inform all and sundry that it was time for the mid morning news.

"This is the BBC. Here is the eleven o'clock news for today Thursday, June the 8th.

Our troops are pushing forward into Bayeux and have made contact with German armoured defences. The town of Caen is the subject of heavy bombing along with fresh targets in the Cherbourg Peninsula. Our correspondents on the ground understand that in a prelude to the beach invasion on the 6th, thousands of Allied paratroops dropped in the dark behind enemy lines to attack and hold strategic locations. Most of those priority targets were secured.

A steady flow of reinforcements and supplies is reaching Normandy by sea and air.

That is the latest official news and sums up the situation thus far this morning. Further news will follow in the BBC's one o'clock bulletin."

Mary, hard at work earthing up potatoes in the vegetable plot, leaned on her spade and wiped her brow. With the back door wide open she'd heard every word of the BBC's broadcast. It all sounded so promising and she desperately wanted to believe that everything was going well for her Chris.

'Cup of tea's ready, Mary! Come along. I've put it in the potting shed.'

She smiled and dug in the spade to let it stand alone. She had to admit the tea would be welcome and walked off down the path of crazy paving. As she did so she slowed to place her boots carefully within some of the more intricately laid slates. Chris had laid the path during a week's leave and she'd made fun of the fact he couldn't lay straight ones.

With a quiet chuckle she reached the potting shed and sat to share the tea with her mother. She sipped and closed her eyes to the sun's warmth. At times like these it was hard to believe there was a war on.

In the heart of London, in an old Victorian three storey town house situated a mile and a half east of the War Office, General Scott Bainbridge stood studying a large map of Normandy.

Bainbridge coughed, cleared his throat and glanced at his cluttered desk. His attention was drawn to the black sheen of a telephone protruding from beneath a stack of paperwork, a telephone now noticeable for its unusually prolonged silence, not something he was accustomed to. He frowned, subconsciously touching the faded scar on his cheek, in two minds over whether it was yet time to make inquiries of Whitehall.

A loud knock on the oak panelled door revealed the chubby round face of Lieutenant Trevor Benedict Ingram, a seldom seen young officer on the General's backroom staff. He slipped inside and drew himself to attention.

Bainbridge smiled at the youngster's look of concern. 'Well, Lieutenant,' he said kindly. 'What can I do for you?'

Ingram held out a sealed envelope. 'This despatch arrived from the War Office, sir. Addressed to you.'

'Did it indeed?' Bainbridge said raising an eyebrow. 'For me you say?' He reached out and glanced at the address. Handwritten.

'Despatch rider, was it?' He moved towards the untidy desk, feeling under the heaped paperwork for his letter opener. There was a hesitancy from Ingram.

'Not exactly, no sir.'

'Then who? Spit it out, man!'

'It was a Captain McCrea, sir. In a staff car.'

Bainbridge had found the knife and was about to slit the envelope. He looked up, curious. 'McCrea, eh? In a staff car?'

'Yes, sir.'

'Mmm . . . , very well. You can wait, in case there's an answer.' He delved inside, removed a single sheet of foolscap and read through. The information given was concise, neatly detailed and without superfluous explanation. It had come via Colonel Douglas Rees-Morton's battle headquarters and only patched through to the War Office after Eisenhower and Montgomery had been appraised of its contents.

A slow smile spread across the General's face, the blue eyes twinkling as he digested an obvious truth. If it hadn't been for Captain McCrea, he might never had received the answer to his request. He folded away the despatch, glanced at the state of his desk and thought better than to leave it discarded to one side. Instead he opened a drawer and placed the envelope neatly inside. He straightened and looked over at the patiently waiting Lieutenant.

'Thank you, Mister Ingram. You should be aware that you were the bearer of a vital piece of information. Hitler's plans to use his heavy armour and prevent us advancing south from the beachheads may well now have received a fatal delay. Much more so than either Rommel or Army Group West ever envisaged.'

The young Lieutenant grinned broadly, his enthusiasm coming to the fore. 'Thank you, sir,' he beamed.

'Very well,' Bainbridge said. 'That'll be all. Carry on.'

The Lieutenant stiffened. 'Sir,' he said and wheeled away to let himself quietly out of the room.

General Scott Bainbridge returned to his chair, lit a cigarette and swung his heels onto the desk. As the coil of cigarette smoke drifted to the ceiling he took another look at the map and nodded. He'd done everything in his power to help the Army move inland. It was to be hoped that the rather ponderous machinery of Allied High Command would take full advantage when the opportunity arose.

He took another lungful of smoke and contemplated the glowing ember. For the first time in years he felt the war was at long last moving in the right direction.

In Normandy, amidst the waving corn south of the Farm Sainte Beaumont, and with the sun climbing ever closer to its zenith, Major Carl Kruger's Kompanie of the 126th Panzergrenadier Regiment set their faces to the north, primed to attack.

Sergeant Bill Cartwright stood with his back to the farmhouse and cast an eye over the sloping southern approach. The existing features offered an obvious line of defence. The barn sat to his right, solid, a bulwark against a right flank attack. Then came the fenced paddock with the odd drinking trough and bits and pieces of farm machinery. Behind him, central to it all was the farmhouse, defensible up to a point but a main target for the enemy. In the middle was a small ornamental pond and next to that a woodpile. A low wall sat this side of the veg patch and finally the workshop acted as a left flank guardian. With Greene's Section watching for any movement out front, it gave him No's.1 and 2 Sections to play with. Not a lot but he'd long since learnt to live with the hand you were dealt, and in wartime that was seldom ideal.

He quickly decided on two fire points for the Bren guns. Kitchen window for Tillman, and to cover the left flank he'd position Lance-Corporal Rob Carter, No.1 Section's Bren gunner, in the workshop. For the remaining Paratroopers it would be defence in depth, two lines stretching out between the old barn and the workshop.

'Corporal Harrison!' he called.

'Sarge?' the Scotsman answered, appearing from the other side of the woodpile.

'I want your Section as first line of defence. Spread 'em out from the stable door, along the paddock fence to that stack of wood, the stone trough, beyond the pond and over to the workshop. We'll have Carter's Bren gun set up in there. He won't be short of company, one of my lot will be nearby.'

'Seven of us, Sarge. That'll make us pretty thin on the ground.'

'I know it, but needs must.'

'And No.3 Section. Where will they be?' Harrison asked.

'They're out front. Jerry have occupied the woods where we arrived.'

'Right, I'll set 'em up.'

Cartwright held up a hand. 'If it gets too hot, fall back on the farmhouse.'

Harrison gave him a lopsided grin. 'Last line of defence?'

Cartwright gave him a lazy grin. 'Something like that, yeah.'

The Corporal nodded and moved off, and Cartwright looked up to the loft window. 'Miller!'

A face appeared looking down.

'Get your arse down here. Is Tulloch still up there?'

'Yeah.'

'Him too, in the kitchen. Move yourselves!'

Miller's head disappeared and Cartwright made for the cobbled yard. He found the rest of No.2 Section cleaning up.

'Right,' he said, 'listen. For those who don't know, we've got Jerry front and back. So we're digging in. In case any of you are not aware, one of those bastards down there is wearing a black eye patch. So there'll only be two possible outcomes to this. They give up and go home, or . . . .' He left the alternative unsaid. It was fairly self explanatory. There was a general murmur of acceptance. It had already been discussed. If you were going to die, then make it hard on those bastard Germans.

He paused, making choices.

'Brennan, I want you this end of the barn inside the double doors. There'll be someone from No.1 Section down at the stable door.'

Brennan, studiously oiling his knife, nodded.

'Tillman . . . , the kitchen window.' The gunner smiled and patted his Bren.

Cartwright pursed his lips. He needed one of them to back up the workshop.

'Corporal Dexter, find yourself a spot towards the workshop, but not in it. You'll be supporting Rob Carter's Bren.'

He then met Stratton's inquisitive gaze. 'Sitting room window for you.'

Stratton gave a small nod, and Cartwright looked round to find Miller stepping out from the kitchen. 'You got anywhere in mind?'

The sniper pointed. 'This end of that pond, where they've built the bank up. Those reeds make a good screen.'

Cartwright thought it was too exposed. 'If you say so,' he said and shrugged. He turned to look at the windows. 'Wouldn't be my first choice.'

Miller tilted his head. 'No good in the house, that's the first place a sniper looks. Hopefully, the reed bed won't be their choice either.'

Cartwright accepted the logic. 'Point taken,' he said.

Tulloch had remained standing in the kitchen doorway. 'You want me in here, Sarge?'

'Yep, and that'll be the command post and first aid station.' He then swept an eye over them. 'Questions?'

Tillman had one. 'Any chance of reinforcements?'

At that moment Major Wingham strode out from the gloomy interior of the barn and gave an answer. 'Tanks are on their way.'

'How long, sir?'

'Soon,' Wingham said. 'Not long.' It was a half lie but he thought it better that the burden of truth remain on his shoulders.

Cartwright rubbed his hands. 'Right then, let's be having you.' And the men split up to go their separate ways.

Wingham caught his eye and with a jerk of his chin beckoned him across. 'You heard the shells going over?'

'I did, yes.'

'That was for the woman. She was our contact and I passed her info to Lane. There was a Château south of us full of wireless stuff, a communication centre for Rommel. It kept him in touch with all the Panzer divisions.' He grinned.

'Not any longer. Our artillery gave it the once over, turned it into rubble, so in a nutshell we're done. The brass hats ordered us back to HQ, soonest, and I told Lane we were surrounded. That's when he said tanks are on their way so I decided to hold and wait. We have to safeguard the woman if we can, but I have to say she's no slouch with a weapon. Where to use her? That's the question.'

Cartwright was emphatic with his answer. 'Kitchen for now. 'There'll be wounded.'

In the cornfield to the south, Major Carl Kruger's radio operator stiffened to an incoming call. He listened briefly and then acknowledged the message.

'Schröder takes up position, Herr Major. He also reports seeing two or three British Paratroopers on the north side.'

Kruger tightened his lips. So be it, he thought. It was time to crush these invaders.

'Good,' he said. 'That is good.' He straightened to his full height, checked the readiness of his command and leaned over the front.

'Lehmann!' he shouted. 'You will advance!'

The young Leutnant nodded and gave a sharp order to his men. The extended line of Grenadiers moved off and Kruger's half-track growled into life, advancing at walking pace, holding the interval between men and machines. The second half-track eased forward and headed fractionally right, widening the gap between itself and Kruger, a text book manoeuvre to split enemy fire. The order went out for the remaining Panzergrenadiers to disembark, and they piled out from the trucks to form slim columns behind the protective armour of the half-tracks.

Kruger raised his glasses in an attempt to find signs of the enemy's deployment, but to no avail. The half-track pitched and swayed to every undulation, too much for stable focus and he lowered the binoculars. But the thin smile remained. There could be no doubts as to the outcome of this attack. He had more than enough firepower to subdue such poorly equipped forces, and his reserve of ammunition would outlast anything the British Paratroopers could carry.

In the heat of a mid-summer sun, Kruger's Panzergrenadiers trampled the ears of ripening corn and advanced in time honoured fashion.

Tillman hurried into the kitchen and checked his view from the window. At first glance he thought it gave him a solid field of fire. But what passed for a window ledge was too narrow for the Bren's bi-pod feet. Without hesitating he smashed the glass, removed a few last remaining shards and let the barrel rest on the frame. Raising the offset rear sight, he bent slightly, aimed the weapon and traversed left to right. Satisfied with the result he relaxed against the upright of the window frame and glanced round the room. Prominent in the centre stood a large scrubbed wooden table surrounded by four rough hewn solid backed chairs. Jed Tulloch had his radio on it, fiddling with the dials. A window out to the front allowed Tillman to see the northern approaches along with the wood from where the Old Man had originally launched his attack. Cartwright had said that Jerry were out there too, and Tillman grimaced. Rats in a bleedin' trap, he thought, and grinned. No one said it would be easy. Not that he was particularly concerned, after all, the Major had said tanks were on their way, just a matter of holding out. If that was good enough for the Old Man, it was good enough for Lofty Tillman. And anyway he joined the Paras for a bit of adventure, and all of this was a sight better than being a butcher's assistant back in Leeds.

He turned his attention back to his own window. So let the bastards come, he felt more than ready.

Hidden in the barn, Keith Brennan lay in straw beneath the cart. The cart had been constructed of thick oak planks and the chunky spokes offered both concealment and limited protection. At the same time it allowed him to cover both the far end of the barn and the cobbled yard between himself and the farmhouse kitchen. Down at the stable door one of Harrison's lads watched the far tree line. Cartwright had said something about it being the 'first line of defence.'

Brennan cocked his Sten gun and rummaged in a pocket. He popped a boiled sweet in his mouth and shifted it to the hollow of a cheek. The juices ran and he savoured the sugar rich tang. Watching the yard his thoughts drifted, remembering the girl in Richmond. He'd met her at the County Showground behind a big marquee, fetching sheep for her dad. He frowned. What was her name? He could see her eyes and taste her lips; they were sweet too. Her name escaped him. He'd been on leave for a long weekend and then reported back for duty. Nice while it lasted.

The frown faded as he remembered his older brother, Jack, killed in the fighting at El Alamein. Later, he heard it had been Rommel's Africa Korps, and going by Miller's description of a pennant on a half-track, the one with a palm tree on it, this could be the same mob. A chance encounter on a different continent, and Brennan hoped he might get the opportunity for revenge. He felt for his knife, thumbed the blade and pressed it back into the scabbard. Easing an elbow in the straw, he watched and waited.

14 Stand To

Mike Stratton hurried to the living room and moved to the big sash window. He was surprised to see it still intact. Without hesitating, he smashed the glass and made himself as comfortable as he could. He might be there for a while. But he'd only just settled when a movement to the south caught his attention. He narrowed his eyes. And there it was again, the top of a German half-track advancing up the slope. He leaned out of the window and yelled a warning.

'Half-track coming!'

Tillman heard the shout and repeated it. 'Half-track, sir.'

Wingham nodded. 'Very well,' he said, and stepped outside the kitchen door. He planted both hands on hips and took a final glance round his defences. As always he mused, Bill had done a good job in setting up the defences. Harrison's Section had taken up their positions roughly thirty yards beyond the farmhouse. They formed the first line of a 'defence in depth', a poor one Wingham conceded, but better than none. Push came to shove, Harrison's Section would fall back on the farmhouse, at which time the Platoon's remaining firepower could then be concentrated.

He scuffed a boot through dirt and swore. So many 'ifs', 'buts' and bloody 'maybes'. He lifted his chin and took a lungful of air. Indecision, he remembered, was the scourge of command. Part of a leader's role? . . . yes. But only in as much as it took to weigh the alternatives, not to dwell. An officer took the responsibility and, right or wrong, must make a choice and stand by it. He became aware of the Cartwright's arrival, looked round and met his gaze.

'As ready as we can be.'

Cartwright inclined his head. 'We are, sir.'

Wingham threw off his misgivings and grinned. 'What's the odds?' he asked, 'six to one?'

Cartwright's weathered face broke into that familiar, lazy smile. 'Yes, sir,' he said, and the smile broadened, 'but those odds do not necessarily favour the enemy. . . . Do they?'

Wingham chuckled. 'No,' he said, 'indeed they don't. And I'm betting they haven't a bloody clue of what's about to hit them.'

He stopped short. Cartwright's expression had become sombre. The forthcoming battle wasn't just about "black patch" and avenging their fellow Paras. It was also the moment when each man recognised the other's unspoken resolve to play their own small part in 6th Airborne's overall strategy; now their mission was over they could help hold the enemy away from the Allies left flank and the bridges over the Caen and Orne waterways.

Cartwright stuck out his chin and bared his teeth. 'Time to show 'em what for.'

The Sergeant's parade ground bark rang out over the defences.

'Stand to!'

Wingham nodded and turned back for the kitchen doorway. He stopped to turn and stare out over the sunlit paddock, and felt the last lingering doubts fall away. With the enemy in sight, and advancing in strength, he knew the die was cast. His watch showed him it was 11.35 hours.

At an old abandoned farmhouse in this ancient land of Calvados, his under strength Platoon must fight and hold, or die in the attempt.

Corporal Steve Dexter, No.2 Section, found an ideal spot half way along the low stone wall to the rear of the vegetable garden. It wasn't much but better than nothing. He cleared away some loose pieces and tried it for size. In the kneeling position he was pretty much hidden, but he added a little depth by scraping away some soil. When he was done he stood for a last look around. Twelve yards to his right, the muzzle of Stratton's Lee Enfield jutted from the farmhouse window. In the workshop to his left, he'd seen Rob Carter of No.1 Section enter with his Bren. Dexter frowned. They were a bit thin on the ground. Then he saw Cartwright striding towards him from the front of the house. The Sergeant brushed through the veg patch and looked at the wall and the shallow scrape.

'Bit exposed out here, think you can manage?'

The Welshman nodded. 'I'll manage.'

'All right, but if it gets too hot fall back to the house. Nothing rash. Just do what you can and get out of it. Clear?'

Steve Dexter heard the concern in his voice. 'Right,' he said. 'I wasn't looking to be a bloody hero.'

'Good,' Cartwright said, and gestured towards the workshop. 'I'll be in there with Carter.' He turned away, but called back. 'And keep your head down.'

Dexter grinned, then slowly went down on one knee before 'assuming the position'. Kneeling in his hollow with Sten gun poised and grenades to hand, the man from Cardiff prepared to fight a battle.

Cartwright made it to the workshop door and warned the Bren gunner.

'Coming in!'

Twenty-one year old Lance-Corporal Rob Carter glanced his way. 'Feel free,' he said, acknowledging his presence, and returned his gaze to the window. He leaned comfortably over the workbench, the Bren pointing through smashed glass.

'They're on the move,' Cartwright said. He shifted past behind him, skirted the forge and anvil, and eased up to the iron door. He leaned head and shoulders out of the opening and peered to his right. What met his eyes was an unrestricted view of the southern approach and the distant apple orchard. He grimaced and slipped the Sten from his shoulder. Standing there at the end of the workshop it struck him that he'd just become the Platoon's left flank guardian. If the enemy took this building, the Major would be outflanked. He thought how handy a heavy machine-gun would be. As it was, Carter's Bren would have to do.

He relaxed against the door jamb and waited to open fire.

Almost due north of Wingham's precarious position, approximately five miles south of 'Sword' beach, where British elements of 2nd Army had made landfall, tank reinforcement for the Paras had almost reached open country. But minefields on that side of the River Orne had yet to be cleared with too few Sappers from the Royal Engineers able to get forward. Adding to the scarcity of tanks for the extreme left flank, the majority of armour clearing inland from the beaches had been urged toward the right flank in order to support Field Marshal Montgomery's push for the strategically important city of Caen. Inevitably the Paratroopers holding out on the left flank became increasingly isolated.

But a single Troop of three Sherman tanks managed to 'thread the needle' between two minefields when their 22-year old commander, Lieutenant Matthew J. Summerton, dismounted and personally took the initiative to walk ahead down a footpath. In normal circumstances the narrow path would have been deemed unsuitable for armoured vehicles, but Summerton felt that 6th Airborne's call for tank support dictated he take a chance. Fifteen minutes on, having checked numerous suspect areas of freshly disturbed earth for mines, and finding none, he remounted.

Inevitably, it was late that morning before the three Sherman tanks of 2 Troop, 'C' Squadron, 8th Battalion King's Own Royal Dragoons, finally crossed two bridges over the Caen Canal and Orne River. It should have been the entire Squadron but Lieutenant-Colonel Terence H. Wheeler, the Regimental commander suddenly found himself ordered to move into some woods where he unexpectedly came face to face with a half battalion of the 12th SS Division.

As far as Summerton was aware, the Caen Canal and Orne River bridges had been the first battle fought by British Paratroopers in the early hours of D-Day. Secured and held. It was that very success that now allowed his Troop to head for the besieged remnants of 6th Airborne in Ranville. Lieutenant Matthew Summerton stood in the cupola of the leading Sherman and willed his driver to increase speed. But as flat as the terrain appeared it was too rough to sustain a top speed of twenty-five miles an hour. Patience, he knew, was a virtue. It would do no good to berate the driver. It was a difficult enough job without having the man up top shouting in his headphones.

At the farm, twenty-year old Private Douglas 'Jock' Stewart, one time honoured member of the Black Watch, but now a proud 'soldier-from-the-sky' of No.1 Section, found cover behind a three-bladed horse plough. The machine had been stored neatly outside the paddock fence, but the steel had a haze of brown rust, as if it had been left unused for many months, and a cracked leather apron lay draped across the handles. It acted as a partial curtain, the lower portion touching the grass. Stewart dropped to the ground, chest and belly supported on his elbows and angled his rifle around the blades. It gave him a reasonable field of fire while keeping him fairly well hidden. He prepared two grenades and placed them to his right, ready when needed.

Stewart was under no illusion as to what was coming. He'd fought in the battle of El Alamein against Rommel's Africa Corps and had seen a blood bath. Casualties on both sides had swiftly mounted, many of the wounded left untended until after the battle. Yes, he thought, it was a victory, but afterwards, from where he'd stood to survey the carnage it hadn't felt like one.

'Alright, Jock?'

He turned his head to glance left at Jim Harrison who lay a few yards away behind the ruined remains of a chicken coop.

Stewart grinned. Putting aside the difference in rank, they'd been mates for a long time. 'Could be better. You?'

Harrison smiled slowly, a lazy, easy smile. 'Well,' he said, 'if lying in a load of chicken shit and waiting for a bunch of Germans is your idea of, 'could be better', then I'm absolutely fine.'

Stewart chuckled. He saw him cock the Sten gun and then lay two magazines and a couple of grenades neatly to his left close at hand. They gave one another a meaningful look. If it got so close that hand grenades were involved then they were probably in trouble.

Rifleman Mike Stratton watched as the half-tracks revved and squealed their way up the slope. A dozen or so Grenadiers weaved ahead, slowly closing the distance. He readied himself, feet apart for a little more comfort. This was the first wave. Beyond the half-tracks more Grenadiers appeared half hidden from view. The second wave, he thought, and God only knew how many more besides. He grinned. For a brief moment it reminded him of the Old Kent Road. A double-decker would pull up to take on passengers and the waiting queue would surge forward and blend together, much the same as the Germans down the slope. Remembering the Old Kent Road he glanced at his watch. Helen would already be at work where he'd first met her, serving from behind a ladies wear counter in Woolworth. They'd become romantically attached shortly after and whenever he had a spell of leave they were inseparable.

A sudden change in the German formation brought him back to the present. Half way up the slope a pair of Grenadiers peeled off from a small group and set up a machine-gun. Stratton dismissed his memories and concentrated on that pair. He watched and waited. The Old Man would call it soon.

Wingham watched the German skirmishers as they neared the trees, watched them spread out as they crested the gentle rise. Close on their heels came the armoured half-tracks, the squealing grind of steel on steel echoing in across the paddock. He raised his binoculars at the leading vehicle and gave a tight smile. Whoever was in command wasn't shy about announcing his presence. Two triangular flags fluttered in the breeze, an incongruous splash of brilliant colour at odds with the dull grey of muted camouflage. The armour glinted to a shaft of sunlight, beyond which Wingham could see the twin mounting of 20mm machine-guns.

He transferred his gaze to the second half-track, no flags but a similar array of weapons. And following on behind the vehicles, dismounted Panzergrenadiers advanced in two columns ready for the main assault.

Wingham lowered the binoculars and raised his voice to the *Ruffians*. 'Wait for my command!'

Tillman at the kitchen window cocked the Bren. 'Brave or stupid, sir?'

'God knows,' Wingham said, surprised by the sheer audacity of such a frontal attack. 'I think they've underestimated our strength.'

'They've stopped.' Tillman pointed.

Wingham raised a hand to shield his eyes from the sun's glare and squinted at the widely dispersed enemy line. Now what? And then he realised . . , the second half-track was making a slow turn away. It came to a halt parallel with the workshop and half a dozen Grenadiers dismounted and went to ground. But Wingham was intrigued by a few men still standing in the back. They were bent at the waist working on something hidden beneath the vehicle's side plates. He raised the field glasses for a closer look. Only then did he realise what they were up to. They were a mortar team preparing for a shoot.

He called towards the pond. 'Miller! Half-track, eleven o'clock. Might be a mortar crew. Feel free.'

The sniper acknowledged with a terse, 'Sir,' and inched the rifle a few degrees left. He located the half-track, centred his lens on one of three men at the tail end. It was a long shot, even with a telescopic sight. He firmed the rifle butt into his right shoulder, took up the slack.

He held the target, head and shoulders, and ran his tongue over dry lips. Then a deep breath, slowly released with pressure on the trigger . . . , he squeezed.

The Lee Enfield's recoil thumped his shoulder, and the magnified lens caught a .303 bullet slamming into the German's chest. Blood sprayed and the man's face contorted. Then he was gone. Miller smoothly ejected the spent shell, engaged the next round in the breech and rotated the bolt into its locked position. When he looked again there was no sign of the other two. Miller aimed at a vacant spot just above a steel panel and waited. It didn't take long. Seconds. A camouflaged helmet, a face. He fired. The bullet snapped across the void. It struck above the left eye beneath the helmet's rim. The face disappeared.

Smoke belched from the half-track, the noise of the engine rising to a snarl and the squealing tracks fled south down the slope.

Miller eased his cheek from the butt and lowered his head behind the tall reeds. One more added to the tally; he accepted the other as a possible.

Wingham, who'd watched it all through his binoculars, marvelled at the sniper's skill. Two shots, two hits, and at that range one British Paratrooper had relieved a considerable threat to the Platoon's well being.

'Nice work, Miller,' he called, and the sniper gave the faintest of nods.

Not that it would alleviate the situation for long. But ranging for the mortar would have to be called in from an observer. If it now became a scratch crew, accuracy might well suffer. And every little helped.

Kruger was surprised to see his mortar half-track retreating from the long outbuilding. Then his radio operator acknowledged a call.

'Sniper, Herr Major.'

Kruger grimaced. They'd not heard the sound of shots over the noise of the engine and he quickly appreciated his vulnerability. Maybe the flags weren't such a good idea. He ordered the driver to reverse and backed off three-hundred metres before venturing to again move forward and take station behind a convenient line of poplar trees. His Grenadiers reacted by halting, and lacking leadership the skirmishers went to ground.

With his half-track concealed by a dense thicket of hawthorn and a line of imposing trees, Kruger looked down at Schwartz.

'Time to show me your shooting, no? Our mortar team reports a British sniper. He must be killed, Schwartz. Killed, you hear me? Let us see if you can live up to your reputation.'

Otto Schwartz looked up and grunted. His pale grey eyes latched on to Kruger's and a quiet smile twitched his mouth.

'You wanted me, Herr Major, and now you have me. And yet now you question my skill. It is strange.' He patted the Mauser. 'I know my expertise, I hope your battle skills are equally as good.' He gave Kruger an insolent salute, dropped to the ground and as he moved into a patch of undergrowth, faded from view.

Kruger momentarily found himself lost for words, taken aback by the sniper's insubordination. Next time, he thought, next time he will pay for such impertinence, but now? He looked round his command, there were more important things.

Straightening to his full height he yelled across to the men.

'Panzergrenadiers! Do you hear me?'

A guttural shout from many throats acknowledged his call.

Krause grinned. 'Are you with me?'

A grizzled veteran came to his feet. 'We're with you, Herr Major!'

'Then show me how you fight.' He pointed at the farmhouse. 'Forward!' he shouted. 'We attack!'

The soldiers came to their feet and with a roar of defiance stormed ahead. From the half-track down the slope, a mortar fired, the shell lobbed high, immediately followed by a second and a third. They detonated short of the farmhouse, shrapnel scything the walls. It was the opening bombardment of

Kruger's assault, no going back. The Englanders must be wiped out, no survivors.

15 Open Fire!

Wingham lowered his binoculars and tucked them in their leather case. He slid the Sten from his shoulder and moved to lean against the open kitchen door. He forced himself to wait, willing the enemy closer. It was the hardest part, the waiting, always the waiting. Another salvo of mortar shells erupted, this time all over the paddock. When the dust and smoke evaporated the advancing wave of German skirmishers were forty-yards closer.

Major Paul Wingham, M.C., took a last look round his defences and gave the order.

'Open fire!'

Mike Stratton, slightly elevated inside the window of the sitting room, had kept a wary eye on the machine-gun crew. With his Lee Enfield aimed on the dark silhouette of the gunner he caressed the trigger and squeezed. The soldier jerked to the hit and fell to the side. His assistant grabbed the gun and squirmed backwards into a hollow, out of sight.

Stratton found a Grenadier running in a crouch. He centred the sights on the man's body and squeezed. The man hit the ground in a tangle of arms and legs. Stratton looked for another. A soldier pointed, gesturing at others, an NCO maybe. He steadied the sights and fired. The man twisted sideways and grabbed his arm, sagged to one knee. Stratton gave him another and saw him go down.

A machine-gun hammered and bullets chipped stone. The window frame splintered. Stratton grunted and spun to one side. He grabbed his right arm. The muscle had been sliced and he felt the warm flow of blood. He also felt the exit wound. For a moment he was left dazed by the shock of impact. A second machine-gun opened up right of centre and tracer fizzed. A bullet ricocheted down and slammed his left thigh. Stratton groaned. A spurt of blood and he sank behind the wall. The noise of battle increased, rifles, Bren guns, Mausers and Spandaus.

He managed to lift the rifle. Glowing tracer whipped in from the left, and bullets chewed granite. He caught the movement of a Grenadier's camouflaged uniform, sighted the Lee-Enfield and fired. The patch of camouflage fell sideways.

Stratton shifted weight to his right leg and again raised the rifle. The pain from his thigh set his teeth on edge but he levered the bolt and chambered another round. A stick grenade tumbled through the air and landed outside. Face to the wall he prayed. The explosion showered the aperture with dirt and smoke, and then he winced as a deflected piece of shrapnel sliced his left hand. He shook his head free of dust and peered through the smoke, seeking another target.

Mike Stratton, ex barrow boy from London's Smithfield meat market, propped himself against the window sill in the midst of battle and wondered how long he could last. Blood pooled from his wounds and began to congeal. He spotted a running target and fired. Missed.

Over in the barn down by the stable door, Lance-Corporal Ben Fletcher, 2i/c of No.1 Section, gritted his teeth. The undergrowth beneath the line of poplar trees lit up to the flash of machine-gun fire. A dozen enemy bullets pinned him behind the right wall. He blew out his cheeks. Sticking your head out into that lot, he thought, was bloody suicide. For a second he closed his eyes, steeling himself to brave the onslaught. Tracer fizzed and hissed, bullets gouging chunks from the doorframe. But then the firing slackened and he risked a look. Through smoke and dust he thought he saw a tank. Not an entire tank as such, but the tracks of a tank. Then he heard the squeal and metallic clank, his eyes had not deceived him. Thick smoke thinned, and he saw it again, only this time he found a standing officer brazenly wearing a peaked cap. It was a half-track, roughly eighty-yards range and he breathed out. Not a Panzer or the feared Tiger, just an open backed personnel carrier. He slipped back out of sight and checked his Sten gun. He loaded a fresh magazine of thirty, 9mm rounds, relishing the opportunity. He remembered the age old saying, probably something first coined in the Napoleonic Wars. Always take out the bugger wearing a big hat. The metallic squeal from the tracks stopped, engine ticking over, growling in response to the driver's accelerator pedal.

Ben Fletcher swung into the open, brought the Sten to his shoulder and hammered a few aimed bursts at the officer. Tracer glowed, sparks flying and the officer dropped from sight. But the gunner in the back was no slouch, quick to react, the twin mounted machine-gun latching on to Fletcher's position and he lunged for cover. Again the upper and lower panels of the stable door took a pounding, lethal splinters torn asunder. Crouching behind the wall, sweat trickling down his face, he grimaced. It was hot. He risked another glance outside. This time what he saw worried him. A long barrelled Pak Anti-tank gun had been unhitched from the half-track's towing eye and manhandled into position. Fletcher stuck his head outside and shouted a warning to Harrison by the paddock railings.

'Anti-tank gun!'

Harrison yelled an acknowledgement and Fletcher heard him detail a rifleman to give harassing fire. At the same moment, three Grenadiers jumped clear of the half track and began leapfrogging one another towards the barn.

Ben Fletcher decided enough was enough and took them on with his Sten. He wasn't about to let anybody through this neck of the woods.

Behind the cracked leather apron hanging from the plough, Jock Stewart had a German NCO in his sights. The man had walked straight out from beneath the row of poplars and was urging a section of Grenadiers to hurry. They hung back, doubtful. He wriggled his elbows into the dirt until he felt rock steady, sighted again on the NCO's chest and gently squeezed. The rifle barked, thumped, and the German keeled over. His section of Grenadiers hit the deck, content to wait, no NCO to push them on.

Stewart bared his teeth in a grin. One shot and a section out of action . . . , for the moment. He cocked the weapon and looked for another victim. But with his attention fixed elsewhere he failed to notice when two of the Grenadiers begin to wriggle forward.

As Bill Cartwright had ordered, the remainder of No.1 Section had taken up positions in a rough line either side of the woodpile. Rifleman Norman Taylor, a twenty-one year old from the small village of Tintagel on the north Cornish coast, knelt behind the rough hewn timber with his Lee Enfield supported over the top. Most everybody called Taylor 'King', because Tintagel was where the legendary King Arthur had held court. He took the ribbing with good humour and the name quickly stuck.

Taylor had no trouble finding targets. He aimed and fired at will. His targets were running Grenadiers and he scored hits, seeing blood. He paused to recharge the magazine and then steadied himself for the next shot. The not unfamiliar smell of the woodpile reminded him of life before the army, when he was a young apprentice carpenter. His particular forte had been hand making wooden coffins. He hoped he wouldn't be needing one yet.

A machine-gun opened up from the trees. Bullets tore at the woodpile. He ducked and moved left to the other end of the logs. Tracer buried itself in the peeling bark, and flames flickered. He lifted himself up ready to fire. A Grenadier rose from the ground and weaved forward. Taylor picked him out and the man went down clutching his side.

He heard Harrison yelling. 'Tree line! Anti-tank gun!'

Taylor coughed from the wood smoke, eyes streaming. He wiped them clear and peered at the trees. A gun crew were hauling an artillery piece into position, the same line of trees that No.1 Section had used earlier, but further away. He reckoned the range as 300-hundred yards, made an adjustment. A man looked small at that distance and he knew the post in the foresight would almost obscure his target. So he aimed low, eased the sight smoothly up to the German's torso . . . , and squeezed. The rifle kicked his shoulder. The gunner flailed backwards.

He found the next man, but he was stooping and turning as he tended the gun. Then, for a vital couple of seconds, he stopped to peer over the curved shield. Mistake. The Lee Enfield cracked . . . , missed.

'Bastard!' Taylor snarled. Another round, try again. But the man stayed low out of sight. A separate movement beyond the shield caught Taylor's attention and he fired. An arm jerked into the air and disappeared. A grenade exploded near the barn. The ripsaw buzz of a Spandau resounded across the field, tracer whipping towards him. He ducked. Bullets bored into the log pile, gouging splinters. He wriggled to the right, back to his original firing position. Risking a glance over the logs, he ducked down with a grim smile. The anti-tank gunners were pulling back from their exposed position.

The Spandau's stream of shells slackened and ceased, moving to another target. Taylor again levelled the rifle over the woodpile. It was time to hurry the gunners on their way.

A bullet slammed into his left arm and he gasped. It passed through the soft tissue of his bicep. The gun jolted from his grasp. He collapsed away from the line of sight and grabbed at the arm with his other hand, eyes screwed shut. Pain. A burning agony. Blood poured from the open wound, but he recognised it for what it was, a flesh wound. In one side, out the other. He let go the wrist and fumbled for a dressing, awkwardly one handed. Tearing the cover off with his teeth, he unfurled the roll and bound the muscle. He finished by tucking the loose end under a wrap. More bullets zipped and whined round the logs.

Taylor felt for his pistol and then managed to ready a Mills grenade. He wasn't done yet. He reached for the rifle, raised it awkwardly to his shoulder one-handed, and then tentatively forced his left arm and hand to give it support. A searing pain shot through the muscle and he clamped his teeth against crying out. But he held on, forcing himself to ignore the pain. Gradually the arm obeyed and he managed to hold onto a target.

Five feet to the left of Taylor's woodpile, Private Chris Jamison lay behind what might once have been a miniature rock garden. It was really no higher than a veg box from his local market, but he'd managed to scrape out some earth, and down on his belly he felt pretty well hidden. He picked out four Grenadiers weaving towards him from the trees. Aiming at the nearest he opened fire. The Lee Enfield cracked and a man staggered, crumpled. He hit another who lurched sideways clutching his shoulder, then missed, and missed again. The last pair dived to the side and one returned fire, accurate, enough to make Jamison hug the ground.

Over to the right Harrison saw what happened, took careful aim at the Grenadier and loosed off with his Sten gun. The man's body jerked as bullets tore into his ribcage. He attempted to roll away but Harrison's last round found him and blood gushed. He lay still.

Jamison nodded his thanks to Harrison and looked for another target. Three mortar shells detonated one after another. The last shell exploded behind him, the blast jolting his body. He lost the sound of battle, a deafening high-pitched ringing in his ears. Dazed, he squinted through dust, clawing for his rifle. Gathering it to his shoulder he rubbed dirt from his eyes and blinked. The noise of battle returned and he desperately searched for a target. He found one, a German wielding a stick grenade, his arm going back for a throw.

The rifle cracked and the bullet hit flesh. The man went backwards and the grenade exploded. A severed arm spiralled into the air, blood spraying. The ragged remains landed close.

Jamison moved on, found another target, engaged. There was no time to dwell.

Wingham could clearly see Harrison's men taking heavy fire, casualties mounting. Either he reinforced them or pulled them back. He glanced round. Paratroopers everywhere were fighting hard, and he had no real reserve to call on. He made up his mind and called for Tillman's Bren.

'Covering fire for No.1 Section. I'm pulling them back!'

'Lofty' Tillman waved a big hand in acknowledgement. He changed targets and gave the oncoming enemy a sweeping burst. Others added to the fusillade. The Grenadiers hesitated, and some dived to the ground. It gave Wingham the opportunity to race forward and he shouted for Harrison to withdraw his men.

The Corporal heard and yelled at the Section.

'Smoke grenades!' A couple were tossed forward and smoke billowed. 'Withdraw!' The men responded, extricating themselves one by one. Bent double they weaved their way back towards Tillman. One limped badly, shot in the thigh, another had his left arm hanging loose, blood streaming from the elbow. Yet another ran from the protection of the logs, a bloodied bandage round his upper arm.

Wingham held his ground, firing aimed shots with his Sten. A bullet snapped past his head, and a tracer round hit his right boot. He winced. Near the paddock fence one of Harrison's men lay prone, not moving. The Scotsman moved to his side and appeared to check for signs of life. Wingham thought it might be Jock Stewart. The smoke began to drift, swirling, no longer opaque. Harrison lunged to his feet and made a dash for safety, bullets plucking at his heels. Wingham urged him on, willing him to go faster.

Harrison was running hard and ten yards from cover when the bullets tore into him. Blood sprayed from his chest, and the force of impact slammed him into the ground. An arm moved, and Wingham saw him turn his head, eyes wide. For a moment their eyes met and Harrison appeared to give a faint nod. Then came a tortured, hacking cough and crimson blood trickled from his mouth.

Jim Harrison of Fort William shuddered and breathed his last.

Wingham scrambled back into cover and mouthed obscenities. So near, he thought, shaking his head. It was a bitter moment.

Norman Taylor made it into the kitchen and leaned his back against the wall. He was breathing hard, partly from the run, mostly from pain.

'All right, mate?'

He recognised 'Lofty'. The gunner stared at him, concerned.

'I'll manage. Hot work.'

The Bren gunner grimaced. 'Just a bit,' he said, and seeing Taylor didn't need his help, returned to the window. The light machine-gun hammered.

Rifleman George Morgan, twenty-one, from the Isle of Wight, shifted position along the farmhouse wall. There was a broken section where he could lie and fire without exposing himself and he wriggled on hands and knees until he lay along its length. Peering cautiously round the end, he brought the rifle to his shoulder and cocked the weapon. Through swirling dust and explosions, Morgan spotted a Panzergrenadier crawling forward with a sub-machinegun. He gauged the distance as two-hundred yards and adjusted his back sight. He hesitated as a mortar dropped and blew up half way between the two of them. Unsighted, but confidant his target would re-emerge from the smoke, George Morgan watched and waited.

16 Against All Odds

A heavily camouflaged German sniper crawled out from dense bushes. Otto Schwartz had taken the time to add a leafy halo to his helmet with more entwined in his draped scarf. He could see Kruger standing in the half-track urging his men forward. He thought it was a suicidal move, taking on an unknown number of enemy who had established themselves in a fixed defensive position. As if to add weight to his thoughts, Grenadiers began to fall as they reached a fenced paddock.

Unconstrained by any specific orders, Schwartz pushed out to the right, circling round towards an old dung heap. Bullets zipped and hissed, too many to ignore and he went to ground, crawling, head down. He reached the heap of manure and pushed aside rotting straw. With care, unhurried by the urgency of battle, he prodded and poked near the top until he'd made himself an untidy hole that a K98k Mauser sniper rifle and telescope could reach through. He removed his helmet and scarf, discarded the carefully chosen twigs and leaves, and then draped the entire light-brown net scarf over his helmet and face. He then rolled aside onto his back and stripped a protective Hessian casing from the breech and 'scope. A 7.92 bullet was loaded, the bolt closed, and he rolled back to his firing position. Teasing the scarf into a final position, he cradled the butt to his cheek and focussed the telescopic sight.

Only then did he begin a methodical search of the enemy positions.

Mortar rounds exploded beyond him, smoke spreading. It partially obscured the buildings and he cursed the mortar team. Somewhere to his left a Spandau ripped bullets at the farmhouse, and the noise of gunfire reached a crescendo. Schwartz closed his ears to the cacophony and concentrated on finding the enemy.

In a low brick building with a rusting steel chimney, away to his front right, he thought he glimpsed movement behind a window facing his dung heap. He studied it but all was still. He moved the 'scope further right, until he reached the end of the building. There appeared to be an open door, far enough open for a man to be watching in case of a possible flanking attempt. He waited for a minute but no-one appeared, so he switched focus to the farmhouse, searching. The window in the loft showed nothing. He lowered the scope to the upper floor but all windows proved empty. And then he trailed the weapon down to the ground floor at the right side.

Schwartz froze, and allowed himself a thin smile. There at the window he found a British Paratrooper waiting for a target. A twist of the knurled power ring and he could see the man's eyes. A check of the range, and no need of 'windage', there was none. He slipped a finger inside the guard, took up the first pressure, found resistance, steadied his breathing . . ., and squeezed.

Mike Stratton felt the burning pain of a bullet whip his right cheekbone and grunted in disbelief. He felt like a target at a fairground stall; pop your head up and you're there for the taking. He twisted sideways and leaned against the wall, out of the line of fire. But he was weakening and knew it. A body couldn't go on losing blood indefinitely. He hopped awkwardly over to a big chair in the corner and sank down into leather bound comfort. He felt for his grenades and laid two on the arm. Lifting the rifle he propped it across the other arm of the chair and waited. The barrel covered the door and two windows and he half smiled. Jerry would pay dearly if they stormed this room.

The sound of battle grew louder.

Jock Stewart opened his eyes to a veil of pink and deeper reds. His head throbbed, dull aches, his forehead hammering with pain. He could feel that his right cheek was lying in grass and he lifted his head. The pain in his forehead transferred to his temples, pounding at his senses. He screwed his eyes tight shut in an attempt to alleviate the spasm and it eased, a little. He opened his eyes and this time brilliant sunlight filtered into his right eye, partially tinged with red, and he realised blood had obscured his sight. His rifle lay under his right hand, finger on the trigger guard and he tentatively moved his arm. No additional pain and he took his weight on that elbow and rubbed his left eye. It was sticky and it took a couple of passes but then with a deliberate blink he found his full vision had returned. So too did the harsh sound of battle.

George Morgan put two bullets into the Panzergrenadier and shifted target. A Spandau had set up in a fold of the ground, a gunner and loader tending to its needs. He fired three shots. The first kicked dirt in front of the machine-gun, the other two he had no idea, just that they missed. Mortar rounds came in, two . . , three . . , four of them, shrapnel flying, acrid smoke and fumes drifting. The Spandau's gunner must have had an idea where Morgan was and opened up with a sustained burst. Stone walling took the brunt, bits of granite sparking. The tracer moved away lifting towards the kitchen and Morgan came up onto one knee. It allowed him to see a bit more of the Spandau's gunner. He raised the Lee Enfield and aimed.

Otto Schwartz reloaded. He ejected the shell and slipped another round into the breech. He'd seen the result of his shot, saw the instantaneous splash of blood on the man's cheek. When he looked again there was no sign of him and he traversed left to find the next window. No good dwelling on a missed opportunity, move on, find another. As the scope travelled along the wall an out of focus movement stopped him. He backtracked and then found a single soldier kneeling below a window on a patch of flattened flower garden behind a low stone wall.

Schwartz steadied, focussed the sight, aiming for the chest. But the British Paratrooper changed position, dropping to his belly, rifle supported on his elbows. Schwartz sighed, gathered himself, and again took aim, this time at the man's face, just above his nose. He squeezed. The Mauser thumped, kicked his shoulder. The bullet struck the soldier's camouflaged steel helmet and ricocheted off.

Morgan felt the blow, the impact throwing him off balance. He fell sideways, stunned, shocked, head thumping, a sharp pain over his right temple.

He blinked, desperate to clear his vision. The helmet had twisted with the hit and he fumbled to pull it back into position. A deep breath helped steady him and he opened one eye. The stone wall appeared in front of his nose and he reckoned luck had been with him, doubly so.

The violent pain eased, the shock wearing off. He realised that other then the strike on his helmet he was unharmed. Time to rejoin the battle.

Otto Schwartz frowned in annoyance and cursed. It should have been a kill, an easy unsuspecting target, a certainty. Two shots in a row without the correct result. He shook his head and slowly withdrew the rifle from the hole in the straw. Lying on his side and with the battle raging around him, he carefully inspected the Zeiss 3x telescopic sight and mounting. This particular scope was one he'd acquired nine months ago from a friend at the Zeiss factory, and Schwartz had then persuaded an armourer of great skill to adapt the Mauser so it would accept the new scope. Hours were then spent on the ranges fine tuning the sight to suit varied weather conditions. In his opinion it was the finest combination of telescope and rifle that he'd ever had the pleasure of handling. He ejected the casing and checked the breech, found no hint of debris. A thin residue of Ballistol oil was still evident from the last time he'd cleaned it. He closed the bolt and gingerly felt the sight to see if it was properly attached.

And his fingers discovered the issue. The sight's forward securing mechanism had come loose and was no longer firmly affixed to the rifle. He removed the scope completely, blew hard on the fixings, then replaced it into the clamps and made sure it was tight. He reloaded, eased the barrel back through the straw and searched for another target. Whether his previous strip and reassembly that morning was at fault, he would never know. All that mattered now was that his next shot was clean. And anyway, Major Kruger had his hands so full with his own problems that he would never have noticed a couple of near misses from his esteemed sniper.

Otto Schwartz grinned to himself and squinted through the scope. The next British Paratrooper he shot at would be in need of a deeply dug grave.

Jock Stewart realised he was alone. Left and right there was no one to be seen. So carefully, staying within the confines of the draped leather apron, he turned to look back at the farmhouse. The Bren gun was still in action at the kitchen window and he caught the glint of tracer spraying out from the workshop. Panzergrenadiers everywhere were edging forward in twos and threes. Smoke, explosions and small arms fire were keeping them partially at bay. A half-track had peeled away towards the workshop, a dozen Grenadiers following in its wake. Another half-track had trundled forward from the trees, triangular pennants adorning the wheel arches.

He turned his head back to look at the row of poplars. The undergrowth hid most of the Germans moving around beyond and he wondered exactly what he should try and do? He was twenty yards from the stable door and that would be across open ground. To retreat to the kitchen was asking for trouble, nearly fifty yards and no cover. He decided to stay put until there was no choice but to risk everything in saving himself. He wasn't about to sacrifice himself for no good reason.

In the blood soaked kitchen Sarah looked up and saw Taylor leaning against the wall, head down, blood dripping from a roughly applied bandage. She went to his side and reached for the arm.

'Let me see that,' she said, and led him across to one of the wooden chairs. He sat heavily, his arm outstretched along the kitchen table. She found where he'd tucked away an end of the bandage and gently teased it out. The wraps had acted like a sponge, soggy with blood.

'I'm Sarah,' she offered. 'What can I call you?' She prised away the remaining length of bandage.

Taylor winced and clamped his teeth together.

'Norman,' he muttered. 'Norman Taylor.'

She discarded the bloodied bandage into a tin bucket, chose a clean square of white cotton sheet and dipped it into a bowl of water.

'Well, Norman,' she said with a gentle smile. 'I have to clean the wound. I'll be as careful as I can but I expect it'll hurt.'

'You go ahead, miss. I'll be okay.'

Sarah began to swab away the worst of the half congealed blood and felt him tense as she cleaned down deep into ragged flesh. Taylor swore, twice, shook his head by way of an apology and stared determinedly at the ceiling.

Wingham worried about his left flank. If the Germans moved enough men out towards the workshop it might only be a matter of time before Cartwright and Carter were over-run. The Platoon already had casualties and looking around he could see that he had no-one in the way of a reserve to lend a hand. Steve Dexter was nearest the workshop, maybe Cartwright would call on him.

A glance at his wristwatch told him it was 10:30 a.m., and then suddenly the sound of exploding mortars filled the air. He peered through the detonations attempting to see what prompted the attack. As the smoke rolled away it was immediately obvious. The next wave of Jerry infantry had joined in the attack. A two pronged assault, head on. Farmhouse and workshop. The mortars were just the opening salvo. And the Panzergrenadiers had fixed bayonets. That could only herald the expectation of hand to hand fighting, close quarters intended.

Behind the stone wall, Rifleman George Morgan shrank down to avoid the worst of the mortar fire. The last mortar out of four exploded close, a lethal cocktail of stones and steel splinters scything overhead. Then he raised his eyes to peer at the slope. As the dust cleared, onrushing Grenadiers came at him, bayonets fixed to rifles. They were fifteen yards out when he shot the first, less than ten when he got the second. Then with no time to reload they were on him.

A bayonet was thrust at his chest and he instinctively smashed it aside with the Lee Enfield. He stepped to his left and jabbed at the man's torso, felt the moment of contact. He screamed his defiance and plunged the blade in harder. The Grenadier grunted, gasping with the pain. Morgan jammed it further and gave the sticker a violent twist. The German cried out, eyes bulging, and dropped his rifle.

Another Grenadier lunged and there was the clash of rifle on rifle as Morgan deflected the bayonet. He tried to twist the point into the German but the man was strong and forced his bayonet back towards Morgan's face. The Englishman summoned up all his strength and with a powerful jerk reversed the pressure. The man's bayonet clattered his grey helmet. Morgan stabbed hard at the Grenadier's neck. His pig sticker pierced the artery and blood sprayed, saturating Morgan's face and chest. The rifle fell as the German grabbed for his neck but panicked hand fingers would never staunch an arterial flow. He collapsed to his knees, eyes pleading. Tracer zipped past Morgan's head and he threw himself back behind the meagre protection of the wall. When he snatched another look the Panzergrenadier had toppled to one side and gone into seizures. The shaking stopped.

Morgan reloaded and levelled the rifle over the wall. He gave a silent whistle and shook his head. Twice luck had been with him today. How much longer?

Major Carl Kruger swore. He tore off a glove and gingerly extracted a jagged steel fragment from his left forearm, and swore again. Blood oozed and he pressed hard to staunch the flow. Looking through swirling smoke he shook his head in frustration. The Englanders fought well, inflicting many casualties on his Grenadiers. He had thought it would be a walkover, he knew now he'd been badly mistaken in his initial judgement.

'Driver!' he snarled. 'Take us back to the trees.'

The driver didn't need telling twice. He hit the accelerator pedal and hauled round on the steering wheel. Well experienced in handling the Sd.Kfz.251 armoured half-track, the driver knew exactly how far to turn the wheel to engage the caterpillar track steering system. Once engaged the braked track allowed for a much tighter turning circle and the driver was only too willing to push it to the limits. Churning the ground into dust with one stationary track, engine howling, and expelling a filthy plume of exhaust smoke, Kruger's half-track spun round, straightened up and headed for safety.

Blood dripping from his arm, Carl Kruger cursed in exasperation. Twice now it had been advisable to leave the field of battle. There would be no repetition.

At the end of the pond nearest the farmhouse, between the woodpile and a stone trough, Joe Miller searched the grassy slopes for anything that looked remotely like a sniper. He'd checked the trees, a frequent location for German snipers. Low growing bushes likewise proved to be a fruitless exercise, and so he moved on, traversing right to left, from barn to the slope in front of the workshop. Finding nothing that warranted giving away his position, he backtracked slowly, taking great care over every dip, hollow, mound and bush.

A Grenadier appeared in his sights, crawling into a slight depression. He'd been dragging something but it was hidden by his body. Miller focussed the lens and firmed his grip on the rifle. He was rewarded by the slow appearance of a helmet, a pair of eyes, and then the first glimpse of a Panzerfaust. Miller was well aware of the explosive power of what was effectively an anti-tank weapon. The British equivalent was the PIAT and the Americans had the

Bazooka, neither of which had the punching power to penetrate heavy armour. In contrast, Miller had seen for himself how a Panzerfaust's rocket propelled warhead could open up an Allied tank's armour at a range of one-hundred feet.

Miller felt the tension of the trigger, steadied, and fired. The Lee Enfield jolted his cheek and a single bullet flew straight. It struck the Grenadier below his chin. Blood erupted and the man slumped. The Panzerfaust lay unheeded, half hidden beneath his body. Miller reloaded and continued his search. He was convinced that snipers would be playing their games. It was up to him to stop them.

17 The Flanks

Over in the workshop Sergeant Bill Cartwright watched through the window as the leading German half-track again swung away from the attack. But that left a dozen or so skirmishers weaving their way across open ground and Cartwright turned to Rob Carter's Bren gun.

'All yours,' he said, pointing to the disjointed line of Grenadiers.

The Bren hammered into action. And stopped, mid-burst. Carter spat. 'Jammed!'

The attack faltered, Germans diving to the ground, but then one or two warily lifted their heads and eyed the workshop, expecting more. None came.

Cartwright didn't waste breath on the jammed gun and instead moved to the steel door facing the orchard. Outside he edged towards the front corner, cocked his Sten and snatched a glance. The Grenadiers were still hesitant, half hugging the ground. Cartwright dropped to one knee, took careful aim, and loosed off a short burst. He grinned. That got their attention. The difference, he knew, between workshop window and back door might only be six yards, but from the enemy perspective that small change suddenly exposed their right flank to end on raking fire.

Before the Grenadiers could react, Carter's Bren gun rejoined the fight, added to which, Cartwright felt rather than saw that Steve Dexter had also responded to the attack.

Dexter peered out from behind his wall and watched the half-track turn away. That left Panzergrenadiers exposed and he counted five Germans moving his way. They were bent low, swerving this way and that in an attempt to dodge British bullets. He saw tracer whipping out from the workshop, heard the Bren firing controlled bursts. Supporting the Sten over the wall he picked on one Grenadier, watched him swerve right and as he made the next move left, hit the trigger. The man went down, hard. But he wasn't done and fired a burst in return. Dexter ducked as bullets whined, and then gave him another. He thought he saw a spray of blood and changed target. They were closer now, not quite within throwing range but they could hurl a stick grenade a lot further than a Mills grenade.

Two of the Grenadiers went down on one knee, rifles aimed at the workshop. Dexter took advantage and snapped off two rounds at each man, hurried. He hit one. The second turned, went belly to the ground and tracer hummed past Dexter's head. He grimaced, changed mags and prepared to empty the lot. It was all getting too close for comfort.

'Dexter!'

It was Cartwright calling from the workshop.

He lifted his chin, enough for Cartwright to see he'd heard.

'Get in here. We'll cover.'

Another burst of machine-gun fire rattled the workshop's bricks and Dexter steeled himself for the dash.

'Ready!' he yelled, and preyed his legs didn't turn to jelly.

Carter's Bren went into overdrive, sweeping the Grenadiers with gunfire. The staccato bark of the Sergeant's Sten joined in and Dexter lunged to his feet. In a desperate crouching run he powered across the intervening ground and hurled himself through the door. Breathless, he dropped to a knee, struggling for air.

Cartwright towered over him and grinned. 'I thought you were fit, sunshine.' He grabbed Dexter under one arm and guided him over to the anvil. 'Sit there, son,' he said, still grinning. 'And if, in your own good time, you'd care to join our little war, we'd be only too pleased to have you alongside.'

A grenade exploded outside and glass shattered. The Bren hammered and Carter gave a triumphant shout. 'That'll teach the bastard!'

Dexter got his breath back, looked round and saw the back door slightly ajar. With Carter and Cartwright fighting to hold the Grenadiers at the front, he stepped across to the door and slipped outside. Shuffling toward the front corner he risked a glance round the end. That momentary look gave him a view of the entire battle. Outnumbered was his first thought, waves of Panzergrenadiers charging the grassy slope. Tracer flew in every direction, detonating mortar shells walking toward the farmhouse. From over by the barn, along the front of the house, and here at the workshop, German soldiers advanced en masse. The noise of battle rose to a cacophony.

Steve Dexter knelt, checked his mag, and snapped it back. He cautiously leaned to the corner. He found three Grenadiers crouching at the base of the front wall below the window. One had a stick grenade about to be lobbed through the window. He raised the Sten and gave them half a magazine. The bullets wreaked havoc, blood spurting. The grenade exploded in their midst and they went down, lay still. He turned his attention to another German crawling his way and gave him two rounds. He stopped moving.

Dexter lowered the Sten and wiped sweat from his face. For a moment, for a precious, fleeting moment, the slope leading south from the workshop was clear of enemy troops. He sagged back to the door and reached for his canteen. The water was tepid, but he let it roll round his mouth and swallowed slowly.

The harsh thump of a large calibre gun echoed and he witnessed a chunk of stonework explode above the farmhouse kitchen door. As the dust cleared a mound of rubble could be seen partially blocking the doorway. Dexter took another swig from the canteen, re-corked it and slipped it back in the webbing. He snatched a quick look inside the workshop. The Sergeant watched from the window, Carter was counting magazines.

Dexter managed a faint grin. They'd held the Platoon's left flank. Only question now . . . , for how much longer?

Wingham was unsighted by drifting smoke, dust swirling in coils of grey. Fragments of walling piled up in the doorway and he tapped Tillman's shoulder. 'Can't see. I'm going upstairs.'

The Bren gunner nodded and Wingham took the stairs two at a time. He reached the landing, turned into the first room and moved tentatively across to the side of the window. Glass crunched beneath his boots but he grabbed an edge of the blue curtain and peered out between ragged strands of frayed cotton. What met his gaze was more than a little disconcerting. Mortar shells were exploding in seemingly haphazard fashion but creeping closer to the buildings. The Pak anti-tank gun had found the range and what he thought was the half-track in command had come back to the fore, advancing just behind the line of grenadiers. There were a few dead Germans out there but not as many as he hoped. He moved the curtain and squinted across to the workshop. He counted seven dead grenadiers and one or two wounded crawling back down the slope. There was no sign of Corporal Dexter behind the wall which was a concern.

He gnawed at his lower lip and rubbed his forehead. So far the Panzergrenadiers had been held, but holding them couldn't last indefinitely. He needed to come up with something more. The sound of battle echoed around the walls and the concussive thumps of mortar rounds grew ever closer.

And the very next mortar shell hit the apex of the roof, penetrated fragile tiles and detonated in the rafters. Smoke and flames erupted from between the roof tiles. Wingham spun away from the window and headed down for the kitchen. Sporadic small arms fire greeted him at the door.

Over at the barn on the right flank and squatting in the relative darkness just inside the stable door, Ben Fletcher snapped a fresh magazine into the Sten. A proud Yorkshireman from Harrogate, he was determined to play his part in holding off the Germans. There was nothing he could do about the anti-tank gun hidden in the trees, too far away for the Sten, but he thought he could still drop a few more Germans before pulling back. And obligingly two Grenadiers stepped out from the undergrowth, one carrying an MG42. The other had spare bandoliers slung across his body and carried a box in either hand. The Spandau wouldn't lack for bullets.

Fletcher knew instantly he had to stop them from setting up that machine-gun. Once in action its rate of fire would paralyse the Platoon, it had the ability to suppress even the bravest of men. He watched closely, praying they would move into range. It was times like this when a Lee Enfield would have been his weapon of choice. The Sten was accurate enough up to a hundred yards, after that it was all a bit hit and miss, whereas the .303 had both range and stopping power. His prayer was answered. A slight change in elevation about seventy yards out made the German gunner break into a trot and then throw himself down behind the rise. His number two followed suit. Fletcher could see the top of both helmets but little else and he cursed. In one aspect his wish had been granted, they'd come within range. Unfortunately the two men were experienced enough to stay well hidden. A 9mm round hitting a steel helmet at seventy or eighty yards might do no more than ricochet into the distance and leave the wearer with a headache. Not quite what he had in mind. But there could be no doubt as to their intentions; they were preparing to lay down a carpet of machine-gun fire.

Fletcher unclipped two grenades and readied them for use. Looking out into the paddock he'd spotted a slight depression that ran out to a rusting metal water trough. He estimated the trough to be as close as thirty yards from the machine gunners. A good throw with a fortunate bounce or two and the grenadiers would be mincemeat.

He went down on all fours and crawled out of the door. It was just a simple matter of making it to the trough, hopefully without being seen. As he eased out into the daylight a movement to his right caught him by surprise. A pair of Grenadiers sprang at him from alongside the end wall. Fletcher tried to avoid a glittering bayonet, tried to twist his Sten round. Too late. The point of the bayonet drove into his right shoulder and he gasped at the pain. A second bayonet ripped into his right thigh and shattered the bone. Fletcher grunted with shock and collapsed onto his back. The first bayonet twisted and was savagely withdrawn. He looked up at the grim eyes of his enemy. The second Grenadier jammed a jackboot onto Fletcher's knee and tugged the bayonet free. He gave a triumphant shout, ready to strike at the Paratrooper's exposed belly.

But Ben Fletcher managed to finish bringing the Sten round. As the muzzle came into line with the Grenadier's grinning face, Ben hit the trigger. The grinning face instantly turned to a bloody pulp, teeth smashed and jawbone severed. He fell backwards. But the first German's bayonet struck again, this time catching Fletcher in the ribs. But before the thrust finished, the last of the Sten's bullets slammed into his chest. With a shrill scream he collapsed and dragged the bayonet with him.

Fletcher shuddered with pain and clamped his teeth to prevent himself from crying out. His thighbone grated but he forced himself onto his belly and dragged himself to the paddock railing.

The metal trough was out of the question now, he'd never make it. He somehow managed to sit up and changed magazine. The Spandau team were just visible.

Fletcher felt the shock of a bullet smash his left elbow. The bone shattered, splintered, and he grunted in agony. A second bullet tore through his ribcage, slammed him into the paddock fence and left him half hanging over the bottom rail. With his right arm he raised the Sten gun, lifted his head and with a scream of defiance pulled the trigger. The gun wobbled in his weakened grip and sprayed an arc of bullets high into the air. A mortar shell exploded, close. Shrapnel gouged chunks of flesh from his body and Fletcher groaned, strength failing. He dropped the gun. Blood pumped from his chest and his head lowered with pain, helmet falling forward. The chin strap held, snagged, and the helmet hung, swaying.

Lance-Corporal Ben Fletcher was dying, knew it, accepted it. He'd done his best but too many wounds had brought him to a standstill. His only regret centred round his faithful, loyal sheepdog. He and Sky would no longer walk the Dales again, not together anyway. His old Dad would be the one to take Sky for his walks now, and the inviting breeze would still rustle Sky's fur when they climbed the higher peaks. Somehow there was comfort in the thought.

Moments later the proud Yorkshireman from Harrogate shuddered and breathed his last.

Jock Stewart had tried to help. He'd fired off three snapshot rounds at a German who had appeared by the stable door. Too late. The German shied away from the line of fire, but the damage to Fletcher had already been done.

Stewart felt a rage burning inside. He looked away from Ben's lifeless body and cursed, felt the prickle of moisture welling up in his eyes. It had always been Harrison, Fletcher and Stewart, the three of 'em, good mates, knew how to down a pint . . . , or two, or five, and not appear any the worse for wear. Now Fletcher had copped it, Harrison was God knows where, and here he was, Private Douglas 'Jock' Stewart, stuck in a sort of no-man's land waiting to get the chop.

The nearby raucous ripsaw buzz of a Spandau filled the air and he peered round the leather apron to find its source. He found a line of tracer whipping away towards the farmhouse, but the machine-gun and its Grenadiers were hidden from sight. He coughed at the acrid smell of cordite mixed with the pungent stink of fuel from the half-tracks, blue-black exhaust fumes drifting. He cradled the Lee Enfield and waited.

8 Kill or Die
1

North of Ranville, three Sherman tanks had made it to within 500 yards of the small village. Lieutenant Matthew Summerton raised his binoculars and brought the dwellings into sharp focus. All seemed quiet, very still in the morning sun. There was no sign of the Paras and he wondered if he was headed for a trap. Not, he appreciated, that they would want to advertise their presence. He couldn't see much damage and guessed he needed to get closer before they ventured out to greet him. Satisfied, he ordered the driver to proceed.

'Advance!'

The tank lurched and gathered pace, tracks squealing. The others came on behind, single file, guns traversing left and right, wary.

His tank reached a narrowing of the road between two tall hedgerows and at that moment a British officer in a Paratrooper's smock and helmet stepped out and held up a hand.

'Halt!' Summerton ordered. He removed his headset and leaned over the turret.

The officer had a huge grin on his face. 'I'm Culpepper, old man, recently promoted Captain for my sins. Are we glad to see you,' he said. 'But you want Major Lane.' He turned and pointed down the road to an imposing building. 'Turn left before you reach that house then follow the road round the outskirts,' he said, 'but be careful if you go beyond the crossroads. Bit hot round the corner. When you find a bright red door you're there.' He craned his neck to look up the road towards the bridges. 'Any more of you?'

'They're coming. Got sidetracked with a few Panzers, but they'll be here.'

The grin disappeared with a forlorn shake of the head. He was clearly crestfallen. Expectations of armoured support must have been great. But he took a deep breath, stood aside and with a gracious bow, waved them on. Summerton gave him a nod, and the tank growled on down the road. He turned left as advised, led them out on a winding road and finally halted the Sherman level with a bright red door. It opened and a lean, rugged looking officer stepped closer.

'I'm Major Lane,' the man announced. 'I've been waiting.' He produced a folded map, held it higher for Summerton to see. A black circle highlighted a couple of isolated buildings. 'One of our platoons is stuck in that farmhouse, on a special mission. And there's a woman, an English woman. She's high priority and wanted back in London. Be a great help if you could get them out.'

Summerton reached inside for his map board, propped it on the hatch and traced a finger to a grid square. He pencilled a rough outline to indicate the farmhouse.

'Anything else, sir?'

'Only that they're surrounded by a bunch of Panzergrenadiers. No tanks reported.'

Summerton nodded and grinned. 'In that case, we'll be on our way.'

The grin was infectious and Lane smiled. 'And your name is?'

'Lieutenant Matthew Summerton, King's Own Royal Dragoons. At your service.'

'Well, Mr Summerton,' Lane said with a chuckle,' I wish you God speed.'

'Thank you, sir.' The tank's engine grumbled into a higher gear.

Major Freddy Lane checked his watch. It was now 11.30, and better late than never, three thirty-ton Sherman tanks were heading to the rescue. He watched them until they turned the corner and disappeared from sight. It would be rather wonderful if the Tankies reached the farm before the *Ruffians* were annihilated.

At the front of the farmhouse, where the high wall joined the imposing bulk of the barn, Rifleman Dan Clayton of No.3 Section had positioned himself behind the beech tree. Not that trying to get comfortable was without problems. Many of the roots lay above ground, some as thick as his wrist. But eventually he managed to achieve a fairly decent belly down position offering a good field of fire for the Lee Enfield but which also allowed for a fair amount of concealment. Peering round the side of a solid tree trunk gave him a certain sense of security. He checked the back sight for range, let the rifle rest, and then placed three grenades to his right, nestled side by side well within reach.

'Dan! See anything?' It was Greene calling from near the gate.

Clayton peered at the field of corn and the line of trees beyond. He knew how easy it was to conceal yourself in those trees, that's where they'd started their own attack on the farmhouse.

'No,' he said loudly, 'not at the moment. Thought I saw movement in the tree line a bit back. None since.'

Greene was silent for a moment before answering.

'Okay. Keep your eyes peeled . . . , and look out for the trees on your left. Don't want to be outflanked.'

'Right, will do,' he said, and settled back down amongst the roots. He took a quick glance along the low wall and counted heads. Most of No.3 Section were in position, one missing, maybe in the ditch. He snugged the butt of the rifle into his shoulder and licked his lips, mouth dry. It was a familiar sensation, the anticipation of having to fight, always the same before battle.

He waited . . . , watchful.

Out back in the kitchen garden near the door, Paul Wingham ducked away from the blast of a mortar. A line of tracer curved in from the distant trees, lazy mid flight, then whipping overhead to carve chunks from the wall.

'Major!'

The call came from out front and he ducked through to the hallway, keeping himself half hidden by the broken front door.

'What is it?'

'I think they're preparing to attack.' It was Corporal Greene.

'How many?'

'Hard to say. All we've seen is two half-tracks and a lorry. Twenty, maybe thirty?'

Wingham frowned and rubbed his jaw. So now it would be from both front and back. If they did a frontal assault from the wood, then Greene's Section had a chance of inflicting a fair amount of damage. He made a quick check of their placements.

Private Dinger Bell had the Bren gun supported on the wall six feet left of the gate. To his left, ten or twelve feet further on, Greene himself knelt behind a damaged part of the wall, and at the foot of the beech tree he thought he could make out the half hidden figure of Clayton. To the right of the gate, Private Pete Solomon had his rifle levelled over the wall and beyond him Lance-Corporal Nobby Clarke crouched with his Sten gun. Lance-Corporal Patrick Mitchell had settled for the end of the wall and Dawson's head and shoulders could be seen down by the ditch. If the Germans had done a recce of the ditch then some might outflank No.2 Section by coming round the gable end. He needed to warn Stratton.

'Right,' he called. 'Hold them if you can, if not then fall back on the house. Clear?'

'Yes, sir,' Greene acknowledged, and Wingham moved back to the bottom of the staircase.

'Tulloch!' he shouted.

'Sir?' Tulloch came through from the kitchen.

'Greene thinks they're about to attack. We need to warn Stratton in case they come round the end.'

'Right, sir. Leave it with me.'

Wingham nodded and Tulloch turned down the corridor for the sitting room.

Wingham stepped back down to the flagstones. There was blood on the floor. He looked round and saw that the big table had been dragged away from the windows and out of the line of fire. Sarah was tending to a wounded soldier, bandaging his left knee. Her fingers were bloodied. She looked up as he entered and met his gaze. Straightening away from the patient she pushed a strand of hair from her face, and left a smear of blood across one cheek.

He nodded. 'Okay?'

She wiped her mouth, attempting a smile. 'I've been better.'

Tillman's Bren hammered, a short burst. A Spandau returned fire, bullets snapping at the wooden frame. Ricochets whined randomly through the kitchen. Tillman dodged sideways and Wingham crouched below the window, and then lunged for the other side of the doorway. A spray of bullets followed. With his back to the wall he swayed to take a glimpse outside. A Grenadier had knelt to point his rifle at the big barn doors. Wingham stepped into the open, lifted the Sten, aimed, and gave him three rounds. The Grenadier went backwards and lay still.

Wingham flinched as his right thigh was struck a glancing blow. The bullet carved out a chunk of flesh leaving a bloody line. He looked down and swore, deliberately putting weight on the leg. Blood ran from the muscle, but slowed, and though painful he felt certain he could manage.

The sound of small arms fire came from out front and he limped to the opposite window. A pair of half-tracks had entered the field from the far left, machine-guns firing in short bursts. He counted thirty plus Grenadiers advancing, wave after wave, leapfrogging one another to gain ground. The half-track's machineguns laid down a lethal spread of covering fire. He studied the hedge and ditch over on the right side but found no sign of movement.

'Corporal Greene!' he shouted.

'Sir!'

'You're on your own. I've no one spare.'

'Right, sir. Done it before, we can do it again.'

Wingham couldn't help but smile. It might well have been done before, but not necessarily in quite the same circumstances. And right now, he thought, the timely arrival of a squadron of tanks wouldn't go amiss. He hobbled back to the kitchen door and took a moment to take a breath. His neck ached, his thigh was red raw painful, and the acrid smoke made his eyes feel like half the Sahara desert had found its way in.

He knelt in the rubble and picked out another Panzergrenadier. Squinting along the sights he pursed his lips. There were moments when the weight of command fell away and a battle sank to the lowest common denominator, the fight to survive. This now was a killing field, kill or be killed.

Major Wingham squeezed the trigger.

In the sitting room Jed Tulloch snatched a quick glance at Stratton and moved to the window. There wasn't much to see, all smoke and dust. He turned back to Stratton, almost unrecognisable behind a mask of blood. But the eyes were clear, wide open.

'Where are you hit?' Tulloch asked, finding it difficult to pick out any individual area.

Stratton mumbled something and looked down at his thigh. There was a lot of blood. Tulloch delved in amongst the sodden cloth, peeled away a ragged edge and located the free flowing wound. He grimaced and met Stratton's eyes.

'I need a first-aid pack, they're with the woman in the kitchen.'

Stratton blinked that he understood, and Tulloch hurried out and back to the kitchen. Stratton was losing too much blood and a tourniquet would work best as a temporary solution. In the kitchen he stepped over the injured, found his own pack and with a nod to the woman headed back for Stratton.

He entered the room at the exact moment a Panzergrenadier stuck his head in the window. It was a mistake. Stratton levelled his rifle and blew the man's face away. He dropped to the ground outside.

Tulloch knelt and slid the tourniquet under and round Stratton's upper thigh and then twisted until the blood stopped flowing.

Stratton licked his lips. 'Cheers, Jed,' he said through gritted teeth and his head lolled back.

Tulloch patted his shoulder and let him be, the window needed his attention.

On the road south out of Ranville, a Sherman tank growled slowly along the paved surface towards a large hotel that overlooked a narrow crossroads. Lieutenant Matt Summerton could see his map indicated he must take the Troop around that hotel and head for a wooded rise. Unsighted and not knowing what might greet him beyond the hotel he ordered the driver to halt. Hoisting himself out of the turret he eased down between the driver's hatch and the hull mounted Browning, slithered off the front to the ground and signalled Sergeants Fitzgerald and Smith to wait. Moving with great care he approached the corner, knelt and peered round the end. For as far as he could see, the few scattered houses showed no sign of enemy occupation. The spire of a small church overlooked a graveyard with a gated entrance. Beyond that the road led out between matching tall hedges and wound its way towards the wooded high ground. A woman came out of a door on the far side of the road and hurried off down a side alley.

Summerton kept an eye on the street for another minute, a stray mongrel the only sign of life. The church spire gave him cause for concern, the open gallery an obvious choice for a spotter. Returning to the tank he clambered aboard and gave the order to advance. The three tanks clattered and squealed their way round the corner and pushed warily on past the church. In minutes they had cleared the last house and were moving at pace toward the woods.

A rocket streaked out from behind the hedge and ripped across the intervening gap. The Panzerfaust slammed into Sergeant Ian Smith's tank, the last in line. It hit between upper and lower tracks, exploding on impact, and tore the steel apart. A fireball flashed.

In the commander's hatch Smith swivelled the Browning and sprayed the bottom of the hedge. Bullets snatched at the foliage and a man screamed. But then an internal explosion shook the tank and a jet of flames erupted from the turret. Writhing in agony Smith dropped from sight, flames shooting skywards. Summerton saw an arm reappear and a scorched blackened hand scrabbled at the hatch cover. He willed the Sergeant to climb out but the burning arm slowly sank back inside. He watched squinting, waiting for the crew to emerge, knowing they wouldn't. Ammunition began to explode, tearing the tank apart. The turret suddenly gave a monstrous shudder, lurched from its housing and tumbled ponderously to the road. Nobody escaped that burning hulk, and as ammunition began to cook off their funeral pyre was marked by giant flames leaping from the steel coffin.

Summerton swallowed and shook his head. He called up Sergeant Fitzgerald and ordered him to follow, at speed. It was no time to hang around and the burning tank rapidly receded into the distance. Thick black smoke coiled lazily into the air.

19 A Fury of War

Joe Miller eased the weight of the Lee Enfield, backed off from the telescopic sight and raised his eyes for a hard look at the battlefield. A stray bullet slapped the reeds and he winced. Ignoring the chaos he blinked and peered through a bank of drifting smoke. Experience told him that any sniper worth his salt wouldn't bother with the tree line at ten o'clock, it was all too obvious.

He let his gaze travel left, to twelve o'clock, and rechecked the low wall that divided the ornamental fountain from the surrounding grass. For an instant he thought he had an answer, but through the scope the dark figure revealed itself to be a dead German. He moved on, to three o'clock . . . , and frowned. A heap of manure, old in appearance, and just high enough to cover a man in the prone position.

Miller wondered why he hadn't noticed it before; couldn't see for looking? It happened.

He settled himself for a slow examination, working his way carefully from right to left. The straw had discoloured over time, had become a sepia-yellow heap of light and dark patches. But even so there was a sort of continuity to the haphazard nature of the pile. And all he needed was that faint, almost indiscernible discrepancy in the strands of straw. A drop of sweat trickled down his nose. A twig lay discarded, a leaf shrivelled in the warmth, brown. He traversed the lens across the top, clumps of straw silhouetted against the cloudless sky. And with that movement a shiver coursed down his back. A disturbance in the pile. There could be no mistaking an irregular upheaval to the topmost layer.

A shell exploded, the blast wave robbing him of breath. He almost lost his grip on the rifle. He blinked dust and coughed, spat into the pond. He re-gathered the rifle and brought the sight back up to meet his eye. Steadying, he refocused on the top few inches of rotted manure. And there it was, the disrupted mess of dried straw. And something more. The muted sheen of gunmetal.

Miller flicked the safety and checked the range. Barely moving he adjusted the scope, windage irrelevant, and elevation. Satisfied, the sniper braced his elbows, drew his right knee forward for extra stability and caressed the riser with his cheekbone. The cross hair settled on the patch of disturbed straw and he turned the ring for precise magnification. Pin sharp, the sheen of gunmetal became the muzzle of a rifle, strips of Hessian camouflaging the barrel. A negligible lift to the Lee Enfield and Miller found a German eyeball, the other eye hidden behind a telescopic sight.

He centred on the soldier's nose and steadied his breathing. He saw the eye blink, a bead of perspiration drip, a living being.

Joe Miller breathed in, let it out . . . , slow, and then in that placid moment between breaths, stroked the trigger. Blood erupted. The German's head twisted under impact and sagged sideways. Miller let a wicked grin ease his tension, ejected the shell case and reloaded. Alive one minute, gone the next. Sniper to sniper and he'd come out on top. There was something really satisfying about beating an opponent with similar skills. He looked up for another target, an officer or NCO, he didn't mind which. Just so long as he could add to the tally.

Over at the paddock fencing Jock Stewart caught fresh movement between himself and the row of poplars. Through the dust and smoke he managed to make out eight Panzergrenadiers edging forward in extended line abreast. One carried a Panzerfaust, and Stewart smiled. Worthwhile getting out of bed for. And three from the right looked to be an NCO, all swagger and arm waving. It really had been worth the wait after all. At the same time he was under no apprehension that he'd be giving away his position. And an old worn piece of leather apron wasn't going to be much protection against what was about to come his way.

Stewart set himself and aimed at the Grenadier with the Panzerfaust. He was the greater threat, better to leave the NCO for later. He judged the range at a hundred yards, centred on the soldier's chest and squeezed. The bullet struck low and right, tore through his innards and lodged next to his spine. The force of the hit drove him down, the Panzerfaust knocked from his grasp. It bounced once and lay unheeded.

The Paratrooper switched targets, reloading as he did so, and picked out the NCO. The Lee Enfield steadied in his hands, foresight following the German's movement. He stroked the trigger. Blood erupted from the Grenadier's belly and he cartwheeled into the dirt. But one of the German's had seen the Paratrooper and pointed, shouting. A dozen bullets rent the air and Stewart thought it was high time he made himself scarce. He lunged to his feet and sprinted for the farmhouse, weaving as he went. Bullets kicked dirt, hissed past his head. He saw Tillman's Bren thumping rounds at the Grenadiers, the Old Man covering from inside the doorway, Sten gun juddering. Enemy tracer whipped past and he cringed.

Then a single bullet creased his left cheek. A burning pain made him grunt, and then he was through the open doorway. He went left behind the wall, panting with the enforced exertion. Lungs heaving, he stood and grinned. Quite how he'd managed to escape that lot was beyond him. Not even a serious injury. He touched the raw wound to his cheek. Even that was no more than a scratch.

The Old Man stepped back away from the opening and gestured with his Sten. 'You up to taking my place?'

Jock Stewart nodded. 'Yes, sir.' The doorway was a bloody sight more protected than when he'd been out there lying behind an old piece of leather. He moved to the side of the door and reloaded.

'Alright Jock?' It was Tillman voicing his concern.

Stewart gave him a wink. 'Aye, bastards ain't got me yet.'

Tillman gave the Germans a short burst. 'Long may it last,' he said, and fired again. A Grenadier staggered.

Stewart aimed and fired and the man dropped.

'Nice,' Tillman said, and the two Paratroopers found new targets.

At the front of the farmhouse No.3 Section took the full force of a head on attack. Two half-tracks opened up as they pushed out into the field, raking the defences with a withering storm of fire. Dinger

Bell did his best to give as good as he was taking but as soon as he fired he became the default target. Two steady streams of tracer raced over the fields, the bullets hammering at the low wall. It was all he could do to pull a trigger let alone aim at something. He ducked again and glanced to his right.

'Pete!' he shouted above the din. 'Bloody Spandaus.'

Rifleman Pete Solomon from Maidstone on the River Medway looked his way and gave a lopsided grin. 'You're not wrong.' He aimed towards the trees and fired.

A mortar shell detonated. The explosion blasted a crater, and dirt and shrapnel tore across open ground. A wave of hot air hit Solomon and with it a steel splinter struck him. He stared open mouthed. His left thumb and forefinger had been severed at the base and he looked at the stumps in disbelief, blood pumping. He grabbed the wrist to compress the flow, squeezed hard. It slowed.

Dinger Bell saw what was happening, and dragging the Bren gun with him, slithered across to help. He flicked the bipod into place and gave the Panzergrenadiers a quick burst. They scattered and dived for cover. He turned to Solomon and pulled open a bandage. He slapped a wad over the end of the stumps and bound the whole lot together as tight as he thought right. It needed something better but he didn't have time.

Pete groaned, the pain hitting him. Bell pointed at the front door.

'Go!' he shouted. 'The kitchen! They'll see to you in there.' He shoved him away and turned back to the Bren. Already the Germans were back on their feet. Dust swirled, cleared, and he gave them a short burst. They weaved, one staggered. And then tracer found the Bren gunner again and he flattened behind the butt.

From left and right he heard the crackle of Sten guns and tentatively raised his head. Corporal Dave Greene had the enemy under fire from the left and Lance-Corporal Nobby Clarke had them pinned from over to the right. Bell slapped in another magazine and lifted the butt.

'Come on you bastards!' he yelled, and pulled the trigger. The gun juddered beneath his hands and he began firing controlled three and four round bursts at the running Grenadiers. His accuracy began to take effect. A man staggered, dropped. Another lurched forward, lost his footing, stayed down. That was better, he thought. In with a chance now.

Private Greg Dawson, 19, a Liverpudlian born and bred, had set himself up close to the end of the ditch, where Miller had killed the lone lookout. He lay half hidden beneath a mass of hawthorn branches, and a low dirt mound to his front helped with concealment. It was an ideal spot for a Rifleman to fire into an enemy flank as they advanced across the cornfield. He picked out a crawling Grenadier, aimed and squeezed. The .303 barked, the heavy butt slamming his shoulder. There was a spurt of blood and the German rolled onto his back, writhing in pain. Another Grenadier knelt to help him and Dawson put a bullet into his side. Two down injured, out of the battle and he grimaced. The more the merrier, he thought. Bit like target practice on the range.

A trio of soldiers appeared through smoke, all with MP40's firing from their waists. One of them paused mid-stride to prepare a stick grenade and

Dawson shifted his aim. The man's arm went back to throw towards the farmhouse and Dawson fired. And missed. The grenade tumbled in a high arc and landed short of the broken front door. The lethal explosion brought a shout of pain.

A line of tracer buzzed in over the yellow heads of corn, the foliage above the ditch twitching and swaying as bullets thrashed leaves. The tracer searched the hedge towards Dawson and he squeezed himself into the earth. Praying. This was his baptism of fire, first contact with a real enemy. He didn't think today was his day to die, hoped it wouldn't be. Bullets hissed over his head. The tracer moved off towards the front wall of the farmhouse.

A sixth sense made him turn. Behind him, looming large from out of the ditch, came a lunging Grenadier. His face was contorted with the effort, a misshapen row of nicotine stained teeth protruding from an unshaven jaw. The gleaming bayonet flashed in the sunlight and for a split second Dawson found himself transfixed. But the instinct for survival kicked in and he twisted to avoid the point. The bayonet caught his smock at the waist, ripped the cloth and momentarily snagged the blade. The German snarled his annoyance and with a violent tug ripped it free. But now Dawson reacted and jabbed savagely with the Lee Enfield's muzzle.

'Bastard!' he shouted, and the tip of the barrel rammed hard into the Grenadier's solar plexus. He hit the trigger. The rifle cracked and the bullet tore through the man's belly. Blood erupted from his back as the bullet exited flesh. He dropped the Mauser and staggered backwards, clutching his belly. With an agonised groan he sank to his knees.

Glowing tracer slashed past Dawson's head and he dived for the ditch. He landed, rolled, then steadied, up on one knee. His helmet had dislodged and slipped to one side. He was breathing hard and he deliberately slowed the intake of air, releasing it with control. His eyes were below the top of the ditch and he gingerly eased up until he could see across the field. Bullets raked the foliage overhead and more kicked dirt in front. The bullets walked in a line and suddenly the Grenadier jerked to hits. Dawson shrugged. The German was dead now, if not before.

A lone bullet whipped in from across the field. It struck Dawson a glancing blow to his exposed temple and he went down like a rag doll.

From the corner of his eye, Mitchell saw Dawson go down and made a dash for the end of the ditch. He found him in the bottom of the ditch unconscious and bleeding from a head wound. Mitchell was tough, not big, but lean and wiry. He knew he couldn't leave him, placed his Sten safely on the top of the ditch, and then hauled Dawson off the ground and bumped him up over his left shoulder in a fireman's lift. He gathered up Dawson's rifle, picked up his Sten and shouted for covering fire.

Nobby Clarke heard the yell and called to Dinger Bell. He nodded and they both watched for Mitchell's signal. They saw him nod and opened fire together, sweeping the near side of the field with tracer.

Mitchell sensed a lessening in the rate of enemy fire and took his chance. He lunged out of the ditch and scampered for the low wall. With an awkward leap he cleared the stones and rushed up the path and in through the door. Blowing hard he staggered into the kitchen. The girl was helping a casualty off the table and lowering him to sit against the wall.

Mitchell hesitated. She straightened and pointed at the table.

'Put him there,' she said, and helped to lie him on his back.

Mitchell undid the chin strap and pointed. 'Grazed him, miss. Not sure what you can do.'

'Leave that to me. You're needed out there.' She bent to check the wound and Mitchell made for the front door. Each to their own, he had a job to do.

At the base of the beech tree, Dan Clayton smoothly levered another round into the breech and closed the bolt. The enemy were moving down his side of the cornfield with what he felt was an overconfidence in their invulnerability. They were visible from the waist up and the nearest were already only two-hundred yards away. Behind them, advancing at walking pace, was a half-track, its pedestal mounted twin machine-guns raking the wall to Clayton's right. He found the gunner standing behind the cab and aimed low, for the man's midriff. He fired, missed. Open the bolt and eject the case, fresh round in the chamber. Close the bolt, aim--fire. Missed. Reload, and this time it was third time lucky, and Clayton saw the man stagger and fall backwards. Behind the open hatch he picked out the driver, aimed. But with the momentary pause in the volume of machine-gun fire, Dinger Bell's Bren gun rejoined the battle and Clayton saw bullets hammering at the armoured cab.

'Dan! To your left!' It was Greene shouting.

Clayton wriggled back from the tree trunk and swept the Lee Enfield round to cover his left. There were three Panzergrenadiers closing on him with sub-machineguns, one firing from the waist. Chunks of wood splintered from the tree, bullets whining. Clayton aimed and fired on the move, coming up on one knee. It was point-blank range no more then twenty yards. Blood sprayed and the German's face slammed into the dirt. The other two split up, diving for cover, and Clayton dropped to his belly clear of the tangled roots. A German jackboot showed from behind flattened corn and he aimed at the toecap. The rifle cracked followed by a shout of pain, the bloodied boot withdrawn. Corn swayed and bent as the Germans crawled away. He chased the unseen enemy with a couple of rounds and let it be. There were more obliging targets coming down the field.

Lieutenant Matt Summerton waited for his tank's gun barrel to protrude fractionally from the leaves and brought the tank to a halt. According to the map the farmhouse lay about twelve-hundred yards ahead beyond the two fields immediately to his front and through to the far side of that wood. By the sound of it there was one hellish fire fight going on beyond the trees. Black smoke coiled menacingly into the sky. He turned to look at Fitzgerald's tank sitting fifty-yards to the right. It was similarly positioned half hidden by undergrowth, the barrel raised in anticipation.

Summerton lifted the binoculars and took a minute to thoroughly inspect the woods. Oak and hornbeam and brambles and pines, and as hard as he looked he found no sign of Germans. Time to make a move. He raised a hand to Fitzgerald and waved in the direction of the wood. The Sergeant's tank throttled up and edged forward into the open, following the line of a tall hedge on his right side.

Summerton gave the word to his driver and the tank crawled out onto the field. Fifty yards apart the Shermans pushed ahead, both commanders straining to catch a glimpse of enemy activity. After a hundred yards they rode up and over a shallow embankment that divided the corn field from what now appeared to be a meadow, and then continued to advance steadily towards the next tree line.

Fitzgerald came up on the net. 'Three graves in this corner. Helmets look like they were Paratroopers.'

Summerton took his eyes off the trees and glanced across. The helmets did appear to be the same as those worn in Major Lane's headquarters.

'Probably from the platoon we're looking for,' he said. 'The farmhouse is the other side of this wood. You see the smoke?'

Fitzgerald said he too had seen it and asked if his Troop commander had a plan of attack.

'No,' Summerton answered truthfully. 'We'll just take it as it comes. My only advice is keep your distance and watch for Panzerfausts.'

Fitzgerald acknowledged. 'Wilco, out.'

Summerton spoke to Gledhill. 'Driver advance.' The engine grumbled, rose in volume and the Sherman jerked forward. Summerton eyed the approaching trees and found what he thought was a thinning of trunks at two o'clock.

'Left stick . . . , more . . . , now straight for that gap in the trees.' Gledhill eased the tank to the left and they rolled on. Fifty-yards to his right, Summerton caught sight of Fitzgerald's tank nosing into the fringe and he nodded. He'd committed what was left of his Troop. Good bad or otherwise it was time to intervene, and in Summerton's personal opinion his armoured cavalry were the ideal weapon with which to take on a bunch of Nazi Panzergrenadiers.

The Sherman advanced cautiously across the clearing and came to a halt where the thinning trees gave way to a rutted track. And it was from there that Summerton caught his first glimpse of the embattled farmhouse. From his elevated position in the turret he could clearly see the German positions, and spotted a mortar section lobbing shells at the front of the farmhouse. He raised his binoculars and focussed on what he thought were members of the Platoon. A Bren gunner came into view, tracer searching out over the corn. He found two riflemen and a sub-machine gunner, all putting up a stiff resistance. The most obvious enemy positions were a pair of half-tracks sat at this edge of the cornfield and unleashing a steady stream of suppressing fire from their twin mounted machine-guns.

Summerton ordered his driver to advance five yards. Unseen by the Panzergrenadiers and unheard over the noise of battle, the squealing tracks brought his Sherman to a halt at the verge of the trees. The barrel of the armoured vehicle traversed a little to its right and Lieutenant Matthew J. Summerton gave the order.

'Fire!'

The gun bellowed and a shell whipped across the void. It exploded against the half-track's rear doors. The detonation tore apart the troop carrying compartment and hurled the vehicle into the air. It somersaulted end over end and came to rest upside down. The driver, caught by the steering wheel was cut in half by the impact. Oberleutnant Hans Schröder was flung over the front. His crumpled remains lay half buried under the weight of the engine, bloody wounds marking his violent exit from the back.

Two Panzergrenadiers who had only advanced fifty metres into the cornfield heard the crack of the Sherman's gun and looked round in stunned amazement. But their astonishment didn't last long. One of them freed off a stick grenade, primed it, and hidden by the tall sheaves of corn wriggled closer to the tank. An officer stood in the turret's open hatch and the Grenadier prepared to throw. The main gun fired again, blasting a shell towards a mortar team. The Grenadier lunged to his feet, took a pace forward and hurled the grenade. He was twelve metres from the nearest track, too far to be certain of accuracy. The stick grenade struck the curved armour of the turret and bounced off to explode harmlessly out of sight beyond the tank's hull.

The officer had seen the soldier's movement and grabbed for the hatch mounted Browning machine-gun. The gun hammered a dozen 0.5-inch rounds in the Grenadier's direction and he went down in a heap of flailing arms and legs. But his comrade was quick to react. He came up from hiding and sprayed the turret with his sub-machinegun.

Matt Summerton was caught by surprise but swivelled the Browning and jabbed the trigger. At the same moment a bullet grazed his left cheek, and he winced at the throbbing sting. But the burst from the Browning hit the target and the second Grenadier fell backwards.

Summerton cursed and sagged, white hot pain lancing up his cheekbone. He blinked and took a sharp breath. Through the pain he saw the mortar crew still served the tube.

'Target eleven o'clock. Mortar.'

The turret traversed left. Stopped. The gunner confirmed.

'On.'

'Fire!'

And the gun belched smoke and flame. In a split second the mortar crew disintegrated in a flaming explosion, a boiling ball of fire.

Summerton sought a fresh target, his left eye watering. To his right Fitzgerald's tank advanced at a slow crawl, the Sergeant manning his Browning in search of Panzergrenadiers.

Over in the trees, hidden in the undergrowth, a single Panzerfaust Grenadier saw an opportunity to target one of the Shermans. To have any chance of success he knew he would need to get within sixty-metres of the tank. The corn was tall and he began to crawl.

20 Hand to Hand

In the workshop, Sergeant Bill Cartwright sat with his back against the anvil and let his helmet drop to the floor. He knew he was wounded and hurting, but exactly how bad he couldn't tell. He'd been hit in the left leg while defending the door to the orchard, a glancing blow to his thigh. And then an exploding grenade had ripped up both shins with steel fragments. A bullet had also deflected off his ribcage. Now he faced the same door and waited for the next bastard to show his face. Outside, six Panzergrenadiers lay dead or dying, each man having been foolish enough to charge that end of the workshop. One man, hit in the thigh was dragging himself away towards the orchard. A trail of blood marked his passage.

Rob Carter still lay across the workbench with the Bren gun propped on its bipod. Rob came from the cathedral city of Canterbury in Kent. It was a place that had not seemed very exciting as he grew up so as soon as he reached the requisite age a recruiting Sergeant was only too pleased to sign him up. At this moment he began to wonder if he'd not been a little hasty with his decision. Right now he thought, a bit of peace and quiet wouldn't go amiss.

His stack of spare magazines had dwindled until only three remained. By his reckoning there were fourteen rounds left on the Bren, that of course was if he'd counted correctly. In battle that wasn't always the way. He too nursed a wound, a bullet entering his right shoulder and exiting cleanly. Blood congealed on his smock, the injury feeling more like a burning sensation. And he'd sprained his left wrist. Quite how he didn't know, only that it felt more painful than the bullet wound.

He glanced round at Cartwright. 'Alright, Sarge?'

Cartwright gave him a twisted grin. 'I'll manage. You see any more out there?'

Carter returned his gaze to the grassy slopes. 'Not this minute. The buggers are pushing towards the farmhouse.'

Just inside the brown door nearest the farmhouse, Steve Dexter leaned heavily against the door jamb. A fragment from a grenade had lodged in his neck and turning his head was difficult. His breathing had become laboured and he felt faint, struggling to stay on his feet. Importantly though, his vision was unaffected and he had a clear view of enemy movement all the way across to the barn. Right now, with a pile of bodies stacked outside, it seemed that the Panzergrenadiers had had their fill of attacking the workshop.

Dexter managed to slowly turn his head and look towards the forge. He picked out Cartwright sat with his back to the anvil watching the far door, and Carter at the window. Dexter smiled. The left flank had held.

In the line of poplar trees beyond the paddock, Major Carl Kruger urged on his Panzergrenadiers. Inwardly he admitted to being surprised by the vigorous defence being displayed by the Paratroopers. At the same time he knew their ammunition stocks had to be running low while his own men had plenty of reserves to call on. The only concern he had was the lack of contact with Hans Schröder's half-track. He'd heard the muted explosion from beyond the front of the house, and after that Schröder had ceased to transmit. Without his reports Kruger was blind to how that frontal assault was going.

He raised his binoculars and made a more considered inspection of the battlefield. He found many more Grenadier casualties lying out there than he had first imagined but at the same time it appeared that there was a slackening of the British firepower. Sheer force of numbers had probably served to overcome much of the enemy's stubborn resistance. Maybe now, he thought, was the time for Major Carl Kruger to join the battle. His presence would give a boost of confidence to his Grenadiers. They would see the blood stained uniform but be buoyed by the knowledge their commander still came ahead to fight alongside.

'Driver! Forward!' he ordered.

The half-track rumbled as the driver engaged gears and throttled up, and the vehicle broke out into the open.

Miller came alert to the growl of the half-track's engine and took the time to search around the slope. Panzergrenadiers were everywhere, bounding forward in small groups, dodging fallen comrades. But a steady stream of British tracer was keeping them at bay, only the bravest or most foolhardy prepared to risk getting to within grenade throwing distance.

And then Miller found a half-track emerging from the row of poplars and a thin smile crossed his face.

'You beautiful bastard,' he mouthed and snugged down tighter to the rifle's butt. He may have missed his chance earlier when that vehicle with its pretty flags was out of range, but this time . . . , this time he would make sure.

Focussing carefully through the telescopic sight he sighted on the engine cowling and wriggled until his elbows and knees were well braced. With one finger he pushed the helmet back from his forehead and then chambered a cartridge into the breech. Closing the bolt he settled again, and then found the bloodied uniform of the officer in charge.

The half-track's twin mounted machine-gun spat flame beyond the officer's shoulder, the gunsmoke rising. Miller saw it but ignored it, concentrating only on the officer's peaked cap. The man gesticulated at his Grenadiers, urging them on, mouth open as he shouted orders. The black patch over his left eye swam in front of the lens and Miller gritted his teeth. It was the hated sign of treachery, a tale that had spread like wildfire, and here was his chance to right a terrible wrong. The half-track came to a halt. Filthy smoke from the exhaust wafted across the lens but as it cleared Miller found he had the perfect shot. He set the range. Then aligning the sight on the man's chest, he took up first pressure on the trigger, steadied his breathing and gently, so very gently . . . , squeezed. The Lee Enfield kicked back. At a velocity approaching 2,500 feet-per-second, the .303 bullet whipped through the air and slammed into the target. Miller caught the moment of impact, the left shoulder taking the hit, a small splash of crimson.

He cursed and swore, muttered and mumbled. He'd bloody well gone and missed. The shame of it.

Yeah, he'd skimmed the man's arm but that was six inches wide of the mark, and he shook his head in frustration. How on earth had he missed by that much? He'd aimed for the left breast pocket. The man must have moved, that was the only feasible explanation. He levered another round into the breech and looked to make amends.

Major Carl Kruger staggered from the force of the hit, but his right hand grip on the armour plate was strong enough to prevent him from falling. A surge of pain swept through the muscle and his arm hung useless, with not enough strength left to raise it. His face screwed up in torment and he sagged against the side. Blood soaked his uniform and he involuntarily reached over with his good hand to support the arm.

Behind him a Grenadier saw him slump sideways and then spotted the blood. The man reached for a box of sterile dressings and bandages and found a bottle of antiseptic. Without ceremony he cut away Kruger's sleeve, found the point of impact but then also an exit wound. Smothering the lacerations in the yellow liquid he then applied a dressing and wrapped a bandage round the injuries. He produced a sling, tied it, and manipulated the arm inside. He looked inquiringly at the Major.

Kruger nodded, wincing. 'Ja,' he managed, 'that is good.'

The Grenadier returned to the rear of the compartment and Kruger hissed at the driver.

'Forward!' he snapped. 'Forward!'

The driver jammed the half-track into first gear and stamped on the accelerator. There was a jolt as the tracks engaged drive, and Kruger grunted as the pain resurfaced. The driver hid a smile at the Major's discomfort. Always the man shouted his orders with no respect. He should learn some manners. He wrestled with the steering as the front wheels rode over a fallen Grenadier, the lower torso squashed to a bloodied pulp. It had happened before and it would happen again, and the driver pushed on. There was no blame, not his fault, it was war.

Miller watched as the half-track become partially obscured behind smoke. It was advancing to his right, heading for the courtyard between barn and the kitchen. If he tried to follow up with another shot he would have to come out from hiding and that would leave him exposed to any Panzergrenadier fancying his chances. No, he thought, a sniper was too valuable an asset to allow himself to be caught so cheaply. He pushed all thoughts of pursuing the officer to one side and settled back to the job in hand. A faint smile crossed his lips. He'd cook some other bastard's goose instead. He traversed the lens and found a Grenadier crawling towards the workshop. It was only the man's head and shoulders but something indicated a worthwhile target. The man's awkward movements seemed to show he was pushing and dragging a heavy object. Then beyond him Miller caught sight of another helmet, just the top, bobbing along in the same undulating manner. He adjusted the telescope, clarified the image. Both targets stayed low, hugging the ground in what could only be a shallow gulley, and all the time they were closing the gap to the workshop.

Miller settled his elbows and brought the butt tight to his shoulder. The first target wasn't an ideal shot, the man's erratic movement not giving the sniper much confidence in his ability to make a hit. But there was more to shoot at than just the top of a helmet.

Then both targets stopped moving forward, the helmets coming together. Miller frowned, still uncertain as to what he was dealing with. And then slowly, deliberately, the muzzle of a Spandau machine-gun protruded up from the gulley. The Grenadier's head and shoulders steadied, and the weapon became horizontal in his hands, aimed directly at the workshop.

Miller pursed his lips, finally understanding. A machine-gunner and assistant, a weapons team. He centred the scope on the gunner's cheekbone. At two-hundred yards it wasn't a very big target. An inch too high and the bullet would strike the steel helmet, too low and it would be the shoulder. Both would incapacitate but a clean hit on the cheekbone or temple would kill. He heard the ripsaw snarl of the Spandau, saw the Grenadier's jaw vibrate with the gun's rapid recoil, spent shells tumbling to one side.

And Miller fired. It was a clean hit, an instantaneous blood-red patch half an inch above the cheekbone, and the soldier's head disappeared. The Spandau stopped firing and the assistant's helmet dropped from view. Miller congratulated himself and reloaded.

Only then did he see the three oncoming Grenadiers. They were running directly for him and one threw a stick grenade. It fell short and landed in the water. The pond erupted with the force of the explosion, mud and reeds flying in all directions. Drenched, Miller desperately cleared moisture from his eyes. A Grenadier splashed knee high into the pond, sub-machinegun fired from the waist, bullets spraying wildly over Miller's head. The sniper lifted the muzzle of the Lee-Enfield and hit the trigger. The Grenadier screamed and doubled up, grasping his belly. Miller came up onto his knees and went to reload, the next Grenadier almost on top of him.

Jed Tulloch was looking out from the sitting room window and saw Miller about to be overrun. He gave the German a short burst and saw him stagger, down on one knee. Another burst knocked him over.

The other Grenadier had Miller at his mercy and the MP40 hammered. The sniper took two hits, left hand and elbow, the fingers torn off and his elbow smashed, jagged bone exposed. Miller dropped the rifle and grabbed for his pistol. In that instant Tulloch fired again. The German pivoted away and toppled off the bank. He splashed heavily into the water, stayed under.

At the kitchen door, Wingham saw Miller come to his feet, left arm a bloodied mess and hanging limp. The immediate threat of attacking enemy had lessened and it was obvious the sniper needed help. Wingham didn't hesitate. He clambered over the heap of rubble and limped towards the pond. A few tracer rounds fizzed in but not enough to deter him and he made it to Miller's side. The half-track's gunner saw him and swung the barrels, tracer chasing towards Wingham. Tillman intervened, the Bren gun juddering under his big hands. The German flinched at a near miss and brought the muzzles round until they lined up on the window. Too late. A bullet from the Bren caught him high on the helmet. It didn't penetrate but the force of impact knocked him down.

Wingham took advantage of the lull. Without a word he grabbed Miller under his good arm and giving physical support to the badly disorientated sniper, managed to get him back into the kitchen. Only once did he moan and that was when Wingham hoisted him almost bodily over the broken rubble.

The girl already had a patient on the table so he sat the sniper gently against the wall and carefully placed the damaged left arm across his stomach. A pair of red rimmed eyes looked up at him and through a face full of grime the Paratrooper managed a tentative smile.

'Thanks, Major. Couldn't have made it on my own.'

Wingham grinned at him. 'And as always, Miller, you'd have taken far too long by yourself.'

The sniper winced at a stab of pain but showed his teeth in a grin.

'Slow but sure, Major. Slow but sure.'

Wingham nodded, gave Miller's good shoulder a squeeze and straightened up. Sarah met his eyes. He inclined his head towards the sniper.

'When you get time,' he said and she nodded. He thought she looked a bit shell shocked, but said only, 'Thank you,' and left her to her gruesome chores.

As he left the room he glanced back at Miller a feeling of helpless frustration coming to the fore. The sniper had done so much to help them and now he was paying a terrible price. That arm might never recover, his dexterity forever impaired. Wingham looked away in sorrow. So many good men were now suffering, and all because he'd let the *Ruffians* get surrounded.

Jed Tulloch watched the Major help get Miller into the farmhouse, changed his magazine for a full one and returned his concentration to the grassy slope. What he saw gave him reason for concern. The enemy to his front were attacking with increased strength, and at a glance he estimated more than twenty converging on this left flank. They came on in the manner of typical infantry, small sections of Grenadiers leap-frogging one another, covering fire protecting running groups. The trouble for Tulloch was they were more than two-hundred yards out and a Sten didn't hurt much at that range. He turned and moved over to Stratton.

'I need your rifle,' he said, and offered him the Sten. 'You'll be better with this.'

Stratton hesitated, not willing to give up his personal weapon. But he realised it made sense, his gun being limited inside a room and unable to fire into wide open spaces.

Tulloch scooped up the rifle, managed to unwrap one of Stratton's .303 bandoliers with the spare clips, and then handed over the Sten and his three remaining mags of 9mm rounds.

'Cheers, mate,' he said, hefting the Lee Enfield. 'I might have the range now.'

Stratton grunted and managed to warn him, 'One up the spout.'

Tulloch nodded his understanding, shrugged into the bandolier and stepped back across to the window. Standing to one side he thumbed the safety catch to 'off', slid the barrel round the splintered frame and picked out a kneeling Grenadier. With the rear sight set to 'battle', good enough for up to three-hundred yards, Tulloch aimed for the German's torso and squeezed. The gun barked, rapped his shoulder, and the soldier hit the ground face first.

Better, he thought, and selected his next victim. The rifle cracked and a German stumbled and fell. Tulloch levered another round into the breech and braced against the wooden frame. He grimaced and picked out a third target. At this rate, he thought, he could put himself forward to take Miller's job.

21 Gun Up

In the leading Sherman, Lieutenant Summerton squinted at the mayhem. It dawned on him that the heaviest fighting was taking place on the other side of the farmhouse. Under the withering fire of the Brownings, the sound of return gunfire subsided and it became all too apparent the Shermans were needed beyond the house. He could hear mortar rounds exploding, the distinctive rasp of Spandaus, hand grenades thumping and the incessant chatter of small arms fire. Dirty blue smoke mushroomed from two or three locations.

He looked for a way to dodge the building and spotted a tall hedge to the left of the house. Further left still he could see an old stovepipe chimney protruding from some sort of outhouse. There was more than enough room between the two buildings for the tanks to make an attack. He raised an arm to Fitzgerald, pointed at the hedge, and made a chopping motion with the edge of his hand.

The Sergeant nodded vigorously, gave a 'thumbs up', and his tank made a move to join Summerton.

Paul Wingham heard a shout from out front and headed for the front door. He passed the girl administering first aid to a man's thigh, blood smeared up her bare arms. He made it to the doorway and called from inside.

'What is it?' he shouted, ducking from a stray bullet.

'Tanks, sir! Shermans!'

Tracer hissed past Wingham's head and he pressed himself back against the wall. It stopped and he risked a look.

A grin spread across his face. He could see two Shermans with both their turret machine-guns raking enemy positions. In the middle of the cornfield a half-track lay upside down on fire, flames flickering round the engine. Thick black smoke curled over the trees.

The rattle of gunfire faded across the cornfield and he saw that the tanks were swinging towards the hedge and the workshop. Whoever was in command of those two Shermans had quickly understood the tactical situation and there was no need for Wingham's advice. He glanced round the cornfield and picked out some of No.3 Section's Paratroopers, including Corporal Greene.

He called across. 'Hold your positions and keep your eye out for any more.'

Greene raised a hand and nodded. 'Will do, sir.'

Wingham took a final look down the field and caught sight of two Panzergrenadiers fleeing into the trees. A third Grenadier rose suddenly from the far end of the field and sprinted into the undergrowth. He was carrying a Panzerfaust. A Bren gun chattered, a short burst to hurry him on his way. It looked to Wingham that No.3 Section had things under control, at least for the time being. He turned back for the kitchen and the sound of Tillman's Bren gun.

Over in the workshop, Corporal Steve Dexter heard the squeal of tank tracks and frowned in consternation. The sounds came from his right, over the other side of the tall hedge and he levered himself away from the door jamb to look out towards the gable end of the house. The growl of the engines reached him and he cocked his head on one side. Those engines didn't sound anything like a German Panzer. German engines had a distinctive rumble, these he felt sure sounded somehow smoother. If so he thought, peering hard at the hedge, these were more likely to be Allied tanks.

Seconds later two long gun barrels appeared over the top of the hedge. Then the foliage shuddered and twigs and leaves disintegrated under the armoured weight of two 30-ton Shermans, ploughing through the greenery in their role as temporary bulldozers. The nearest tank clanked towards the workshop before slewing to a halt.

Dexter made himself visible in the doorway and only when he was sure the tank commander recognised his uniform did he hobble across to make contact. A British Lieutenant stared down at him, a bloodied cheek bone evidence of a recent wound.

'What's the score, Corporal?'

Machine-gun tracer zipped in to ricochet off the Sherman's armoured nose. The other Sherman also began taking hits.

Dexter ducked before pointing across in front of the driver's goggles at the grass covered slope and the row of poplars.

'Panzergrenadiers, sir. Must be at least half-company strength. Couple of half-tracks, mortar teams and a gun, a Pak anti-tank. In that line of trees.'

As if to underline his explanation a mortar round whined in and exploded half way between the two tanks.

'What's your strength?' the Lieutenant asked, raising his voice to be heard over the noise.

Dexter nibbled his bottom lip, squinting at the farmhouse and barn.

'I think we're down to eight or nine. Mostly in the farmhouse with Major Wingham.' He gestured with a thumb over his shoulder. 'Three of us still holding out in this workshop.'

The Lieutenant nodded and pursed his lips, eyes taking in the extent of the battlefield.

'Right,' he said forcefully. 'Let's see if we can't help you sort these bastards out.' He looked over to the other tank, spoke into his handset. Dexter saw the other commander nod and answer. They both then raised a hand and the engines rose in volume.

The Lieutenant looked down and gave Dexter a grim smile. 'See you when we're done, Corporal.'

As the noise of the engines increased yet again, Dexter wished them all the luck. Both tanks manoeuvred out onto the grass covered slope, the gap between them widening. Two Browning machine-guns hammered into action. Grenadiers desperately began to seek cover.

Sergeant Cartwright wanted to see the tanks. It was an almost child like need. After all this time he had to see for himself. He twisted round, grabbed the anvil and hauled himself to his feet. The leg burned, his ribs ached and breathing was difficult. But even as the grenade fragments stung his shins Cartwright forced himself to hobble towards the pock marked steel door. Limping through he stepped gingerly over a dead Grenadier and stopped to catch his breath. He leaned against the wall, the noise of the tanks drawing him on. Tentatively, painfully, he made it to the corner and looked round, and there they were. Two Shermans, Browning machine-guns hammering, raking the grass covered slopes.

A slow smile lifted his worn features. Shot up, bleeding and in considerable pain, for Sergeant Bill Cartwright this was still one of the best moments of his army career. Slowly, awkwardly, he lowered himself down against the brick wall and sat with his legs outstretched.

A long way north, back across the English Channel in West Sussex, Flying Officer Ronald "Ronnie" Hart, a twenty-four year old graduate from R.A.F. Cranwell, strode over to his Hawker Typhoon fighter-bomber, clambered into the cockpit and began pre flight checks. His ground crew signalled 'chocks away' and with the engine ticking over and the propeller on fine pitch, Hart taxied to the end of the temporary runway. The Sommerfeld Tracking well served its purpose in enabling the squadron to operate from what, until recently, had been a farmer's winter pasture for his dairy herd. The interlinked steel mesh matting gave substantial reinforcement to the field and added one more Advanced Landing Ground to the R.A.F.'s operations. This airfield sat only two miles inland from Bognor Regis on the south coast and reduced the distance to Normandy to as little as twenty minutes flying time.

Through his headphones came the voice of Squadron Leader Allan J. Carson.

'All sections . . . , on our way.'

Ronnie slid the hood closed, brakes off; he eased the throttle forward, heard the engine rise, the Typhoon trembling, and then as the snarling roar of the Napier-Sabre howled into full power the fighter surged up the runway. The tail came up and moments later he inched the stick back, and the wheels rotated free of terra firma. Airborne again. Undercarriage up, a check in the mirror and a quick glance around. Twelve fighter-bombers banking south in a tight formation. They levelled out and gained height, climbing to Angels one-five. And the distant sight of a smoke shrouded French coast came into view.

At the small thatched cottage near the coast, Mary stopped her weeding as a squadron of Typhoons roared out over the English Channel. She'd seen similar aeroplanes flying around her home for almost two weeks now so she guessed they had an airfield somewhere close by. But for the last three days there'd been a noticeable difference in their markings. Instead of the usual pale underside and camouflaged fuselage the Typhoons had been painted with very visible black and white stripes. And they weren't alone. From what she'd seen, every single aircraft flying off towards France had the same markings.

She lifted a hand to shield her eyes from the sun's glare and watched as the fighter-bombers climbed ever higher before becoming mere specks over the sea.

Mary turned back to the weeding, the afternoon sun warm on her back. She worked the hoe up and down the rows and then bent to pull a particularly stubborn plant. As she leaned, the silver locket hanging round her neck swung out, the delicate chain touching her chin. She smiled and lowered the hoe to the ground. Carefully she prised the locket open and for a long moment looked down on Christopher's smiling face. The photograph had been taken four years ago when he was still comparatively young. But since then the years of war had lined his face, the crows feet round his eyes etched deeper.

She clipped it closed and sighed, let it gently hang. Glancing again at the sky the thought struck her that the very same pilots that had so recently flown over the cottage might well be flying over wherever Chris now patrolled.

Mary picked up the hoe and chopped at a clump of weeds that finally succumbed to a more determined attack. A quiet growl from behind made her look round to find 'Bob' sat with his head on one side fixing her with an inquisitive look. She checked her watch and saw it was mid afternoon. Time to check on Snowy and the growl was Bob's way of reminding her. She returned the hoe to the potting shed and walked off down the crazy paving. The privet hedge made her go left round the chicken coop and it was there, six-feet beyond the chicken wire fence, that a sturdy iron gate made of metal tubing served as an entrance to Snowy's paddock. As she slid back the bolt and pushed, Bob bounded through and took off for the other end where Snowy lifted her head and shook his mane.

Bob barked with excitement and raced in circles round the pony. In reply, snowy tossed his head and neighed loudly, a front hoof stomping the grass.

After a minute Snowy calmed, snorted, and walked head down towards Mary. She reached out to stroke his mane, at which point, as always, Bob made a last circuit round the pair of them and then dropped to his belly between Snowy's legs.

Mary smiled gently and ran her fingers down Snowy's silky smooth neck. The ears twitched and a big brown eye followed her every move. The smile lingered and she thought of Chris. Whenever he came over on leave he always spent the late afternoons with Snowy and Bob, and just like now, the two animals would come and stand quietly at his call.

She hoped and prayed that sometime soon, she would once more stand at the paddock gate and watch them do it all over again.

Wingham watched Tillman aiming short bursts at a slow moving half-track, the same half-track that bore the Regimental pennants. There looked to be an officer stood behind the driver. Wingham limped to the rubble piled in the doorway and added a burst from his own Sten. In the back of the carrier, the Grenadier on the twin machine-guns latched on to the kitchen window. Tracer zeroed in, flint and granite chips bouncing out of the wall. The bullets chewed the wooden frame, splinters flying.

Tillman gave a sharp grunt and took a faltering step back from the window, the Bren gun sagging in his hands. For long seconds he stood with his head bowed, breathing hard, but as Wingham ventured to help him, the man from Leeds straightened and secured the Bren back on the window ledge. A Grenadier breaking out from behind the cover of the half-track took three rounds in his chest and dropped.

Tillman ignored the taste of blood and found a fresh target.

From the woods facing the barn's small window, two Grenadiers made a dash for the wall. They made it in one piece and slammed their backs into the brickwork. Having caught their breath they edged toward the front of the barn and paused before summoning up the courage to move out into the open. To their relief, the few Englanders remaining were watching the woods at the far end.

Without a word they both crouched and moved forward until they reached the adjoining wall. The house and nearest window were tantalisingly close, a few paces. Neither German had any stick grenades so it would be a matter of sub-machineguns. With two-metres between them they made their decision and crept forward. The first reached the window, cocked his MP40 and levelled it over the sill.

Sarah sensed a shadow at the window, glanced up and saw the gun barrel appear. With a scream of defiance she grabbed her Schmeisser and hit the trigger. As the German's MP40 sprayed the room, Sarah's bullets lashed the window, a dozen rounds. Three caught the Grenadier and blood sprayed, spattering the wall. The contorted face disappeared and she waited, down on one knee.

Wingham saw it all and lunged past the table. Sten gun pointing he reached the window, thrust his head and shoulders through. A German crouched and he gave him a burst. The man flailed backwards, throat and chest turning crimson. He caught sight of

Corporal Greene turning to see what had happened and he gave him a thumbs up. Back inside the room Sarah struggled with the next Paratrooper, and shouldering the Sten gun, Wingham stepped over and lifted him bodily onto the table. He groaned and swore and then remained still.

Sarah ripped a fresh square of linen and compressed the leg wound, staunching the blood.

He touched her arm acknowledging her quick reactions. It was doubly impressive that she switched from nurse to killer with no hint of hesitation.

'That was well done, Sarah,' he said over the noise of gunfire. 'Good work.'

She looked up and managed a strained smile. 'I never really thought I'd ever make a nurse, too much blood. How wrong can you be?'

He patted her shoulder and walked away. Only when faced with such dire circumstances did a person find out the true extent of their ability to cope. It seemed likely that Sarah had met the test and passed with flying colours.

Choking smoke from the upstairs fire coiled along the corridor and he knew it was only a matter of time before they would need to evacuate. Bullets pinged and ricocheted off the door and he ducked to a near miss. The wound to his leg troubled him, a strange cold weakness causing it to almost give way. He limped back to the doorway and up onto the heap of rubble.

From over by the workshop heavy tracer swarmed down across the slope. It was the opening foray from the tanks and Wingham couldn't help but grin. Those Germans not caught in that lethal fusillade instantly went to ground, desperately seeking cover where none existed. Further down the slope the mortar team changed targets, and high explosive detonations walked towards the tanks. The tank nearest to Wingham veered right, its turret gun traversing left, and fired. The mortar team's half-track erupted in a flash of orange-red, steel splinters and shrapnel whirling through the air. Men screamed, torn apart, dying, reduced to bloody lumps of flesh. Machine-gun bullets thrashed at the remnants, like crows picking at the leftovers of some medieval feast.

A ragged cheer went up from the defenders as each man in turn realised what was happening and took in the longed for sight of Shermans. It gave each man that little extra impetus to fight to survive.

Standing next to his Pak anti-tank gun, well hidden in the row of poplars, Oberleutnant Erich Ritter raised his field glasses and made a quick study of the two Shermans. A young man with an exemplary record and already the recipient of a much heralded Iron Cross, he was only too pleased to be presented with such prominent targets. From a gunnery officer's standpoint the tanks were fairly straight forward. Not that he had ever personally encountered a Sherman. But he was well versed in their armour and where that armour was particularly vulnerable to penetration. He lowered the glasses and eyed his gun. It was a 5-cm Pak-38 anti-tank gun with a proven history of being able to take on Russian T-34's and coming out victorious.

Ritter looked again at the Shermans and a knowing smile passed across his face. They seemed oblivious to his presence, advancing at pace, the range already down to less than three-hundred metres. He clenched his teeth in anticipation. The gun could be loaded with Armour-Piercing-Ammunition that utilised a hard tungsten core easily capable of overcoming the frontal armour of a Sherman.

Unfortunately, only two of his original four man gun crew remained to tend the loading and laying, the other two he'd brought in to replace the wounded. Nonetheless they were more than equal to the task of fetching, carrying and clearing the expended shell cases.

He turned to the prime crew who had just loaded with high explosive. He could fire it at the soft target it was meant for, but that might give away his position to the tanks. He thought better of it.

'We change ammunition. Load with Armour-Piercing!'

The breech block slid aside, H.E. shell extracted and a 'Panzergranate 40', the purpose made solid shot anti-tank shell, was rammed into place. Breech block closed, the gunner confirmed.

'Ready, Herr Leutnant.'

'The nearest tank?'

'Jawohl. On!'

'Feuer!'

The gun cracked, recoiled, the spread legs digging in. The high velocity shell screamed across the intervening gap and slammed into the Sherman's frontal sloped armour. With a thumping clang it ricocheted.

Sergeant Fitzgerald caught the muzzle smoke.

'Target! Anti-tank. Traverse right. Two o'clock, tree line!'

The turret moved, the gun barrel sweeping round. It stopped, lifted.

The tank's machine-gun opened fire, tracer slashing the tree line.

'On!' from the gunner.

Fitzgerald called it. 'Fire!'

The gun barked, recoiled, and the shell whipped away across the field. It missed, high over.

'Reload!'

But now the German gunners had reloaded and Ritter gave the command.

'Feuer!'

And again a shell screamed across the void. This time the high velocity at the moment of impact punched in and half penetrated. Internally the armour shattered. Red hot fragments flayed the crew compartment. The gunner collapsed over the breech block, his abdomen lacerated. One of the Sherman's shells had been exposed for quick use and the cartridge case suffered a direct hit from a glowing shard. The explosive charge ignited, began to burn, and in seconds flames engulfed the interior.

Sergeant Fitzgerald felt the moment of impact and then the swirling heat round his legs.

'Bail out!' he yelled into the intercom, and hoisted himself from the turret. A hail of enemy bullets whined past his ears and he tumbled to the ground. Crouching low he made for the rear of the tank and collapsed down on one knee. Tracer from a Spandau zipped angrily round the Sherman. The driver, half in and half out of his seat took a bullet to the head.

A third shell from the Pak whipped in, hit the rounded turret and bounced off.

The radio operator managed to wriggle out of the turret and throw himself rearwards onto the engine decking. He bellied to the back and rolled off to join Fitzgerald.

He jabbed a thumb back at the turret. 'It's bleedin' hot in there!' he said, and slapped down a patch of his smouldering tank suit. They both waited for the gunner but he failed to make it. Incinerated. Leaping angry flames shot from the open hatches and red tinged oily black smoke billowed skywards.

Fitzgerald glanced about, saw that the workshop was nearest, and pointed. The radio op nodded and Fitzgerald shouted.

'Go!'

22 Hell Let Loose

In the other tank, Summerton had witnessed it all, and more by luck than judgement, had spotted the smoke from the gun's second round. He found the curved shield through his binoculars.

'Target! Two o'clock. Gun. Beyond the paddock rail!'

The turret traversed a touch right, steadied.

'On!'

'Fire!'

There was a stab of flame, the crash of gunfire. Recoil. Extract and reload. The acrid stench of cordite.

'Ready!'

Summerton had ignored everything but the end result and gave a small smile. The shell had hit the Pak's front shield and blasted the gun into a twisted wreck. The gun crew were scattered by the force of the strike, the split trail gun carriage wreaking havoc on soft flesh.

Oberleutnant Erich Ritter was hit by a spiralling steel trail and hurled to the ground. Soft leaf litter cushioned his fall. Lying on his back he felt an agony of pain in his left leg. He levered himself up into a sitting position and bit his tongue in shock.

His left leg was no longer attached and lay a metre away. He looked down and the ragged stump pumped blood with every beat of his heart. And then came waves of excruciating pain, pain that he wouldn't have believed a man could endure. It was white hot, lancing into his groin. His belly contorted, more pain. He looked and trembled with horror. His intestines lay open to the elements, partially unravelled.

Ritter shook his head. This was not to be braved, no future worth the living. He scrabbled for his Luger. The pistol came free and he thumbed the safety. So much for future prospects, a promising career gone. What price now an Iron Cross First Class? Tears of frustration came to his eyes, unbidden, and he screwed his lids tight shut. Leg torn off, his belly ripped open, what chance of a recovery? None. He felt the end of the cold barrel against his temple. Another ferocious stab of pain. End it, he pleaded silently. Reluctantly? Yes, but better than a life of crippling pain, terribly disfigured, nothing to live for now . . . . He summoned up the last of his failing courage and pulled the trigger.

Oberleutnant Erich Ritter, a proud Officer of Panzergrenadiers toppled sideways, relieved of his misery, dead by his own hand.

Kruger heard the heavy blast of gunfire and turned, astonished to find Shermans on his doorstep. The nearest had already been neutralised, oily red flames flickering from the turret hatch, but a second manoeuvred freely in front of the far outbuilding. He turned to look round for Ritter's Pak and cursed at the sight of smoking wreckage, the long gun barrel pointing haphazardly skywards.

Seeing a white star on the side panels, he automatically concluded they were American panzers. This he could report immediately, must report. But only two? They must surely be the reconnaissance unit of an armoured thrust, perhaps an initial attempt to encircle Caen. No commander in his right mind would send out feelers without major reinforcement close to hand. Kruger made his decision and nudged his wireless operator.

'Get me headquarters.'

The man flicked a switch on the transmitter, listened carefully and spoke into his handset. He waited, nodded with a 'Jawohl', and handed earphones and handset to Kruger. 'It is Captain Buschmann, Herr Major.'

Bullets from a Bren gun hammered the half-track's door and tracer hissed overhead. Kruger hunched lower.

'Buschmann?' he queried, voice raised above the din. 'Get me Fredrickson.'

'Major Kruger,' came the calm, cultured tones of the Regimental Staff Officer. 'Major Fredrickson is not here. What can I do for you?'

'American panzers, Buschmann! I am in contact with American panzers!'

'Where are you, Major?'

'We're up at the Farm Sainte Beaumont, where we had our Observation Post. I think they are the forward elements of an armoured battle group. You must warn the Colonel, put the Regiment on alert.'

There was a short pause before Buschmann replied. 'Major Kruger, I must tell you that recently we lost all contact with Oberst Kohlberg. We cannot raise the Château Fontaine. It is as if it never existed. I have sent two men to investigate, a motorbike and . . . .' A crackle of the airwaves interrupted his reply.

Kruger hesitated, momentarily at a loss as to how to proceed, but then remembered his orders.

'Are you still receiving me?'

'Jawohl, Herr Major.'

'Then get word to General-Feldmarschall Rommel. He is the one who ordered us to carry out this patrol. He wanted up to date information. You understand, Buschmann. It is vital you inform Rommel.'

'I will do my best, Herr Major. But all landline communications are down and the wireless-telegraphy office does not always receive an answer.'

Kruger cast a glance round the small field of battle. He could fight Paratroopers, but panzers? No. Not without the Regiment's full compliment of men and weapons. And the information he needed, Rommel needed, had fallen at his feet. There was no necessity to continue with the reconnaissance; he could quite legitimately call off the attack and return to Colombelles. Live to fight another day.

Or, he thought, if he could just get back to the row of poplars he might yet make these impudent Englanders regret ever having had the temerity to try and resist Kruger's attack. And what he wondered, a hard smile crossing his lips, what if he ordered 'B' Kompanie to reinforce his own Grenadiers? Buschmann was hardly in a position to refuse. With the Colonel out of contact, seniority meant command of the Regiment fell to Kruger. Buschmann would have no choice but to obey.

'Right, Buschmann, do what you can. We are not done here yet. I will regroup and strike again. In the meantime you will send 'B' Kompanie as my reinforcement. Have them join me soonest, you hear?'

There was only a slight hesitation before Buschmann answered. 'So be it, Herr Major. Soon.'

Kruger passed the set back to the operator and leaned to the driver. He pointed.

'Enemy panzers. Get us back behind the barn. Schnell!'

The driver nodded vigorously, stamped on the accelerator and hauled the half-track round to the south. Vicious lines of tracer rattled the thin armour plating. Grenadiers watched him retreat and he waved an arm towards the poplars. He passed the mortar team hidden in a fold in the ground.

'Smoke!' he shouted. 'Smoke! We're regrouping.'

In seconds mortar rounds began to thump from the tube, lobbed high to detonate in the gap between the Sherman and Grenadiers. Smoke rose into an impenetrable wall, lingering in the still air. Germans scrambled to their feet and fled down the tree line, wounded stumbling after the uninjured as they made the dash for safety. Tracer snaked after them and some fell, mowed down by British Paratroopers firing blind through the fog. As the smoke drifted and thinned those Panzergrenadiers who'd made it to the trees threw themselves into the undergrowth and the shallow ditch. And although appearance suggested a panicked rabble in headlong retreat, as soon as men made it into the scant safety of the trees they quickly turned to face the farmhouse.

Kruger's half-track took the shortest route. It smashed headlong through the paddock fencing, made a violent turn to the right and disappeared behind the far end of the barn. Safely out of the line of fire from the one remaining Sherman, Kruger gave orders to prepare for another assault.

23 The Raid

Wingham had watched the half-track turn away and crush the paddock railing as it went. It moved rapidly down to the far end of the barn, a burst from Tillman's Bren giving it added momentum. Convinced the half-track belonged to a German officer who commanded the entire operation, Wingham decided to take a chance. Nothing ventured, nothing gained, as the saying went, and he looked about for manpower.

Inside the pair of barn doors he caught sight of Brennan hidden beneath the old cart, and he could be certain sure 'Angel' would be keen to join him. And there was Tillman. The big man would make an ideal candidate. But if he took Tillman someone would have to replace him. He checked the wounded.

'Anyone fit enough to cover the door and window?'

Two hands went up.

'You can stand?'

Both nodded and levered themselves to their feet. Rifleman Pete Solomon, one hand wrapped in a pink-stained white bandage showed he could support the rifle. And Norman 'King' Taylor, an improvised triangle of grey supporting his left arm, stepped forward and slipped his arm out of the sling. He too demonstrated that, push come to shove, he could help fill the gap left by Tillman. Wingham thought he looked a bit pale but let it go.

Now all he needed was one more to join the party. He went back to the doorway and peered left past the woodpile. And he found Chris Jamison lying prone behind a miniature rock garden. He was clearly carrying the fight to what few Germans were still left in the open, his Lee Enfield finding targets.

'Jamison!' Wingham bellowed, and the Paratrooper's head turned. 'Here, with me!' He beckoned to emphasize the need.

Jamison raised his shoulders for a better look at the enemy positions, gathered his knees and feet beneath him, and prepared for a dash to the kitchen. He took a last look at the southern approach and shook his head.

'Bollocks to this!' he snapped, lunged to his feet, and sprinted hard for the kitchen doorway. He heard a bullet zip past his ear and another smacked the wall. He made it to the rubble filled doorway and launched himself over the heap. He landed hard, left shoulder taking the worst. He rolled and came up on one knee, rifle cradled.

'You wanted me, sir?' he asked with a tight grin.

Wingham smiled and nodded. 'That was the general idea, Jamison. How'd you like to be part of a small expedition?'

A Spandau opened up from the poplars and tracer ricocheted.

Jamison's head tilted enquiringly. 'An expedition, sir? Me?'

'Four of us. You, me, Tillman here, and Brennan. Will that do you?'

A flurry of bullets splintered wood and pinged off walls. At the kitchen table Sarah swore, vehemently, and every man in the room looked at each other and chuckled. 'That's my kind of lady,' said one of the wounded and found agreement from the others.

Tillman spotted the seat of tracer and gave it a squirt.

Jamison brought them back to the point. 'Where, sir?'

Wingham gestured with his chin. 'The barn. Collect Brennan and get down to the stable door, sharpish. I'm going after that half-track.'

Jamison came to his feet and glanced at Tillman. The big man scowled and hefted the Bren off the splintered frame. 'Time we gave the bastards what for.'

Wingham gave him a look. 'Spare mags?'

Tillman patted his large smock pockets and nodded. 'Four. All that I've got left.'

'Right,' Wingham said, and turned for the door. 'Let's get hold of Brennan.'

They charged out of the door well spaced. Hunched over and weaving, they tore across the cobbles and hurled themselves into the comparative gloom of the barn.

Brennan, surprise etched all over his face, wriggled out from under the cart.

Wingham fixed him with a hard glance. 'Knife and Sten. With me, soldier.'

Jamison led the way, pig sticker clipped in place, rifle waist high, expecting trouble. Tillman followed, the Bren small in his large fists, moving lightly for such a big man. And behind Wingham came Brennan, Sten cocked in his right hand, knife in his left, an insane grin twisting his lips.

At the splintered stable door, the two halves partially open, Jamison peeled left and slid along the wall until he could see out to the right. He instantly lifted a warning hand and jabbed a finger in that direction.

'Half-track!' he hissed.

Tillman dropped to one knee and Wingham stepped round him. He stopped and looked over Jamison's shoulder. As he did so, Brennan went to the right of the doorway and put his back to the wall.

Wingham narrowed his eyes at the sight of the half-track. The vehicle sat facing the trees no more than ten yards away. Exhaust fumes smoked from low left of the engine compartment and he counted five Grenadiers squeezed in the back. Both Spandaus were manned and the gunners looked competent, alert. It wouldn't be straightforward to destroy that half-track. He looked at the tree line, a dangerous threat if his little party were caught in the open. What he needed was cover and some kind of diversion while he attacked with grenades. But what? He wracked his brain to find a solution and then the exhaust smoke caught his attention. If he deployed a couple of smoke grenades between the poplar trees and this end of the barn, then it would be a straight fight between the half-track Grenadiers and his party.

'Who's got smoke?' he queried.

Brennan patted the right pocket of his smock. 'Three.'

Jamison said, 'Two.'

'Good,' Wingham said. 'I want a smokescreen between us and the trees . . . , when I give the word. Then we hit that half-track. Grenades first. All clear?'

They nodded. Brennan and Jamison unearthed a smoke canister apiece, readied themselves.

Wingham held up a hand, eying the Germans in the half-track. They were concentrating on their weapons. 'On my count. Three . . . Two . . . Go!'

Jamison stepped into the doorway and hurled his high and long, and scampered back inside. Brennan's also curved out a similar distance but ten yards to the right. Both detonated on impact and smoke swirled.

Tillman lunged outside with Wingham, a pair of fragmentation grenades lobbed at the half-track. One landed inside with the Grenadiers, the other caught the apron, skidded, and bounced down at the driver. There was a shout of alarm and Germans threw themselves out of the carrier. Men hit the ground hard and not all landed on their feet. An explosion rocked the half-track and a second came close behind. The driver never made it, his torso lacerated by a dozen hits. He fell back into the seat. Three of the Panzergrenadiers had landed facing the stable door and reacted quickly, sub-machineguns hammering.

Jamison went wide towards the smoke. He dropped to the ground, his rifle finding a target. Tillman hit the trigger, firing from the waist, the Bren thumping in his hands.

Brennan sprinted alongside the end wall of the barn. As he drew level with the half-track's rear door a Grenadier ran round from the far side, rifle held low. Brennan swerved left to close him down. Five paces and he was on him. The German looked startled, fear in his eyes. Brennan could have shot him but chose to smash his face with the butt of the Sten. The steel frame hit the man's upper lip and crushed his teeth. He screamed at the pain, his front teeth broken, torn from the gum. Blood filled his mouth. The rifle cracked as he involuntarily pulled the trigger, the bullet flying wide.

Brennan gave him a vicious kick between the legs and the German lost his grip on the rifle. He collapsed in agony, bent forward holding himself, in a world of pain.

The Paratrooper finished it then. He pushed him over with a boot to the shoulder and gave him two rounds in his chest. Brennan grinned. The Panzergrenadier met his end still clutching his 'crown jewels'.

Wingham went past Brennan and rounded the far side of the half-track. He found himself confronted by a motorbike, mounted by an officer wearing a sling. The man saw Wingham and grabbed for his sub-machinegun. Wingham fired as he dodged right, a bullet plucking at his smock. From the corner of his left eye he caught sight of the smokescreen beginning to thin, time running out. He hit the ground and rolled, came to a stop and fired.

The German winced and aimed his MP40. Nothing happened. Empty. He threw it and grabbed for his Luger.

Wingham fired and emptied the magazine, and a single 9mm round slashed the German's right cheek bone. He snarled with pain, ignored the Luger and twisted the throttle. The motorbike roared, and discarding the sling he wrenched the handlebars to the left, his left boot firmly planted to help haul the machine round. As it drew away towards the poplars the bike bounced and shimmied over uneven ground. Motorbike and rider hit the drifting smokescreen, the thinning smoke swirling aside. The officer clung on and squeezed the last ounce of speed from the engine, bursting into the line of trees. He braked hard and swung the bike round to a standstill.

Flames flickered and danced round the half-track's engine compartment, and blipping the motorbike's throttle Major Carl Kruger cursed. This battle was not proceeding according to plan and now his own wagon was out of action. He felt the warmth of wet blood trickle down his face and savagely brushed it away. What, he wondered, would it take to convince these Englanders to give up? He could see the Sherman's gun traversing across the field of battle and knew that would have boosted their resolve. Even so, their limited supply of ammunition must be nearing the end. One lone American Sherman must not be allowed to change what he estimated to be a foregone conclusion. After all, his men were Panzergrenadiers, their particular speciality was killing tanks.

He looked along the tree line at the recovering soldaten. A number of them carried Panzerfausts. If he gave them a chance to take on the Sherman with those lethal little rockets . . . ? And it would not be long until 'B' Kompanie arrived.

The smoke screen had almost thinned to nothing.

Chris Jamison heard Wingham call them back and for a long moment he hesitated. Where the flames leapt up around the half-track's engine bay, he thought he'd seen a Panzergrenadier kneeling with an MP40. The smokescreen had all but disintegrated and the black smoke from the engine lifted clear of the ground. He looked over his shoulder and spotted Tillman gathering the Bren.

'Lofty!' he shouted. 'Cover me!'

Tillman snatched a glance his way. 'Gotcha!' he shouted, hugged the Bren into his waist and hit the trigger. Tracer whipped out towards the trees.

Jamison came up to a knee, fired two fast rounds at the kneeling Grenadier and made a dash for the stable door. Bullets whipped past his head and he felt the hot wind of a tracer round. He and Brennan reached the door together, turned either side of the opening and covered Tillman's sprint to safety. He came in fast and spun round to face the doorway.

'Where's the Old Man?' he snapped.

Bullets thrashed the door surround and they ducked from the line of fire.

Jamison peered round. 'Dunno, thought he was in here.'

Brennan stuck his head out, searching. He found him crawling away from the half-track, struggling on all fours.

'I see him,' he said and skipped back outside. He bent at the waist and zigzagged towards the Major. Bullets ricocheted off the wall to his right but then the half-track hid him from any further gunfire.. He reached down and grabbed Wingham under an arm, hauled him upright.

'C'mon, we can make it.'

Wingham was short of breath, panting. But he nodded. 'Glad you came,' he wheezed, and took a step forward.

'Together then,' Brennan said, and dragged him almost bodily over to the barn wall. From there he could see Tillman's Bren gun sighted at the line of poplars. 'Coming in!' he shouted, and took a renewed hold of Wingham's arm.

'Ready?' he asked looking into the Major's eyes. They were clear enough and his breathing had calmed. He nodded and stood a little taller.

'I'm ready.'

Brennan gave Tillman another shout. 'Now!'

The Bren barked, a fusillade of shots chasing out towards the trees. Brennan shouldered the Old Man's weight and went for the door. He felt Wingham summon up his strength and in an ungainly, stumbling run, they somehow made it without being hit. They fell through the door and Wingham collapsed into the straw. His breathing was noticeably ragged but he levered himself up into a sitting position.

'Well done,' he gasped, and between breaths said, 'Now back to the kitchen.'

'Wait one,' Jamison said and moved from the door to stand looking down at the Major. 'You hurt, sir? What's up?'

Wingham looked up with a wry smile and shook his head.

'Bloody silly really, I think I've cracked a couple of ribs,' he explained and gently touched his side. 'It's alright as long as I don't cough.' He reached up.

'Give me a hand.'

Jamison grabbed a wrist and hauled him to his feet. The Old Man stood for a few seconds, slung his Sten gun and eyed Brennan.

'You okay to hold the fort?' he asked.

Brennan pursed his lips and glanced round the barn as if seeing it for the first time. The answering smile came with a slow nod.

'Consider it done, sir.'

'Good,' Wingham said, 'but no heroics. When it gets too hot, get out of it.'

'Oh,' Brennan said, frowning, and then narrowing one eye. 'You mean a bit like what we've just been doing?'

Tillman and Jamison chuckled.

Wingham heard the irony and couldn't help but reluctantly admit to being guilty.

'Yeah, okay, guilty as charged. But you know what I mean. Don't overdo your stay.'

This time Brennan gave a sober nod. 'Sir.'

And with that, Wingham led them up through the barn, left Brennan inside and then managed to ignore the pain of his ribs to dash across the cobbled yard. The three of them made it through a flurry of bullets and ducked inside the kitchen door.

24 Carnage

In the small provincial town of Colombelles, Hauptman Thomas Buschmann gave orders for 'B' Kompanie to assemble on the main square. He had passed on Kruger's report to the wireless room and instructed them to keep trying Rommel's headquarters. The last resort would be a despatch rider but that would take hours.

In the meantime he prepared to take command. His latest information was that the Kompanie would be at full strength and with the usual experienced cohort of veteran NCO's leading the way. By rights, the Colonel should have authorised the transfer of command from a Major to a Captain, but as the Colonel was incommunicado and the Regiment's 2i/c, Major Frederickson, was nowhere to be found, Buschmann made the decision himself.

After what seemed an interminable wait, but was in fact no more than twenty-minutes, 'B' Kompanie had formed up in full battle order. The roll call was taken and the number of Panzergrenadiers on parade confirmed.

Buschmann strode out onto the square to be greeted by a smart salute from his senior Leutnant.

'All is in order, Herr Hauptman.'

Buschmann returned the salute and beamed at the assembled Kompanie. In his opinion these Grenadiers were the best in the Regiment and it was a proud moment for him to stand at the front of such men, a moment to savour. And there at the head of the assembled unit, an eight-wheeled reconnaissance armoured car waited for him to take command. He personally favoured the armoured car above the half-tracks. It was fast, up-gunned in a revolving turret, and relatively comfortable. As he strode forward to mount up a smile played on his lips. He liked to think of the eight-wheeler as his "chariot", something with which to ride into battle, more befitting his rank.

Having settled himself in the commander's hatch, Buschmann turned to survey the Kompanie. Satisfied that they were ready for war he raised a hand and pointed ahead. He was eager to find out what Kruger had got himself into, what all the fuss was about.

Lieutenant Matt Summerton hesitated. A tank advancing without infantry support was vulnerable to enemy Panzerfausts and he'd had more than his fair share today. And he might yet be in the sights of another anti-tank gun. He scoured the tree line with his glasses but found no obvious signs.

'Driver advance. Left stick.' The tank edged forward and veered left across the front of an outbuilding. Summerton felt the tension but let the Sherman continue to run wide in order to accumulate distance between himself and the poplars. Ten yards out from the neat rows of an orchard he repositioned. 'Right stick. Hard round.'

The tank slewed round to face the poplars.

'Driver halt.'

The Sherman came to rest, engine grumbling, the gunner acutely aware of the need for vigilance.

Far above the fields of Normandy, Flying Officer Ronald "Ronnie" Hart, pulled back on the stick and banked the Hawker Typhoon into a steep starboard turn. He soared effortlessly over the congested invasion beaches of Sword and Juno and levelled off at fifteen-hundred feet. Below him the entire panorama of the Allied beach head stretched away on both sides of the fighter bomber. This was his third day over Normandy and his fourth sortie of the day. But now there was a major difference. This was the first sortie where he was able to use his own discretion in choosing a target. The entire Squadron had been designated as 'seek and destroy', individual pilots judging for themselves whether to attack any given objective. He was free to inflict the greatest amount of damage he could, and Hart was intent on making the most of it.

He eased her up to two-thousand feet and rolled left over the outskirts of Ranville. South of Ranville, not far from the scattered dwellings of a village called Escoville, he caught the signs of an isolated battle, smoke coiling skywards. He throttled back and lost height, dropped a wing and flew down to investigate. A small wood came into view below the starboard wing, followed by open fields and then a larger wood covering many acres. The smoke became three or four separate entities and it centred on what looked like an old farmhouse. He swept over, hauled her into a swift climb and dropped back round for another look.

This time he clearly picked out the American white star painted on a pair of Sherman tanks. A rising column of dirty smoke came from one of those tanks, flames licking out from the turret. But there was no obvious signs of a battle in progress, yet bodies lay scattered on a grass covered slope. With a slight movement of the stick he eased the Typhoon over a row of poplars and banked gently right to come round in a wide circle. For the umpteenth time he glanced in his mirror and checked left and right over his shoulders. From the first sortie of D-Day to this, he'd seen hide nor hare of the Luftwaffe, but that was no reason for a man to drop his guard. Then, as the Typhoon came round on a fairly flat turn, a check over the port wing led to a chance discovery. A column of fast moving half-tracks and wildly swaying German lorries were moving along a road leading out from what he knew to be a town called Colombelles. Heading the column he could see an armoured car, the white face of its commander staring up. Seeing that the road passed the lower fields of the farm, Ronnie Hart put two and two together, guessed they were reinforcements and prepared to give them a passing gift.

His Typhoon's armoury consisted of four 20mm canon, eight air-to-ground rockets, and two 500 pound bombs. The choice was an easy one to make. The enemy were in light skinned vehicles, not something to waste rockets or bombs on. He nudged the throttle back to reduce speed, banked over to align with the hedged road and took off more speed to give himself time to home in. He jinked to starboard for better alignment, the ground a blur.

Nose down, gunsight on, thumb over the button. Less than 500 feet up, fast approaching the target. Upturned faces saw him coming, throwing themselves off the back of wagons. The commander's hatch on the eight-wheeler slammed shut and the vehicle accelerated.

Now! He jabbed the button and his thumb trembled to the thunder of four 20mm Hispanos. Tracer glowed from the wings, lashing the ground, ripping into running soldiers, blasting a furrow through the ranks of Panzergrenadiers. Lorries exploded into flames and a half-track took the full brunt of Hart's scything burst. He released the button, throttled up and raised the nose. The power of the Sabre engine whipped him into a rapid climb and he banked hard left, wing tip down holding his line of sight. Men ran in fear.

Behind the oxygen mask Ronnie Hart gave a tight smile. This second strafing run would be the coup de grâce. A fast look round the sky, mirror behind. Clear. He righted the fighter, jinked left, sights on. He hit the button and tracer flashed, tearing at the road. The glowing lines created havoc, mowing down everything in the way. A motor bike exploded and the last undamaged truck succumbed to the canon shells. He gave it four seconds . . . , four seconds of explosive mayhem, and the last vehicle to take the strafing run was the armoured car attempting to flee up the road. Hart released the button and soared skywards, carnage left in his wake, a bloodied mess of shattered bodies. He leaned into a gradual turn and surveyed his handiwork. Lurid orange flames flickered, oil black smoke drifting through the hedges.

Flying Officer Hart nodded his approval. Wherever that column had been headed at such speed had just become totally irrelevant. There was little left to indicate it had ever been anything of any consequence. He raised the Typhoon's nose and went off in search of something more befitting of his remaining fire power.

Thomas Buschmann was dying. His dreams of glory on the field of battle were never to be realised. It would not be a quick death, but prolonged and unremittingly painful. At the last moment he had tried to vacate the turret, to jump for a hedgerow and the freedom of the fields. Mistake. A fuel tank had exploded when hit by tracer and Buschmann was hurled from the turret. He landed on his back and his lower vertebrae collapsed, partially trapping nerves. It would have been better for Buschmann if the nerves had been completely severed, as it was the pain was multiplied. Flames from the armoured car reached out in all directions, the fire catching his boots. A flicker travelled up his leg and burned bright.

Buschmann tried to drag himself clear but the pain in his back stopped him, a weakness setting in. A box of ammunition exploded, bullets randomly flying wide. He was hit twice, shoulder and throat. He cried out in his agony, to no avail. Burning embers drifted and fell, eyes blinded. He rubbed and managed to clear the right eye just as a burning Grenadier, on fire from waist to head, ran screaming into a hedge. He collapsed into the ditch. Buschmann tried again to move, not knowing why or where, only that the flames had reached his jacket. He attempted to roll over but his legs no longer obeyed. He thought of Kruger, wondered if he'd survived, hoped he hadn't, wished him a painful death.

Blood in his throat gurgled and he desperately tried to draw breath. His belly contracted, flesh shrivelling in the heat. The uniform jacket charred and the cloth shrivelled, distorted. Slowly, so very slowly, death came amidst tortuous, leaping flames, and Hauptman Thomas Buschmann became just another unheralded Panzergrenadier to join the long list of those already killed in action.

At General-Feldmarschall Erwin Rommel's Army Groupe B Headquarters in the Château La Roche Guyon north of Paris, an order was given for Panzer-Lehr to abandon all caution and make a fast approach in daylight to Caen's northern outskirts. On arrival they were to tie in with the 12th SS Panzer Division and act as reinforcement to the city's defence. Deep below the Château's impressive castle like exterior, the five operators in the wireless transmitting-receiving station were busy deciphering a multitude of incoming signals.

One of the operators, the Austrian born Senior Telegraphist tasked with processing the order, had served the Feldmarschall since his days as 'The Desert Fox'. A trusted member of the General's communications staff he had been specifically assigned to maintain contact with the Château Fontaine. With the written order to hand, earphones in place and his right hand fingers poised over the telegraph key, he made a final check on the wireless frequency display. Satisfied with the tuning he tapped out the Château's call sign and waited for a response. Over the next five minutes he made repeated attempts to make contact, even changing to the day's previous frequency in the vain hope someone might have simply not changed to the new one.

Still with no reply, he tried to piggyback his call via an 'in-the-field' mobile station that he knew should be well within range of the Château. It was all to no avail.

He picked up the written message, came to his feet and straightened his tunic. Something serious had happened at the Château Fontaine and this lack of contact was a major breach of operational procedure. He must report the breakdown, if necessary to Rommel himself. With a nod to his comrades he left the room and mounted the lower staircase. Whatever the Feldmarschall's mood, this news would not lighten his countenance.

Carl Kruger sat on the motorbike and counted heads. He estimated seventy-five men strung out along the line of trees awaiting orders, which meant the majority of his Panzergrenadiers had now reformed into some semblance of their original formation. Here and there a Spandau opened up on the farmhouse and tracer hammered the openings. But only briefly. With the Sherman sat threateningly close, it was a case of fire and move before high explosive took them apart.

Kruger dismounted and strode a few metres towards the centre of his troops. He cupped his hands to his mouth and shouted.

'Where are my Panzerfaust warriors?'

'Here, Herr Major,' came a chorus of shouts.

There was movement down the line and seven or eight men raised their tubes.

'Then you must make your "armoured fists" ready,' he called, pointing. 'The Sherman will be destroyed, no?'

There was a concerted shout of approval.

'Jawohl, Herr Major!'

'That is good, my friends. And now we must attack again. The mortars will lay smoke before our Panzerfaust warriors kill the armour. Do you hear me, Grenadiers? Without armour the Englanders cannot hold.'

There was a surge of yelled agreement and men braced to charge the farmhouse.

Kruger turned to face south where two mortar teams had set up in a fold on the slope.

He raised an arm and chopped down. 'Feuer!'

The mortar tubes thumped and launched their bombs, lifting high before plunging to earth. Six in total cracked on landing and white smoke billowed. An enormous shout erupted from German throats and the Panzergrenadiers made their charge.

Lieutenant Matt Summerton watched the smoke rise into an opaque wall and spoke to his driver.

'Reverse!'

The engine growled in response and the tank lurched backwards.

Summerton looked behind, judging the moment when he was safe to stop. Experience told him that any Grenadiers with Panzerfausts would advance into the smoke and attack on sight. And they could be lethal at up to two-hundred feet. He let it run until the Sherman had backed off almost sixty-yards from the smoke.

'Halt!'

They came to a stop and Summerton grabbed the handles of the Browning. The slightest suggestion of a shadow in the smoke was all he needed.

Seven Grenadiers went left and headed for the barn's stable door. The NCO in charge held back and signalled for them to split up left and right. The first got to the opening and was shot from inside. He fell and blocked the entrance. A Grenadier dragged him clear. The same man stuck his MP40 through the opening and sprayed the interior. The next man hurled a stick grenade, flat and low. They waited for the explosion and then went in fast, crouched low, then hesitated in the dim light. Smoke coiled, flames flickering.

At the other end of the barn, back underneath the familiar comfort of the cart, Keith Brennan had heard the beginnings of the fresh attack, another wave of fanatical Panzergrenadiers. He'd wriggled out from beneath the cart and come up on one knee. In his eyes he'd just become the right flank's last line of defence and he gave a tight smile. The only defence more like . . . , and the barn was his to use as he saw fit. So he shifted position to a pair of heavy upright stanchions, rough hewn support beams for the roof. Each beam was ten or twelve inches square and, more to the point, had been built with a small gap separating them. Ideal spot for a firing position. He hefted the Sten, lodged it in the gap and waited.

Not for long. A shadow crossed the threshold of the stable door and the bulky shape of a Panzergrenadier filled the opening. Brennan didn't hesitate and loosed off three rounds. The soldier fell, half in and half out, blocking the doorway. A pair of hands snatched at his tunic and dragged him clear. A sub-machinegun appeared round the door jamb and blasted bullets all over the barn. The shooting stopped and a grenade tumbled inside. The explosion hurled shrapnel but short of Brennan.

A German lunged through the door and dived right, another hard on his heels went left.

Brennan hit the trigger, gave them both a short burst and slapped in a fresh mag. A third Grenadier threw himself inside and dived to the floor. Flames flickered from the grenade's explosion and smoke billowed, dense in the confines of the barn. A machine-gun chattered and tracer whipped at Brennan. He shrank from the uprights and squatted low, firing his own burst in retaliation. The blue smoke thickened, coiling from floor to ceiling, the flames rising. A grenade came out of the smoke, landed six feet from Brennan. He threw himself backwards, hit the floor and pressed his face into straw. The explosion was loud, his ears ringing. He came back up to one knee behind the upright and waited for one of them to show.

The smoke in the barn reached the rafters and Brennan coughed as blue tendrils snaked down to head height. He thought he saw shadowy figures in the gloom and gave them a short burst. Changing positions, he bent low and backed off towards the big doors. By the stone trough he dropped to one knee. The cough hit him again as he tasted smoke, his eyes watering. He tried peering down to where the fire had begun but to no avail.

Then, with no warning, the flames leapt to the rafters, consuming the coiling smoke and bathing the inside of the barn with an orange glow. Brennan saw his enemy and grimaced. There were five unveiled by the brightness of the fire, and they had spread out across the barn. He readied a Mills grenade, removed the pin. Two Grenadiers advancing up the right side were closer together and he didn't hesitate. His arm went back and he threw. Not the classic over-arm a man was taught in training but more the fast return of a cricket ball from the boundary; a flat trajectory. It bounced once, rolled and exploded. Shrapnel hurtled in every direction and both Grenadiers went down. Brennan didn't know if they were dead or wounded, didn't care as long as they stayed out of it.

A stick grenade tumbled the length of the barn and landed short of the trough. Brennan threw himself backwards and then rolled sideways under the cart, making himself small. The grenade detonated and a steel shard sliced his right calf. He grunted at the pain but brought the Sten to his shoulder. The Grenadier to his left was closest and Brennan fired without taking time to aim. But pointing the muzzle in the general direction was enough. The short burst went low and the man was hit in the pelvis. He screamed and fell forward. The remaining pair split up, one giving covering fire while the other crouched low to dodge from one support beam to the next. The smoke from the fire gave them both the benefit of a partial smokescreen.

Brennan had seen enough. The big barn doors offered a way out with a chance to recover, and he launched himself into the open air. His calf muscle protested and wouldn't hold his weight and he crashed to the cobbles. He squirmed round to face the doors, changed mags.

An enormous Grenadier appeared from the dark interior, a rifle balanced in his huge hands. His lips were drawn back in a vicious snarl to display a mouthful of crooked, tobacco stained teeth. He came blinking into daylight.

Brennan squeezed the trigger. His gun misfired and jammed. He cursed and forced himself up to kneel. He reached for his 9-mm pistol just as the Grenadier fired his rifle. Brennan dived left and fired on the move. The German's bullet struck high into Brennan's left collar bone and he hit the ground hard. It jolted the pistol from his grip. He saw the Grenadier wobble, blood appearing on his arm. He staggered towards Brennan and the Paratrooper unsheathed his knife. Ignoring the pain from his calf he forced himself into a crouch, the fighting knife ready to strike.

The Grenadier saw the knife too late, already committed to the attack. He tried to shy away from the blade, twisting his body aside. Brennan was having none of that and lunged hard for the ribs. The Sheffield forged steel, diligently honed and sharpened by Brennan's loving attention, jolted his forearm as he drove it to cut deep between the bones. The man gasped and cried out, impaled on the blade. Brennan grabbed the man's collar, dragging him closer, and twisted the knife. But the effort proved too much for the damage to Brennan's collar bone and he knew he must finish this now. He drove it up to the hilt, twisted it again to crack the ribs and shoved the man away.

As he staggered backwards Brennan followed the move with a fast slash across the man's prominent jugular. His scream of fear turned to a bloodied cough and he dropped to his knees, hands at his throat. The grey eyes bulged and he toppled forward, quivering as death claimed him. He twitched once and lay still.

Keith Brennan paused to look down at his enemy. A thin lipped smile straight lined his lips and he nodded with satisfaction. He felt liberated. It was the first time he truly believed his brother had been avenged. He turned away and struggled to pick up his weapons, his sense of balance all over the place. He was loosing blood and his collar bone grated as damaged ends scraped together. He limped over to the wall and slumped down with his back to the stonework. He lifted his gaze to the barn doors, expecting to see the last Grenadier emerging. But other than a lurid orange glow from the flames inside and a curling wall of blue smoke rolling up out of the doorway, there was no sign of further movement.

Brennan hefted the pistol, ready if necessary. When no-one came through he changed weapons, ejected the jammed cartridge from the Sten, settled a fresh magazine in the housing and cocked the gun. The loss of blood left him weakened, an effort just to load the weapon. To his front skirmishing Panzergrenadiers were getting closer, weight of numbers beginning to tell. He raised the Sten, found a target and pulled the trigger. The gun barked and automatically reloaded. Where the bullet went was anyone's guess.

For Keith Brennan all that mattered right now was that the gun worked again.

25 Waves of War

On Kruger's command a wave of Panzergrenadiers stormed the farmhouse almost dead centre. A smokescreen covered the movement of four Grenadiers with their Panzerfausts. They spread wide and advanced slow, achieving their ideal placement for cornering the Sherman. The smoke hugged the ground, a comforting, thick wall.

In the workshop Carter sighted his Bren on the wave of Grenadiers headed for the farmhouse and estimated he was watching a platoon in action, maybe thirty, tops. But they had advanced in line with one Grenadier nearest the workshop, and the remainder stretched away in a long line to his left. It gave Carter the perfect flanking angle to mow them down. It was an opportunity too good to miss, and taking careful aim on the closest Grenadier, Lance-Corporal Rob Carter squeezed the trigger. The machine-gun juddered in his hands and he gave them an accurate burst. Tracer flew. Blood sprayed and men tumbled. Five or six went down and he eased off the trigger. But only long enough to realign on the next group of charging Grenadiers. He fired again, aiming chest high. The tracer swept into them and he held it on target, tearing into their ranks. But not all the Germans stayed down, some seeing where the tracer had come from. They returned fire, sporadic shots finding brickwork.

From near the trees a Spandau opened up and bullets cracked and snapped at the workshop window frame. Carter winced at a near miss and ducked his head, cursing. The Spandau was doing what it was best at, suppressing enemy fire, and Rob Carter was on the receiving end. The charging Grenadiers took advantage of the lull and surged again.

In the kitchen window, Tillman had seen the Spandau open up on the workshop and made a snap decision. Better to take on the Spandau and give Rob Carter the chance to have another go from the flank. He hit the trigger and his own tracer whipped across the intervening space, the lethal rounds thrashing at the low growing foliage. The Spandau fell silent and Carter took full advantage, finger clamped round the trigger. Panzergrenadiers jerked to the hits, arms flailing as they crashed to the ground.

The Germans hesitated, looking to one another for reassurance. But the line continued to thin as British bullets found their mark. A Grenadier came to a halt, took a backward step. Another followed, the first true sign of a failing German resolve.

At the same time, Major Carl Kruger witnessed three Grenadiers backing away from the barn, something he'd never personally experienced on the field of battle. Not from men under his command, not without orders to retreat. He looked for his Panzerfaust specialists and found none. He checked again for how many Grenadiers were still unscathed and the harsh reality began to dawn. Not many by the look of it, and probably nowhere near enough to launch another attack. And without Panzerfausts the continued existence of that single Sherman had him at a severe disadvantage.

He looked at his watch and shook his head. 'B' Kompanie should be here by now and the first inkling that all was not well made it through to his subconscious.

'Verdammt!' he spat, playing with the bike's twist grip. Suddenly the battlefield seemed to no longer hold the same attraction as he had once imagined. Now might be the time to make himself scarce. Not that he considered even for the slightest moment that defeat was in any way his fault. The Panzergrenadiers lacked backbone, had grown soft in the French climate, should have fought harder. And there'd been blatant disobedience by some, particularly the much praised sniper. So much for the warm words he'd received.

Kruger dragged the motorbike round to his left, gave it a handful of throttle and took off along the row of poplars. Moments later he disappeared into the cool shade of ancient woods.

Amongst the shattered bushes beneath the poplar trees, almost two-dozen Panzergrenadiers watched him flee.

A Tiger tank with its broken right track lying half unravelled barred the way for Jurgen Voigt's Panther IV.

'Left! Hard left!' came through his headphones.

Voigt tugged the left stick and increased the revs, stopping the left track but forcing power into the right track to slew them round. A low hedge of hawthorn gave way to a small copse and he took care to avoid the thick, solid trunk of a tall pine tree.

'Now come right, Voigt.'

He hauled the Panther in the opposite direction and waited for the order to straighten. They had avoided the Tiger with its broken track; time to exit the woods, rejoin the main road and attach himself to the tail end of the column. He hit the accelerator and the Panther IV jerked forward, the tracks biting at the dirt. As Voigt negotiated the first dwellings that formed the sprawling western suburbs of Caen, the dirt track gave way to a paved surface and the going became a smooth procession. He knew from the map the distance from here to where the enemy might be about to attack. Twenty minutes should see the armoured probe making an initial contact.

Voigt let a strained smile pass his dust caked lips. Their gunner was first rate with a string of 'kills' to his name. God help the enemy if he found them within range.

With the leading Panther a half-kilometre up the road the remaining twelve strong unit of armoured reconnaissance pushed on. Panzer-Lehr might well have been delayed but finally the first of its heavy armour would shortly take on the advance formations of the Allied invasion.

No new orders from Rommel's headquarters were received to give fresh impetus to the elite forces of Panzer-Lehr and the main body of the Division, now trailing the reconnaissance unit by almost thirty kilometres, continued to exercise extreme caution when confronted with the Hawker Typhoons of the Royal Air Force. Progress towards the front line was inevitably slow and wireless communications non existent. Grinding sluggishly along narrow forest paths, and only briefly appearing on limited sections of open roads, the armoured might of Panzer-Lehr crept ponderously through the French patchwork of fields and villages.

Ronnie Hart had taken the Typhoon up to two-thousand feet and had joined with a pair of Spitfires in a loose formation searching for worthwhile targets. As he meandered south checking the terrain below, a discrepancy caught his attention. An area of wooded valley appeared different from the surrounding landscape and he side slipped to fifteen-hundred for a closer look.

A faint blue haze drifted from the trees. No sign of battle smoke, just a vague, thin veil of blue. And then it dawned on him. Exhaust fumes! It had to be, and a lot of them. He waggled his wings to gain attention, pointed at his eyes and jabbed a finger at the ground. Seeing a thumbs up from both pilots, he dropped the Typhoon's nose and pushed forward on the throttle. There had to be a lot of vehicles hidden in those woods, and more than likely heavy armour. He decided to make a fast low level pass. There'd either be a strong defensive reaction or he would see the evidence for himself. He dived down in a wide circle and a mile north of the target, levelled out at four-hundred feet. Throttle set at three-hundred he roared across the tree tops.

Tracer erupted.

Glowing streams of anti-aircraft rounds curved up from beneath the green canopy, flashing past his cockpit. He grinned. It was the confirmation he needed. With a push on the throttle he accelerated hard, weaved wildly and then pulled the stick back. The Typhoon responded instantly and clawed her way skywards. As he pushed her ever higher he mulled over what little he had actually seen. Three tanks moving through a clearing, two fuel bowsers that might have been for water, and a pair of half-tracks visible on a dirt lane. Other than that very little.

The Typhoon reached three-thousand so he throttled back and levelled off. He checked controls for damage and found none, ailerons and flaps all working. He looked round for the Spitfires and frowned at an empty sky. He dipped a wing, and there, almost at ground level the two Spitfires had taken advantage of his absence and had quite literally gone in for the kill.

Their canon shells were already wreaking havoc, leaving a trail of burning wreckage. Tracer glowed, green and red orbs chasing the Spitfires. An ammunition truck exploded in a volcanic ball of fire. The swirling multi coloured mass of flame expanded and rolled. Men died.

Flying Officer Ronnie Hart had seen enough. The leading elements of the tanks remained relatively untouched, still advancing towards Caen. Fighter bombers such as the Hawker Typhoon could inflict a lot of damage on such a target. In a moment of purposeful intent he hauled the fighter into a sharp turn, levelled, and then nosed down in a shallow dive. Evil black smoke obscured what must have been the tail end of the column, but the front was all his. He moved his head to align the rocket sight, flicked the selector switch to choose the port wing array and prepared to fire. He picked up a Tiger tank edging out from under the trees and held it in the sight, no side slip, no yaw, waiting. And then, certain the unguided rockets would hit the target, he pressed the tit.

'Tally bloody ho!' he mouthed inside the mask, and watched four fiery tails streak towards the target. With a velocity of 750 feet per second, two high explosive 60-pound warhead slammed into the German tanks. The leading Tiger suffered simultaneous strikes to the front of the turret. One hit low, left side, traversing ring. Its twin detonated on the gun mantle. The combined concussive force of 120 pounds of high explosive sheared the retaining ring and eleven tons of armoured turret slumped sideways. Commander and crew were obliterated. The other pair of rockets missed but blew up in the trees, a fierce fire sweeping the lane.

Hart banked sharp left and climbed to a thousand. He levelled off and veered to port. Thick smoke coiled out from his first strike, marking the way. A mile out he took her down to four-hundred, throttled back until he had a rock steady firing platform and prepared to launch the starboard bank of four rockets. He found a Panther IV trying to squeeze round the side of the wrecked Tiger and latched onto it. It was a tight space, the tank virtually at a standstill. His thumb hovered.

Steady .... Steady .... He deliberately left it late, and fired. This time he couldn't wait to watch them in. Too close. He rolled left, throttled up and made for the sky. A lurid glow from his instrument panel made him glance in the mirror. It showed the tank wreathed in flames, internal explosions venting from the commanders hatch.

And Hart smiled ..., mission accomplished. The progress of an entire column of heavy armour had been severely delayed. Yes, he thought, pulling back on the joystick, he'd also destroyed tanks in the process, but more importantly the troops advancing inland from the bridgehead had gained vital breathing space. He glanced at his instrument panel; enough fuel for another fifteen minutes flying before having to head back home.

Lieutenant Matt Summerton thought he saw shadows in the smoke and hammered them with a dozen rounds. The Sherman's bow mounted Browning next to the driver shuddered as the gunner picked out a movement to his front. Tracer whipped into the smoke, and the shadows were gone. A nervous driver throttled up ready to move.

A rocket streaked out of the smoke. Summerton swivelled the Browning and blasted the area with .30 calibre. And now his original caution paid off. The Panzerfaust hit the ground twenty feet short, but still with enough velocity to explode on impact. Dirt, turf, pebbles and smoke erupted without causing any damage. Summerton ceased firing. He waited, watching, the smoke rapidly thinning. And now, without the cover of smoke, all was revealed. Three Grenadiers lay dead, widely dispersed. A fourth could be seen kneeling and aiming a Schmeisser.

Summerton reacted. The Browning spat shells and the riddled German hit the ground, hard.

With the smoke gone the poplar trees re-emerged and there was evidence of Panzergrenadiers milling around in the undergrowth.

'Driver, advance!' The tank growled, tracks churning.

'Target! All of them!'

The turret traversed. Stopped. The gun elevated. Stopped. 'On!'

'Fire!'

The gunner stamped on the trigger plate. The gun bellowed, and 15 pounds of high explosive shell screamed across the intervening gap. At 2000 feet per second, and loaded with a lethal charge of TNT, the shell detonated on contact. The violent explosion erupted amidst a bewildered and disorientated band of Panzergrenadiers. In the ensuing carnage many died.

'Again!' Summerton urged.

A shell entered the breech and was sealed. The gunner changed target to the next group of Germans.

'On!' he called.

'Fire!'

The gun flamed and recoiled. A second shell whipped into the trees, exploded. Men screamed, struck by splinters. Pounded and burned, faces shrivelled, they frantically sought to escape the tank's retribution.

But Matt Summerton grimly stuck to his task. He'd seen the sorry state of the besieged Paratroopers, had good friends killed in the two tanks he'd lost, and he had absolutely no intention of letting these bastards off the hook.

'Right stick! . . . . Steady!' The manoeuvre brought the tank a little towards the paddock, the row of poplars opening out on his left. The turret rotated.

'On!'

'Fire!' The gun blasted smoke and flame. Summerton grabbed for the handles of the Browning, found fleeing Grenadiers and hit the trigger. The vibration flowed through his hands and arms, hugely satisfying. Blood and sinew, muscle and guts, all succumbed to the violence meted out by the machine-gun.

And suddenly, there was nothing left to shoot.

'Driver come left!' He waited for the tank to pull round.

'Halt!'

All movement ceased and the noise of the engine fell away to rumble quietly in tickover. Summerton watchfully surveyed the trees and bushes, expecting movement, but none came. He looked round at the farmhouse and decoded to pull back, find whoever was now in command.

Wary of a lone Grenadier with a Panzerfaust he gave the driver his order.

'Reverse.'

The noise of the engine rose and the Sherman rolled backwards. Summerton had hold of the Browning, just in case.

In the kitchen Frank Tillman slowly lowered the butt of the Bren gun, lifted the barrel away from the window frame, and with the weight of the gun cradled in his arms, sagged to the floor.

Wingham caught the movement from the corner of his eye and hobbled over to join him. There was a spreading patch of blood on his left shoulder and his eyes were screwed tight shut. Wingham reached for the Bren to remove some of the weight, and Tillman's eyes snapped open, his grip tightening on the gun. He saw it was the Major, but even then, only reluctantly allowed it to be taken from him.

'It's okay, I've got it,' Wingham reassured him, flicked the safety to off and leant it against the wall. Looking at Tillman's face Wingham saw all that he needed as testimony to a battle hard fought. The keen eyes had become red rimmed and stared out from a grey face, rivulets of sweat forming lighter tracks down the stubbled jaw. His breathing was laboured, teeth clamped against the pain. But then, somewhat unexpectedly, the big man grinned.

'Showed the bastards, didn't we?'

Wingham gave him a gentle smile and nodded. 'Certainly did.'

The harsh squeal of tank tracks sounded from outside and Wingham crossed to the door. The Sherman drew up still facing south and halted, and Wingham limped out to meet the man in command.

In the turret, Lieutenant Matt Summerton looked down at the grimy Paratrooper and recognised the man's authority without seeing anything to indicate he was an officer. Nonetheless he needed to know who he was dealing with.

'Lieutenant Summerton, sir. May I ask your name?'

'Major Wingham, Paul Wingham, and by God am I glad to see you.'

Summerton threw up a parade ground salute. 'Glad we were able to get here, sir. Better late than never.'

'How many are you?' Wingham asked.

Summerton made a great show of looking round at the smoking Sherman, finished with a grimace and said, 'Unfortunately, just us now.'

Wingham pursed his lips and looked down the slope. 'I know you cleaned out the poplar trees but could I ask you to check the southern approach. Just to be sure. If there's any left I don't think they'll be back, but you never know.'

Summerton inclined his head. 'Your word is my command, sir.' He lifted the handset and gave the order. 'Driver advance!'

The noise from the engine rose in volume and the Sherman rumbled away towards the trees.

26 A Reckoning

Wingham stood for a minute and watched it go, and then looked over at the workshop wondering who had survived. Wearily now, for the 'after battle' reaction had set in, he hobbled off to see for himself. Passing the pond he glanced over at the dead Germans, one still half afloat in what had now become a crimson pool of diluted blood. Then it was the smoking Sherman, blackened armour round the cupola. As he stepped round the rear engine compartment and faced the workshop he stopped, stunned by the sight that met his eyes.

Bodies. The bodies of Panzergrenadiers scattered outside the windows and doors, dead where they lay from repeated attempts to overrun the workshop. Off to his right down the grass covered slope, more dead Germans. He shook his head at the carnage and limped towards the wooden door.

A tank Sergeant and one of his crew sat slumped against a low bank outside. They smoked in silence and he let them be. The wooden door stood ajar, splintered and pock marked from a dozen or more hits. He limped inside and stood for a moment to let his eyes become accustomed to the relative gloom of the interior.

He picked out Carter in the light from the window. He was supported by a workbench with his torso lying across it, Bren gun still in his hands but his head turned sideways resting on the butt. Empty magazines lay strewn about the bench, a few on the floor.

He found Corporal Steve Dexter sitting propped up against the back wall next to the forge. His helmet lay upside down discarded on the floor beside him and from a face caked in filth his glazed eyes stared unseeing at the opposite window. The dark red patch of blood on his collar showed he'd been hit. Wingham nodded but received only the blink of an eye in return, so he limped on, careful to avoid the anvil, its pewter-grey sheen glinting softly in the afternoon sun. He approached the old steel door with its vivid display of random bullet holes, still without finding any trace of Cartwright. He eased through the opening and paused.

Sergeant Bill Cartwright sat crumpled in partial shade against the end wall facing the orchard. His Sten gun lay pointing across his lap at the workshop's southern corner, his head slumped forward on his chest. Blood had soaked his shins, and his smock appeared more red than camouflaged.

Wearily, Paul Wingham limped closer and managed to go down on one knee.

'Bill?' he queried, 'Bill?' and he reached out a tentative hand to touch his friend's shoulder. The old warrior grunted and raised his chin, eyes narrowed as he struggled to focus. Recognition dawned and a weak smile played across the leathery face. He shifted the Sten, the effort causing him to groan.

Wingham tried hard to identify a serious wound but with the amount of blood everywhere gave up.

'Where's the worst of it?' he asked, desperate to help.

Cartwright coughed and winced, a grin coming despite the pain. 'I think,' he said slowly, choosing his words with care, 'it would be easier to tell you where it hurt the least.'

Wingham smiled. Same old Cartwright, never willing to admit what he thought to be a weakness. Never mind the bodies stacked up outside, their blood forever staining this small corner of Normandy.

The Sergeant reached out a hand, grabbed Wingham's wrist.

'Look out for Dexter. Couldn't have done this without him. He's a bloody giant when it comes to a fight. A lot of those dead Grenadiers are down to him.'

'I've already seen him, by the forge. Bit shocked at the moment but he'll make it.'

Cartwright sagged, his brief burst of energy gone. He managed to stammer a, 'Thank you,' and let his chin sink back to his chest.

Wingham straightened, testing his weight on the leg. It felt no worse and he set off across the sloping ground towards the wrecked paddock fence. Nearing the fence rails he looked across sloping ground and swallowed. Dead Panzergrenadiers lay sprawled in the contorted shapes only violent death brings. Some had died alone, others in groups of two or three. All bore the marks of battle with blood soaked uniforms and grotesque fragments of flesh and bone. Their weapons lay unheeded, smashed and ruptured by the fury of war. He thought back to the young German in the barn and on reflection, his poorly judged assessment of the enemy's fighting qualities. He shook his head and moved on towards what remained of the paddock fencing.

Lance-Corporal Ben Fletcher lay across the bottom rail, his Sten gun still clutched in his right fist, a finger on the trigger, the muzzle buried in the dirt. His helmet hung from the strap, his face a bloody mess and his smock stained dark red. Multiple shrapnel wounds had taken their toll.

Wingham knelt, and tenderly, very gently, he eased the helmet's strap from around Fletcher's neck and laid it to one side. He paused then to look at the man's face, the proud man from Yorkshire. He remembered that Fletcher's world when he was at home revolved around his dog. How the pair of them walked in wild spaces, but no more. Another good man gone.

Wingham straightened and peered towards the row of poplars, beyond which he could see the solid bulk of Summerton's tank guarding the lower slopes. He limped on and headed for where he knew the anti-tank gun had been hidden by the undergrowth.

As he reached the line of trees the dull gleam of a gun barrel came into view. It pointed upwards at an odd angle and Wingham pushed through the last of the bushes to find a welcome sight. The weapon had been well and truly shattered, the curved shield blown asunder. The split trail carriage was broken in two and a dead officer with a leg missing lay nearby. His guts had been sliced open. The gun crew had been scattered by the explosion.

He turned away to limp back to the farmhouse. It was only right and proper that he find Sarah and thank her personally for her hard work.

Wearily now, he approached the kitchen doorway but then paused before attempting the rubble. A strange silence had settled over the Farm Sainte

Beaumont, the sounds of battle fading, only the nearby crackle of burning flames a reminder of the battle's savage fury. A voice from over by the barn attracted his attention and Wingham limped across the cobbled courtyard to stop and lean against the big doors.

Keith Brennan lay slumped against the wall, chin on chest and blood soaking the smock down his left side. He still held the hilt of his fighting knife in his right fist, blood congealed on the blade. His Sten gun lay balanced on his knees pointing at the paddock. He somehow looked as if he was holding off the entire enemy attack on his own. The truth was, 'Angel' Keith Brennan, once a bricklayer from Richmond had succumbed to his wounds and breathed his last.

Jed Tulloch lay with his head on his pack, helmet gone and a blood stained bandaged wrapped round his head and right eye, left eye still visible. His face was filthy, a combination of dirt and sweat, smock torn open at the neck. He saw Wingham and managed a slow wink from the one good eye. Wingham smiled, nodded, moved on. Stratton had been helped out too, lying in the afternoon sun, looking more dead than alive.

'S'all right, Major. I'm still breathing.'

Wingham felt a lump in his throat, found it difficult to reply, couldn't find the words. He managed a nod, a meaningless, inadequate acknowledgement of the man's stalwart defence of the sitting room.

He stared at the bloodied flesh, the makeshift sodden bandages, the bodies of those who'd fought and not made it through. The sacrifice was almost more than he could accept. Was this really what victory felt like? It was he who'd had brought them to this and there'd not been one word of dissent.

From the front of the house Corporal Dave Greene shouted a warning. 'Jerry! In the woods!'

Wingham rushed for the front door and stared at the trees. 'Where? How many?'

Greene pointed across the fields to where the ditch began. 'Over there. Listen.'

Wingham readied his Sten and moved down the short path. He stopped and strained to hear the enemy's approach. Then, clearly heard in the mid afternoon quiet, tank tracks squealed and clanked as they pushed their way ever closer.

Paul Wingham sighed and shook his head. Not again. He couldn't keep asking these men to put their lives on the line against such odds. They'd already sacrificed so much, fought with such tenacity. And he had to consider the wounded, so many in difficulty. But the spectre of death by execution hung over them all, and the *Ruffians* had sworn never to surrender. Then there was the girl too. If anything she needed to be spirited away to the beaches, got back to England. Maybe he could ask for volunteers? Just a few to help get her out. He dropped his chin to his chest and scuffed a boot on the path.

'Sir! Look!' came a shout. 'Look. They're ours!' And an excited cheer spread through the survivors.

Wingham looked up and stared at three Sherman tanks bludgeoning their way through the outskirts of the wood. Paratroopers accompanied them, platoon strength if not more, moving purposefully forward as they swarmed into the cornfield.

Paul Wingham felt his legs go weak and took advantage of the low stone wall. He sat and allowed himself a quiet smile. How on earth had he and his lightly armed bunch of *Ruffians* ever managed to hold off an entire company of German Panzergrenadiers? He rummaged in a breast pocket and found a pack of cigarettes. With great deliberation he extracted one and applied a flame. He took a welcome slow lungful of smoke and let the nicotine work its magic. At last, he thought, a moment to himself.

Captain Gordon Culpepper, Major Lane's second-in-command, advanced through the cornfield at the head of fifty skirmishing Paratroopers. The three Sherman tanks, also members of Lieutenant Matt Summerton's 8th Battalion King's Own Royal Dragoons, had arrived at Lane's headquarters with urgent orders from Colonel Douglas Rees-Morton. To that end, Culpepper, and as many Paratroopers as could be spared were immediately despatched to assist the tanks in extricating however many of Major Wingham's isolated Platoon had survived.

Culpepper himself had his doubts as to whether they'd find many of the '*Ruffians*' still alive. What little information he'd been privileged to access before departing was that their mission had been an unparalleled success and every effort should be made in the attempt to get them out.

Halfway through the cornfield he could clearly see the pockmarked farmhouse and a number of weary looking Paratroopers waiting in various stages of exhaustion. He moved past the smoking wreckage of an upturned half-track, the bodies of a number of Panzergrenadiers scattered in the corn.

'Stay sharp!' he called, a brief reminder to those he led that the enemy might still be close. Behind them the three Sherman's clattered and clanked their way into the field, the tracks mowing down the corn in widely dispersed lines.

Culpepper made it to the far end and nodded to a corporal sitting in a shallow scrape in front of a low wall. A pair of red rimmed eyes stared out of a blackened face, a faint nod acknowledging the Captain's presence. Over to his right a Paratrooper leaned against the trunk of a beech tree, his Lee Enfield balanced in the crook of his arm. A cigarette hung from the corner of his mouth and he too nodded faintly. On the wall by the gate another Paratrooper sat slouched, a Sten gun nursed across his lap, head down and smoking. There was blood on the man's collar and more on a leg and what could be seen of his hands indicated more blood. He didn't make any effort to look up so Culpepper let him be and walked up the short length of path to a door hanging askew.

A murmur of voices could be heard from inside and he followed the sound into what at first glance appeared to be a kitchen. As he stepped down onto the flagstoned floor he heard a muffled groan and looked round the wall to his right. He knew instantly that the sight meeting his eyes would not easily be forgotten. Nor would the smell. At a glance he counted nine casualties and a girl. The girl was tending to one of the wounded and leaning over the table. Blood covered her arms from hands to elbows. More than that the room was a bloodbath. The table and floor swam with blood, glistening darkly as it congealed. A soldier lay groaning quietly. Beneath the table a bucket overflowed with used bandages, a constant drip adding to the mess.

Culpepper swallowed hard and turned to a doorway partially filled with rubble. He clambered over and dropped outside onto the remnants of a once neat flower garden now trampled flat. To his right a cobbled yard extended across to a large pair of barn doors, dense smoke filled the opening. He looked out over gouged lawns at a row of poplars to where a Sherman tank nestled amongst the undergrowth, the gun turret traversing slowly left.

One of Culpepper's Sergeants came out from the kitchen and gave a slow whistle. He glanced to his left beyond the pond and the blackened wreck of a shot up Sherman. But what caught his attention the most was the sheer number of dead Panzergrenadiers.

'Christ almighty,' he said, and pointed to the grass slope in front of a low roofed outbuilding. 'Look how many of the buggers have copped it over there.' He shook his head in disbelief. 'What the bloody hell happened?'

Culpepper, who'd been studying the verges where the poplar trees met low lying bushy undergrowth, could see for himself another area of German corpses.

'I think, Sergeant,' he said, choosing his words with care, 'that Jerry came up against the one thing they hadn't reckoned on.'

'Sir?' the Sergeant prompted.

'This Platoon we've come to help, know who they are?'

'Not exactly, no sir.'

Culpepper smiled. 'It's the *Ruffians'* Sergeant, and of all the bloody minded bunch of buggers you wouldn't want to tangle with, this lot have got to be top of the heap.'

The Sergeant just murmured, 'Ahh,' and continued to stare at the bodies.

Wingham finished the cigarette and came to his feet. He slung the Sten over a shoulder and turned back towards the front door. Before Corporal Greene's shout had interrupted him he'd been intent on finding Sarah. Three of the newly arrived Paratroopers stood hesitantly at the bottom of the stairs, choking blue smoke curling from above. Wingham brushed past, oblivious to their stares, and stepped down into the kitchen.

He found her then, covered in blood, sat slumped in the only serviceable chair, head down and eyes closed. Only two of the wounded remained in the room, one sat beneath the window, the other was laid out on the kitchen table.

Wingham crossed to the chair and bent over until his face was close to hers.

'Sarah,' he said quietly. 'You okay?'

In response she lifted her head and opened her eyes to meet his. Her matted hair framed the blood smeared face and she looked very tired. But she managed a rueful smile.

'Do me a favour?' she asked.

'Anything.'

'Let me have a cigarette will you? They smoked all mine.'

Wingham delved in a pocket, lit one for her and let her take it. She took a deep lungful, the tip glowing bright, her eyes watching him over the smoking end.

'Better?' he asked.

She blew smoke at the ceiling, inhaled again and this time let the smoke dribble from the corner of her mouth.

'Better than you can ever imagine,' she said, and straightened in the chair. 'Is it over now?'

'For the moment,' Wingham offered, well aware it might not be. 'We've got to get back to our lines. No telling quite what that will entail.'

A fleeting smile crossed her lips. 'No more wounded would be nice.'

Unseen by either of them, a Medical Orderly had walked in wearing his Red Cross on the obligatory white armband. 'I can't guarantee that, miss, but I'll take it from here.'

Sarah gave him the biggest smile. 'I can't thank you enough, and you're more than welcome.'

The Orderly peered under the bloody dressing she'd applied to Dawson's temple.

'You've done a good job there. He just opened his eyes.'

She looked at Wingham and shook her head. 'Who'd have thought it. I wouldn't have given a brass farthing for his chances.'

Wingham straightened and reached for a hand. 'Come on,' he said, 'let's get you some fresh air.'

Sarah used his support and came to her feet, pausing to shake off a momentary weakness. Wingham went first and helped her over the pile of rubble. She stepped down and stopped, taken aback by how the once well manicured lawns were now cratered and torn. The scars left by rampaging half-tracks remained deeply embedded in the turf.

But the afternoon sun helped lift her spirits and banished the worst of her fears. The enemy had withdrawn and she'd survived.

27 A Final Wave

Major Paul Wingham took a final walk round the grounds of the farm. With the exception of Bill Cartwright the last of the wounded had been loaded aboard the trucks and he just wanted to reassure himself that everyone had really been accounted for. Near the pond he paused to once again look out over the field of battle and wonder how in hell's name they'd managed to hold off an entire company of Panzergrenadiers. He shook his head and walked back to the kitchen door where Cartwright waited, perched on the pile of rubble.

'I think we're done. Time to get out of it.'

'Yes, sir,' Cartwright said, and struggled to his feet. With one hand holding onto the door frame he too paused for a final look.

'You know something,' he said thoughtfully. 'You remember Churchill's speech, the one about 'never in the field of human conflict' and all that?'

'Of course.'

The Sergeant rubbed his unshaven jaw. 'Well, I don't think we *Ruffians* did so bad either.'

'True,' Wingham agreed, then wracked his brain in an effort to conjure up vaguely remembered words from almost totally forgotten Greek mythology. 'We soldiers few,' he muttered under his breath.

'What was that?' Cartwright asked.

'Nothing important,' Wingham smiled, then turned to reach out a helping hand. 'Come on now, they're waiting.'

And together they limped their way through the house to the narrow track out front where three Bedford trucks sat ticking over.

Culpepper was busy overseeing the task of loading the wounded, distracted by the cries of pain. Stretcher bearers carefully slid their loads into the back of vehicles and went back for more. Bill Cartwright was directed into the back of the second truck and muttering and mumbling was helped to clamber up the tailboard. He squeezed inside and sat on the floor.

Wingham found a seat in the cab of the third truck and eased his leg to help with the pain.

Corporal Dave Greene closed the tailgate of the first lorry and then swung up into the driver's seat. He'd relegated the original driver to look after wounded in the back. There'd been a lot of cussing and swearing before 'Corporal' Greene let his rank do the persuading. He looked at his two front seat passengers and smiled.

'All set?'

Steve Dexter gritted his teeth and nodded. Sarah wriggled to sit a little more upright and gave a vigorous nod.

'Yes,' she said and reached for the door handle. 'Ready when you are.'

Greene started the engine and stuck a raised thumb out of the driver's window. Ten yards ahead, Lieutenant Matt Summerton acknowledged with a wave and the Sherman spat smoke. It lurched forward, the tracks churning on the turn. At the third attempt Greene found first gear and slowly followed on, acutely aware of the need to try and avoid the worst of the track's uneven surface. The three tanks that had recently arrived remained at the farm along with Culpepper's Paratroopers. Lane had passed orders that the farm might well make an ideal jumping off point for a push south. The Sherman tanks of 'C' Squadron, 8th Battalion King's Own Royal Dragoons, could well form the spearhead of an armoured attack.

At Honeysuckle Cottage near England's southern shoreline, Mary wandered into the garden with her treasured hand woven basket. In the vegetable patch she carefully placed it to one side and reached for the fork. A minute later six early potatoes had been brushed off and placed reverently into the basket. A row of radishes beckoned and she bent to pull just enough for two. Lettuce leaves from three separate small plants came next, the luscious green a perfect accompaniment to the firm young potatoes.

The laundry had dried nicely in the sun's warmth so Mary placed the freshly picked veg on the kitchen draining board and while she then gathered the clothes from the line, her mother happily folded them away in the spacious airing cupboard.

Mary then checked the stove was topped up with enough coal for supper and popped the kettle on for tea. Her mother came down the stairs and started to rummage through a drawer where she kept the important bits and bobs.

'Mary,' she said abruptly, 'have you seen my ration book?'

'Yes, mother, you left it on the hall table, but why? You shopped yesterday.'

'I know, but I'll need to get down to the grocery shop. Mister Crawford said he would have more tea arriving by tomorrow and we've almost run out. I'll need your book as well.'

With the two books safe in the confines of her handbag, Mary poured tea and they slipped out into the garden. The afternoon sun was beginning to leave lengthening shadows and they took their cups to the nearby bench.

Her mother looked out over the sea and took a thoughtful sip. 'I do hope Chris is all right, dear.'

Bob the dog wandered over and flopped down at Mary's feet. She reached down to tickle his ears and smiled.

'He'd damn well better be. The chicken coop needs repairing and the latch on the front gate is sticking.'

Her mother chuckled and shook her head. 'I wonder if he really knew what he was getting himself into when he bought your engagement ring?'

Mary laughed, her eyes sparkling. 'Of course he did. Three square meals a day and a very warm bed to sleep in.'

The dog yawned and laid his chin between front paws. A pair of blackbirds swooped in to land in the veg garden and began pecking for worms. Snowy whinnied softly and watched from over the gate.

Mary touched the locket, and pensively nibbled at her lower lip. She looked round at her mother. 'He'd damn well better be alright or he'll get a piece of my mind.'

For a moment they looked at one another, and then both burst out laughing. They lapsed into quiet contemplation, making the most of the sun's warmth.

Beyond the horizon across a hundred miles of blue-green Channel sea, the Allied invasion of Nazi occupied France pushed remorselessly on beyond Hitler's now fatally damaged, crumbling Atlantic Wall.

It was early evening by the time Matt Summerton's convoy made it back to Major Lane's headquarters. On arrival the priority was for the medics to ascertain exactly who needed to be evacuated to the beaches, where intermediate hospital facilities had already been set up. Any further surgical procedures would then be taken care of on board one of the Hospital Ships waiting off shore.

By now a dozen Shermans from the 8th Battalion had taken up residence in Ranville, preparations well under way for a push south to join the reconnaissance troop at the Farm Sainte Beaumont.

Captain Tim Smith of the Royal Army Medical Corps had been attached to Company HQ. More commonly addressed as 'Doc' he'd set up a Medical Aid Post in the cellar of a large town house where he duly carried out a number of critical operations before sending his patients back to the Regimental Clearing Station.

Major Carl Kruger cursed in his fight to control the motorbike. It had not been at its best running over rough terrain, bouncing and scrabbling over the many stony ridges left by long forgotten ploughs. Nonetheless he was nearing the end of a tortuous, winding detour that had kept him free of enemy observation. Twice his front wheel had hit fallen branches buried beneath the litter of leaves in the wooded slopes outside Colombelles, and twice he was almost thrown from the saddle. But eventually he coaxed the motorbike down through the serried ranks of an apple orchard and gratefully rejoined the road running west to east from Colombelles to Escoville. Thoroughly dishevelled by the experience, a short while later he arrived in the quiet square and skidded to a halt outside the hotel.

A young Oberleutnant hurried out to meet him, clicked his heels and flung up a half hearted salute. Flustered by the Major's unexpected arrival, Franz Dornberger stared at the visible accumulation of blood discolouring the Major's tunic.

Kruger dismounted and turned to him. 'Well, Franz. Has the Colonel arrived?'

'Nein, Herr Major. You are the only senior officer here. Major Fredrickson has not been seen, and Capitan Buschmann took 'B' Kompanie out to join you at the farm.'

Kruger winced as pain in his arm lanced down to his elbow. 'Have we had any further orders from Division? Anything from Rommel?'

'A despatch rider came with orders to place the 126th Panzergrenadiers on standby. And before the man left he said that General-Leutnant Feuchtinger had to change headquarters. The countryside is swarming with parachutists. The rider only just avoided being caught.'

Kruger stared at the ground, glared at the sky, and finally took a deep breath. 'Gott im Himmel!' he snapped. 'How many men have we left?'

'No more than three-hundred, Herr Major.'

'Any reports on how near the Englanders are?'

'The rider said he'd seen many tanks north-west of Caen. They had white stars painted on them. Other than that, only what you told Capitan Buschmann.'

Carl Kruger hung his head and worried his bottom lip. It seemed that the enemy were here to stay. They had obviously expanded their beachhead and were landing heavy armour. He looked up and gave Dornberger a tight grin.

'Listen to me, Franz and listen well. The enemy forces will be after Caen and we will be ordered to stop them. Do not allow our Grenadiers to defend fixed positions. Keep moving.'

'But what about you, Herr Major? Will you not be in command?'

Kruger shook his head. 'I must fulfil my orders, Franz. Communications are poor are they not?'

'Ja, many French saboteurs. Lines are down.'

'And that, my young friend, is why I must leave you to take charge. I have the motorcycle as transport and I can personally deliver my report to Feldmarschall Rommel.' He placed a hand on Dornberger's shoulder. 'Do not fear, Franz, you are easily ready for this task and I believe you will not let me down.'

Oberleutnant Franz Dornberger straightened to attention. 'You can rely on me, Herr Major.'

Kruger inwardly smirked at Dornberger's naïve willingness to accept the Major's reasoned advice. The fact that Kruger had volunteered himself for a mission that any despatch rider could have handled never entered the young officer's consciousness.

'Good,' Kruger said. 'Your loyalty does you great credit. I will remember you in my report to Rommel. Now I must leave. There is little time to waste.'

'Jawohl, Herr Major.' He threw up a full salute and received a half wave in return.

Kruger took a last lingering look at the hotel. His time there had been all that he could have wished for and it was a pity the Englanders had again brought war to his door. He throttled up and took off down the nearest road for Paris. It would do no harm to ingratiate himself into Rommel's entourage. It would be a long time before the Allies got anywhere near the Feldmarschall's Paris headquarters. A cruel smile disfigured his mouth. If he took that thought to a logical conclusion, the officer who wore a black patch over one eye would escape any possible retribution for what amounted to a small error of judgement on the field of battle.

Major Carl Kruger heeled the machine round the next bend and pushed on for Paris. He looked forward to renewing his acquaintance with the venerable Erwin Rommel. It would need little embellishment for Kruger to convince the Feldmarschall of a limited Allied breakthrough. And Rommel would appreciate that no man could do more than to risk his life by bringing his Commander-in-Chief such important news. In the meantime, for all his recent battlefield transgressions, Major Carl Kruger smirked as he made good his escape from the clutches of enemy paratroopers. Once again an Officer-of-Panzergrenadiers lived on to fight another day.

Private Chris Jamison came out from the Aid Post and blinked into the sunshine. Tiredness had set in now, the fatigue that crept up unannounced but hit hard. Dan Clayton stood leaning against the wall puffing a cigarette, the odd leaf from the beech tree caught in his smock. Jamison spotted Rob Carter having a smoke nearby, Pat Mitchell next to him in a shaft of sunlight. Pete Solomon lay with his head propped on his pack, a hand heavily bandaged, eyes closed. Dinger Bell was going through the motions of cleaning his Bren gun, a lit cigarette hanging from a corner of his mouth. Nobby Clarke sat cross-legged next to him, his Sten gun glistening from a film of light oil.

Private Douglas 'Jock' Stewart, the wound to his cheek covered in yellow iodine, looked up from where he sat and nodded.

'Chris.'

'Jock,' Jamison said, and wandered over to join them, slumped down with his back to the wall and delved in his smock for a fresh pack of cigarettes. It was slightly crushed but he selected one and teased it straight, flicked his lighter. Smoke curled and he let his eyes close, his thoughts turning to a small cottage and a silver pony. He managed a faint smile as he pictured his home coming. Mary would shed tears of happiness, Bob the dog would start bounding around in ever decreasing circles, and Snowy would trot across to be stroked at the gate.

A distant explosion interrupted his thoughts and he opened his eyes. He could dream all he liked but it might be a long time coming. He took another drag on the cigarette and relaxed. He'd survived, and right now that was more than enough.

Norman 'King' Taylor sat leaning against warm brickwork and sipped at a freshly made mug of sweet tea. His arm had been properly attended to and though painful was resting in a new white sling. A faint smile came and went. He'd avoided the need for a new coffin.

Lying on an improvised stretcher, Joe Miller lay half propped on a pack and watched the rest of the *Ruffians* who'd made it through. He had a note attached to his smock that indicated he was on a one way to Blighty. The arm was strapped and the morphine had worked its magic, and right now he was free of pain. Long may it last.

Frank Tillman lit a cigarette and pulled his Bren gun a little closer. He'd become fond of that weapon. If there was one thing a gunner needed, it was reliability and this Bren gun hadn't let him down, not once all through the day's fighting. He patted the barrel and took another pull on the cigarette. He didn't ask much out of life and at times like these he was more than content with his lot.

Wingham had made a point of overseeing the initial stages of segregating the seriously injured from the less so, but then realised he was more of a hindrance than a help, and left it to the expertise of the medics.

He found Major Freddy Lane had moved his headquarters to a more suitable dwelling with a good view of the adjacent countryside. The usual conglomeration of signallers, clerks and messengers were all easily encompassed within spacious rooms. Lane had his back to the door leaning over a map of the local area.

'Hello, Freddy,' Wingham said as he limped in, 'I see you've been busy.'

Lane straightened from the map and looked round.

'Paul, you old bastard,' he grinned. 'Made it then?'

Wingham pursed his lips and gave a faint nod. 'Skin of our teeth, yep.'

Lane spread his hands, embarrassment written all over his face. 'I'm sorry, Paul, but we were caught with our pants down. The radios wouldn't work, couldn't make contact. By the time you got through to us we were last in the queue.' He raised an eyebrow. 'Except for that fire mission. I gather that had a certain importance attached to it?'

'*La raison principale*, as the French would say. And the artillery were spot on. Made a right mess of the target.'

Lane frowned. 'And the girl? Where is she now?'

'Cleaning up ready to go home.'

'Good, there's a jeep waiting.'

Wingham smiled. 'She'll be pleased with that. I'll let her know.'

Lane nodded. 'Yes, do that.' He seemed distracted.

'What's wrong, Freddy?'

'Nothing, nothing at all. In fact it's just the opposite.' He glanced quickly at the windows and round the room. He lowered his voice.

'I shouldn't be telling you this but I've had it on good authority that your little mission turned up trumps. From what the RAF is reporting, an entire German division has been delayed, milling around like a headless chicken. The Typhoons are already calling it 'bomb alley.'

Wingham took the news with a grim smile. 'Thank you, Freddy. Good to know.'

Lane turned back to the map. 'And you'd better get that leg seen to. We're not done yet.'

'We're not?'

'No. If you're feeling up to it, you're wanted by the Colonel. Briefing here at 18.00 hours.'

'Right. Six o'clock it is.'

He found the jeep with the driver impatiently waiting to head back for the beach, then saw Sarah step out from a house across the road. He raised a hand and she moved to join him. He was astonished by the transformation, amazed by what a quick wash and brush up, and a little lipstick could achieve.

'I came to say farewell,' he said. 'You're going back to England. This chap will take you to the beach. There'll be an officer waiting.'

She nodded and held his eyes. 'Thank you, Major,' she said. 'I don't think you'll ever fully appreciate how much I owe you.' Before he could reply, she leaned over and kissed his cheek.

He stammered something useless, embarrassed by the gesture, and before he could say anything more she clambered into the jeep. The driver glanced round and Wingham nodded. 'All yours.'

The jeep took off and she turned to wave, the evening sun glinting off her hair. He caught the white of her teeth as she laughed and then she gave him a final, lingering wave. The jeep turned a corner and she was gone.

Wingham moved away and directed his footsteps towards the Aid Post. In the crowded gloom of the cellar a medical orderly gave him the once over, cleaned the leg wound and finished off with a well applied bandage.

It was then that a voice called from in the cellar.

'Major Wingham?'

'Yes?'

Captain 'Doc' Smith stuck his head round the corner.

'It's Private Stratton. Sorry, but I couldn't save him. He lost too much blood.'

Wingham blew out his cheeks and half shook his head. He wasn't really surprised. For all Stratton's bravado he'd looked pretty awful.

'Thanks, Doc. I guess you can't win 'em all.'

Smith rubbed his bloodied hands on an already discoloured cloth and nodded.

'That's a fact,' he said bitterly. 'But it doesn't make it any easier. And we're keeping an eye on Private Dawson. He suffered a wound to his temple. He's alive but I don't give much for his chances.' He shook his head and turned away to his operating table.

Wingham pursed his lips in thought. Stratton gone, and Dawson more dead than alive. The cost was mounting. He tested the leg, thanked the orderly and squeezed up the crowded stairs. Outside he walked over to where Bill Cartwright sat with a mug of tea.

'Still with us then?'

Cartwright grunted agreement. 'Yep. I've used up a fair few lives, but I'm not done yet.'

Wingham dropped down beside him and offered his cigarettes. They lit up and watched a fresh batch of soldiers arriving. Some were Airborne, and by the look of them they'd seen their fair share of fighting. A group of Commandos walked through without stopping, immediately followed by a bunch of regulars. Wingham thought it might be the beginnings of a build up.

They sat together for a lengthy spell, content in each other's company, with no need for words, just enjoying the familiar unspoken friendship of two long serving, battle hardened veterans.

With a few minutes to go before the briefing, Major Paul Wingham heaved himself to his feet and prepared to take his leave. But first there was something he needed to do.

With his leg now bolstered by a snug fitting bandage he strode across the road to where many of the Platoon had now gathered. Initially he found it difficult to put names to faces. Dirt and sweat had mingled to leave men unrecognisable. There were walking wounded with blood stained bandages amongst them, but in most cases his *Ruffians*, though visibly uninjured, had been left shocked and dazed by the sheer ferocity of what they had endured. The stress of battle, the fear that accompanied the explosive unknown, and the unexpected relief of still being in one piece at the end of it, all those emotions became indelibly stamped on a man's face. They saw him coming and to a man, regardless of their wounds, respectfully came to their feet. He came to a halt a yard or so short, and looked at each man in turn. A lump rose in his throat. He coughed to clear it and straightened up to his full height.

'I have orders to report to Colonel Rees-Morton. For a briefing. I suspect that means a parting of the ways.' He took a deep breath.

'So in case I don't get another chance, I wanted you to know I'll always be in your debt. More by luck, I had the honour of taking command of the *Ruffians*, and I'm proud to have fought alongside you.' He hung his head for a moment but then looked up with grave certainty. 'Some of us didn't make it today, but rest assured I'll not forget their sacrifice. And I know many of you have been badly wounded.'

He paused as he noticed other members of the *Ruffians* emerge from the Aid Post to limp or shuffle their way over and join the perimeter of listening soldiers.

'But there's something else I want you all to know. The mission we were given achieved everything it set out to do. In addition, and more importantly, few though we were in number, we helped to delay an entire German Panzer Division. And that delay was critical. It left them vulnerable to our fighter-bombers who apparently had a field day.' He paused, gathering his thoughts.. 'Without a shadow of doubt,' he said, leaning on the words for emphasis, 'you've saved the lives of more men than you'll ever know.'

A murmur of appreciation rippled through the gathering and it built to an unrehearsed, ragged cheer, before it slowly faded.

An anonymous voice piped up from the crowd. 'Couldn't have done it without the Old Man though, could we?'

Rifleman George Morgan chimed in. 'Not bleedin' likely. Someone should have warned the poor bastards.'

The laughter rose, loud in the evening quiet, and then to Wingham's astonishment, Dinger Bell stepped forward with his hand outstretched.

'It was a privilege, sir,' he offered and gave him a firm handshake.

'Thank you,' was all that Wingham could manage. Rob Carter and Pete Solomon joined in and the Major willingly accepted their hands. And one by one, all those that had gathered to hear his words, came forward.

For Wingham it was a humbling experience. He felt he didn't deserve their gratitude, not after all his bad calls. That these tough, experienced soldiers wanted to shake his hand . . . , he had no words. Corporal Steve Dexter, wearing a couple of neatly finished bandages came last in line, and Wingham noted he seemed well recovered in comparison to when he'd last seen him in the workshop.

When they were done he gave them an inadequate nod of appreciation and took a step back ready to turn away. But Rifleman Chris Jamison took a half pace forward and came to attention, ramrod straight.

'On behalf of all us *Ruffians*, sir, we just want to wish you good luck for the future.'

Wingham managed a heartfelt smile. 'Thanks, all of you,' he said, and again took in the sight of their familiar faces.

'And I wish you God speed.'

With that he deliberately turned and walked away, broke the ties. Any more and his face of stern authority would have broken for all to see. He'd always found praise difficult to take, from embarrassment as a child, to accepting unwanted compliments from his peers. But the tribute he'd just received from such courageous men, it was all he could do to disguise his emotions.

It took no more than five minutes to present himself back at Lane's headquarters. And this time, as Freddy had warned, the tall figure of Colonel Douglas Reese-Morton stood waiting next to a large empty fireplace. He and two of his staff officers looked round as Wingham entered.

'Ahh, Major,' Reese-Morton beamed. 'Glad you could join us.' He pointed to the table.

'Perhaps you'd care to cast an eye over our next little enterprise.' One of the staff officers straightened out some creases in the map and stood well back. The Colonel jabbed the map with a finger and frowned at Wingham.

'In the early hours of D-Day some of our Sappers destroyed this bridge over the Dives river. We've now had reports that the Germans might be looking to rebuild. I want you to get down there and persuade them otherwise. Two platoons should do it and you'll have a 3" mortar section join you. Major Lane's been organising. The idea is to act as cover for another unit of the Royal Engineers while they place more charges, create a larger gap so to speak. Think you can manage that, Major?'

Paul Wingham eyed Reese-Morton and gave him the faintest of smiles.

'Give me the men, Colonel, and I'll manage.'

'Good man, good man. Never doubted it.' He straightened from the map table and made a move for the door. He paused there and glanced back over his shoulder. 'By the way, Major, reference that little skirmish of yours down at the farm. Good show, couldn't have done better myself.' And with that he was gone.

Wingham stared after him and then grinned. That was the sort of back handed compliment he found perfectly acceptable.

He then took time to give the map another once over before Freddy barged in with a list of men getting prepared. The realisation dawned that the

Paras would still be in the thick of it, after all, the battle for Normandy had only just begun. Having made notes of all the relevant information Wingham wandered back outside. He found a pleasant spot to stand in the warmth of an evening sun and let his thoughts drift back to the day's action. The battle for the Farm Sainte Beaumont might well be over, and he had no doubts it would quickly become no more than a footnote in some dusty Regimental archive. But for Wingham, the courage, the devotion to duty, and the selfless sacrifice of those who had endured such never-ending waves of a bloody war, would long remain etched in his memory.

Major Paul Wingham shouldered his weapon and prepared to meet his new command. As he did so a broad grin flickered across his weathered face.

Somewhere back in Portsmouth Dockyard, Lieutenant-Commander Richard Thorburn would be well advised to keep that bottle of gin on ice.

Printed in Great Britain
by Amazon